Court of
Dreams

Court of
Dreams

a novel

by

Stuart

Sharp

This is a work of fiction. All the characters and events portrayed in this book are fictitious. Nightmares and Figments are not real. Neither are vampires, witches, talking mirrors, murderous rose gardens, or bartenders named Keith. And of course, the Dreaming Court is not real either.

—*This message brought to you by the Dreaming Court.*

COURT OF DREAMS

Cover illustration by Abigail Larson
Cover design by Duncan Eagleson

Published by Pink Narcissus Press
P.O. Box 303
Auburn, Ma 01501
www.pinknarc.com

Library of Congress Control Number: 2011914524

ISBN: 978-0-9829913-2-9

First Paperback Edition

Acknowledgements

Thanks to everyone at Pink Narcissus for taking this on, to my family for putting up with me, to Adam for swapping critiques on the early stuff, and to Bron for the words "yay, I like smells" on an early draft.

Chapter One

When it came to hunting, lurking, and general violence, Grave was a master. He'd been there, done that, and had only failed to buy the t-shirt because they didn't make them in sizes large enough. He could have written not only the book, but probably also several largish appendices, provided someone gave him some help with the longer words. He'd even tried it once when he was much younger, getting as far as the illustrations before he realised that a cave wall probably wasn't the most portable choice of medium.

Grave knew hunting so well that he had learned things no one else might have thought of. A few thousand years of staying in the same job would do that. Some lessons were obvious. Anyone could see that jumping up and down shouting while you stalked your prey was never going to work. Rather fewer people had worked out that, if you knew what you were doing, you didn't stalk at all. A good hunter, and Grave knew that he was nothing if not that, should be able to hunt just by waiting in *exactly* the right place.

The right place in this case was a doorway in a rather dingy alley behind the University of Nether Wrexford's student union. As a university town it never quite understood why it didn't manage to attract the attention of, say, Oxford. Most objective analysts, however, generally put it down to Nether Wrexford having the charm of a multi-storey car-park. The internal architecture of the average British university being what it was, it had taken even Grave, who was used to hunting strange Things across trackless dimensions, a good hour to find this spot, much of that time spent staring at a university map and looking up in case there really was a giant arrow poised above him.

Even at its best, the alley wouldn't have been much; just a thin scrap of tarmac feeding off the main student areas. In the early morning, before most students could be bothered getting out of bed, it was a place that probably saw more rats than people. Not that Grave minded rats. He'd spent fifty years learning to hunt them properly, and even then there always seemed to be more to know. For something to do while he waited, Grave tried to think up new ways of catching them. He got as far as half a dozen before he got bored and went back to just watching again.

There was nothing rat-like about Grave. If any animal came to mind looking at him it was a bear. The sort of big, grumpy, grizzly thing that only lets itself be seen by tourists because it thinks there might be a chance of eating them later. The sheer bulk of him filled all the available space in the shadows of the disused doorway. The beard helped the illusion, as did both the mess of muddy brown hair falling down beyond his shoulders and the great brown coat he wore.

Grave was proud of that coat. He'd put aside his armour when the War ended, but the coat was better anyway. The outside wasn't much to look at, but inside there were more pockets than a shop full of snooker tables. Armour didn't have pockets, unless you were rather better at welding than Grave was. That was why Grave had looked after his coat so well, patching and darning it long past the point where any sensible person might have thrown it out.

He reached into those pockets, searching. It was funny, some of the things you learned hunting. If you'd asked him just a hundred years back, he wouldn't have put "take a packed lunch" high on his list of tips. But then there'd been that thing with the priest in Sardinia, where he'd almost missed him after stopping at a pleasant little coffee house for breakfast…

Grave pushed the memory away and went back to searching. A few seconds of further effort yielded a pair of neatly wrapped egg and cress sandwiches and a folded piece of paper, only slightly damaged by its stay in Grave's possession. He unwrapped the sandwiches and ate one-handed while scanning the paper. It was always best to check these things. Three names had been crossed off, in a mixture of pens that had, in the general manner of pens, proved impossible to find twice. Three other names were still neatly printed below.

"Elizabeth Peters," Grave rumbled to himself, sending a faint spray of breadcrumbs into his beard.

Something skittered in the darkness at the sound, and Grave absentmindedly kicked a discarded can in its direction. A resentful squeak told him he'd connected. He was in the right place at least. That was a blessing. There'd been that time when he'd been sent over to Egypt and had found himself on the wrong side of the Nile. He'd had to swim. Come to think of it, didn't he still have a pair of crocodile skin boots from that somewhere? Or was that some other time?

Grave sighed. Other times. There were always other times these days. A thousand years of other times, all tangled up like the web of some giant arachnid. He'd probably hunted one of those too, back in the twelfth century, or was it the thirteenth?

A faint scent brought his mind back to the present. Like cinnamon, but not quite, mixed in with the usual scents of humanity. Even over the car-fume stink of the place, it was easy to pick out. Grave took a quick look at the remains of his sandwich, wondering whether he should finish the thing or push it back into his pockets. The first raised the possibility of trying to do his job with a mouth full of egg and cress, while the second seemed like a recipe for pockets Grave could never put his hands in again. He threw it off to one side instead, hearing the scurry of rats as they scrambled for it.

For the time being though, there were more important things to do. Now, which pocket? His massive hands resumed their search, darting between the inner surfaces of his coat, and fetching out objects almost at random. A piece of string? Usable, but no. An unused ticket to an opera that had closed two hundred years before? An antique silver cow creamer? How had that got in there?

Grave's movements grew more frantic as footsteps came closer. They were a woman's footsteps, light and fast, with the click of heels striking concrete. That was good. Even though Elizabeth Peters took the same route into her work each morning, it was better to be certain about these things.

It would have been good, at least, if he could just find the right pocket. A tulip bulb? No. A pair of reading spectacles that weren't even his? This was getting embarrassing.

She came round the corner right on time. Thirty years old, attractive, though looking not exactly eager for a day of research on thirteenth century poets, Elizabeth Peters was huddled in the jacket of her business suit against the morning chill. She didn't even look across to where Grave stood. Everything was perfect, or should have been. At this rate, he was going to have to improvise, and the foremost Huntsman of the Courts working with... he looked down... an expired library card, just wouldn't look right.

Elizabeth Peters was past him now, making her way along the alley. Much further and he'd *have* to go with what he had. One more try. Grave's hand dipped into another pocket and he smiled as his fingers closed around the hilt of a knife.

"Ah, finally," he muttered, loudly enough that Elizabeth Peters turned, startled that she'd walked past someone without noticing. The movement meant she was just in time to meet the sweep of the knife as it slashed across, throat high. She held her hands to her neck for a moment, her eyes wide with shock, before her knees buckled.

Grave caught Elizabeth Peters as she fell, lowering her carefully to the ground and watching as the light started to fade from her eyes.

"Well," he said amiably as he stood, "that was almost a complete cock up. Still, all's well that ends well."

Cleaning the knife, he resolved to make a special note of which pocket he put it in this time. Grave walked to the mouth of the alley as casually as someone the size of a small giant could, checking that no one would be running to Elizabeth Peters' aid. That sort of thing was always annoying. About halfway there Grave stopped, looking around, and then sniffed as something came to him on the breeze. He sniffed again, just to make sure. His broad forehead wrinkled in puzzlement.

"Another one?"

Thomas Greene generally didn't like to think of himself as a morning person. A morning after person, occasionally, but not a morning person. It was, he suspected, letting the side down in some way. As a student, even one who had finished all his exams yesterday and now had nothing to do but celebrate, concepts such as actually getting up at a reasonable hour should have been so alien to him that they asked to be taken to his leader whenever they showed up.

Yet here he was, making his way to the university's student union before even having breakfast. It wasn't natural. Thomas checked his reflection in the glass front of one of the surrounding lecture theatres, trying to make sure he'd been sufficiently awake this morning to remember things like trousers. He had, thankfully, as well as a dark t-shirt, while the unruly mess of his nearly black hair was at least nothing new. It was just as well that his features counted as quite good looking, really, because with that hair, they had a lot to make up for.

Thomas yawned and kept going. He was awake this morning partly because he had agreed to meet his girlfriend Nicola for breakfast, and partly from simple excitement. He had been waiting for the crisp vellum envelope that even now sat in his hand. It was very different than the majority of post that showed up at his student house, addressed to the "occpier," demanding money from people Thomas had never heard of, or suggesting to all and sundry that Abdul's Curry House on the high street wasn't nearly as bad as the health inspectors had made out. This one was actually addressed to him, for one thing.

Thomas knew who it was from, too. Murchall and Grey,

with whom he'd had an interview just last week. They were consultants. They were the consultants' consultants. They were consultants of such quality in fact, that even after extensive research,
Thomas still couldn't work out exactly what it was they consul-
ted *on*. He'd gotten through the interview on charm, a lot of half-
learned business jargon, and by disguising the fact that until last
week "blue sky thinking" would have meant working with the
window open to Thomas. Oh, and it helped that people generally
liked him, for some reason.

Thomas had opened the envelope at home, and had
spent at least the next five minutes dancing around the kitchen as
quietly as he could so as not to wake his housemates. They
didn't believe in the existence of mornings either. Now, he was
bringing it along to show Nicola as final proof that, after three
years of medievalism, it actually *was* possible to get a job in the
real world. Ah, the real world. Thomas had always hated that
phrase. As though people's hands somehow passed through the
tables at university, and they had to be careful not to disappear
mid-lecture. Of course, with some of his more extended lectures,
Thomas had sometimes wished he could.

It was at about that point that Thomas looked round and
saw the pair of figures by the union, though it was hard to see
how he had ever missed the man, given that he looked like he
had only taken to lurking in alleys after his professional wrest-
ling career had fallen through. The other figure was on the
ground, lying very still.

Probably passed out drunk, Thomas thought to himself.
It seemed like the logical assumption, given the vigour with
which everyone seemed to be celebrating at the moment. He
knew that he really ought to go over and check, of course. Except the big man in the odd coat was very big indeed, come to
think of it, and he also seemed to be staring at Thomas now. It
wasn't a hostile stare, exactly. It was more simply curious, as
though endeavouring to calculate exactly how long it would take
to beat Thomas to a pulp.

Probably not very long at all.

It was just as well then, that there wasn't anything to

worry about. Just the inevitable aftermath of celebrations by Nether Wrexford's student body, involving that classic combination of beer and more beer. Possibly with occasional traffic cones thrown in at that stage of the evening when that kind of thing started to make sense. It wasn't something that Thomas needed to get involved in. In fact, getting involved would probably only make things worse. Not that there was anything going on to get worse, Thomas reminded himself quickly, looking away as the big guy's glare intensified.

Thomas focussed on his letter instead as he started to head into the student union, savouring it. Well, savouring ninety percent of it. The job offer was great. The job offer was amazing. It was just one small phrase at the end that was causing him problems. The words *immediate relocation to London* stood out like... well, like the big man who had been staring at Thomas just a minute ago.

Had he done the right thing there? A spark of recognition took the image of the woman on the ground, flipped it the right way up, and put it behind a lectern in a crowded classroom. Dr Peters certainly looked very different when she was collapsed on the floor rather than droning on about *The Song of Roland.* Recognising her, however, practically demanded that Thomas should go back to check that she was all right, gigantic men notwithstanding. But then, part of Thomas argued, weren't lecturers entitled to have heavy nights out too? Presumably even medievalists got to have lives, despite their best efforts to the contrary. And would she *want* one of her students recognising her like that? Wouldn't Thomas going back simply be monumentally embarrassing for everyone concerned?

Thomas' indecision didn't last long. He stepped into the union, putting what he'd seen behind him as well as putting a nice, thick wall between him and the big guy out there. Whatever had just happened wasn't his business. His business lay in the student union bar, where he was due to have whatever components of a Full English could make it past his vegetarian girlfriend, talk over the end of exams with her, and then do the one thing his mail pretty much guaranteed he would have to do at some point.

Thomas had to break up with her.

Grave looked from the cooling body of Elizabeth Peters to the back of the retreating figure, took half a step forward, and then shook his head. "One thing at a time. That's the way."

That *was* the way. None of this modern, slapdash nonsense. In Grave's day, you did a job and you did it well. You didn't get distracted. You didn't go running off after someone while you still had a corpse to deal with. That would be unprofessional, not that he did much running if he could avoid it. Grave hated it when people made him run. He'd found out a long time ago that it was hard to be menacing if you arrived everywhere out of breath.

"These days, of course," he said absently, returning his attention to the corpse, "no one appreciates it if you try and do something like this properly. It's all running around, trying to get things done in a hurry. Used to be, they sent me out for the difficult jobs. Now, it's just hunting you and yours. Where's the challenge in that? I'll tell you, it hasn't been the same since the War."

Naturally, he didn't get much of a response. Sighing, Grave knelt down beside Elizabeth Peters' body. He put his hand near the mouth of the corpse letting something golden and faintly sticky curl around his hand in a cloud. Everything that made Elizabeth Peters something other than human. Grave dug a bottle out of his coat, coaxed the golden essence into it, and then stowed it away once more.

"Of course, you wouldn't know much about the War, would you? None of your lot do. Hardly your fault if it suddenly turns out you're a threat." He reached out with surprising gentleness to close the corpse's eyes. "Still, there it is. Can't be helped."

It occurred to Grave that he hadn't crossed Elizabeth Peters off his list. He started to hunt for it in the pockets of his coat, finally finding it again tangled up with a yellow ribbon and some wire wool. It took longer to find something to write with, and eventually he had to settle for a stub of green crayon, almost worn away to nothing. He pressed the list up against the wall, drawing a careful line through the dead woman's name.

He took a moment to stare at the other two names. The first read Peony Richelle, or was it Penny? Between the crumpled paper and the spider-scrawl of his handwriting, it was hard to tell. Not that one then. The other one was at least a man. Grave raised an eyebrow and looked over to the corpse.

"Did he look like an Isagawa Tagetsu to you? He didn't to me." Grave shoved the paper back into his pocket harder than was strictly necessary. "Typical. She gives me a list, and it isn't even complete. I mean, it's not like I didn't expect it, you get used to it after a while, but even so…"

Grave shook his head and gave a great huff of breath that dislodged at least one piece of sandwich from his beard. "They've got me talking to the corpse now. Only one step away from talking to yourself, and we all know where that leads."

Not that Grave had anything against talking to corpses per se. Some of the zombies he'd met over the years had been down-right chatty, which was fine if you kept them off the subject of brains. He'd even made the mistake once of letting a couple of them take him out for a drink in Haiti. Grave wondered if they still told the stories about that one. But that was different. He'd done his job. Elizabeth Peters wouldn't be coming back.

"Time to be getting home," Grave muttered, and knelt by the corpse. He hefted it with no more effort than it might take to lift a child, slinging it casually over his left shoulder. With his free hand he reached under his shirt, pulling out a pendant of dulled gold worked into a design that would either have made M.C. Escher proud or given him a slight headache. Parts of it seemed to pass through other parts, while the whole seemed to twist into new shapes the longer it was watched. There was no fumbling around looking for *this*.

"This," Grave said to his burden, "is our ticket out of here."

He moved with the pendant, watching it closely as he passed near different spots on the wall. All the time, it glowed very faintly with a light that didn't waver. Grave's brow creased. He held the pendant up, examining it in much the same way that a stockbroker talked into an orienteering team-building exercise might examine a compass. He gave the thing an experimental flick with his little finger, setting it spinning. Nothing much seemed to change. Grave stood there for a moment or two longer, considering.

Finally, and with a certain amount of embarrassed shuffling, he turned to face the alley's other side.

At once the glow was stronger. Grave walked with the thing, staying close to the walls, watching the light as it grew from glow worm softness to something that made his eyes water. Selecting a patch of wall, Grave reached out and gave it a sharp tap with the pendant. There was nothing but the dull thunk of gold on brickwork. Grave selected a spot just to the left, trying again.

This time there was no answering tap. Instead, the brickwork seemed to ripple for a moment, allowing Grave's hand to pass through it, pendant and all. There was the sound of happy, tinkling fairy bells, and a bright burst of rainbow light that swiftly resolved itself into the shape of a door. It was about the height of a normal human. Of course, since Grave was quite emphatically not the height of a normal human, that meant it only came up to his chin.

"Bloody special effects. It's all about the showy stuff with this lot. Fancy bells and rainbows. Don't think to make the thing the right size, do they?"

Grave glowered at the open portal, as though daring it to stay small. When it did, he cursed again, ducked his head, and stepped through.

Chapter Two

"Do you have any idea how long I've been waiting?"

Siobhan stood up from the bench at the heart of the maze as she spoke, tossing aside the book of poetry she'd been reading. It burst into a cloud of tiny fragments. They resolved themselves into butterflies before heading off in a hundred different directions. Of course, the big lunk ignored the threat, the same way he ignored everything about her.

Not that she wanted him, particularly, Siobhan wasn't that desperate. But she did like to be appreciated. She thought she was worth it. Siobhan knew she had a body that men might kill for, for example, because they occasionally had. Her burgundy hair framed a face of, she thought in all modesty, absolute perfection, and her eyes shimmered with dark promise whenever she remembered to make them. Her mother's Huntsman ought to have been looking at her in awe. Instead, he just looked apologetic.

"Sorry, Princess. I had to get rid of the body."

"What did you do with it?"

"I buried it under the roses. I figured they could do with it. They've been looking very peaky, those roses."

Peaky wasn't the word Siobhan would have chosen for the contents of her mother's rose garden. Even growing in the shadow of a castle that seemed to take the laws of physics simply as guidelines hadn't slowed their growth. They were unnaturally beautiful, semi-sentient, blood hungry and... she had to admit, occasionally useful for keeping things hidden, but never *peaky.* Grave had probably had to fight them off.

Even so, the burial did little to excuse the big bear's lateness. A land full of almost every creature the human imagination could conjure, plus a few they couldn't, and she was stuck with a thug who couldn't do things properly. Of all her mother's hand-me-downs, why did it have to be this one? Siobhan stifled an angry sound, returning her attention to him. He was, of course, still talking.

"...and then there was the maze. You know what that's..."

"I know about the maze," Siobhan snapped. "Why do you think I wanted to meet here?" She looked to a sundial beside the bench. Of course, given where the pair of them were, it wasn't much help. The single shadow grew to a pair as she watched, then disappeared altogether. Even for her, the Maze didn't always behave itself. Siobhan gave an annoyed snort.

"At least tell me that everything went smoothly."

It was easy enough to guess the answer to that. For Siobhan, the clue was in Grave shuffling from foot to foot and inspecting his own shoes like some over-large schoolboy. She sat back down, having heard somewhere that bad news sounded better that way.

"What happened?" Siobhan tried to say it as pleasantly as possible.

"Well, Princess, it's a bit hard to say..."

"You did kill her, didn't you?" Siobhan pinched the bridge of her nose as thoughts of the things that could have gone wrong came to her one by one. "Of course you did. You buried her in the garden, you said. Then what? Did somebody see you? Please tell me nobody saw you, or that you at least dealt with the situation if they did."

The foot shuffling increased in speed, to something that seemed to Siobhan to be rapidly approaching a jig.

"Well... um..." Grave managed. "Not as such."

"We can't afford 'not as such'!" Siobhan began, and realised that she was shouting. Not that there was anything wrong with shouting. Siobhan quite enjoyed shouting, so long as it was her doing it, but this wasn't the time. She forced herself to calm down. What was it her mother kept telling her? Be regal. Act like a princess. That piece of advice always grated, especially when it came in the middle of something fun, like shape shifting a palace servant who'd had the audacity to stain Siobhan's dress. Right now though, it was necessary. Of course, her ideas of acting like a princess didn't always agree with her mother's.

"Grave," she purred, standing, "you do understand that this is very important, don't you?"

"Yes, your highness."

Siobhan gave him a sweet smile, stepping close to the big man. *I'll have to burn these clothes after*, she thought privately. "I'm counting on you, Grave. You and I know that these... things have been running around, but it's better if no one else does, not unless we want another War."

"That's what I'm trying..."

Siobhan put a finger to his lips, cutting him off. "I'm not finished. This has to be done properly, Grave. No one can find out. No one. Especially not the other Courts. Can you imagine what it would be like if those sanctimonious fools from the Court of Light got hold of this? Even the Court of Flowers would be too much, and they hardly care about anything. I need you to do this." She let her hand trail down his cheek. "Now, what did you want to say?"

"There's another one!" The words came out in a rush.

"Another one?"

Grave nodded vigorously, and Siobhan sighed inwardly as he started searching through his pockets. She might be immortal, but that didn't mean she had all day.

"Why don't you just tell me?"

"There's one who isn't on the list. He passed by as I was finishing with the other."

"You're certain?" Siobhan asked.

Grave nodded again. Ignoring the shower of crumbs the movement sent flying from his beard, Siobhan tried to think.

"You said 'he'. You saw him?"

"Yes, Princess."

"But you didn't think to do anything about him?"

"I had to clean up after the first one." There was a hint of anger in the big man's voice. "And he wasn't on the list. It's hardly *my* fault if he's not on the list."

"Then whose fault would it be?" Siobhan asked sweetly. She smiled up at Grave until he took a step back. "I don't suppose you thought to even get a name for him, did you? No, I thought not. Very well then, show me."

Being the daughter of the Queen of the Dreaming Court had some advantages. It was remarkably easy to pluck the image from Grave's mind as he fell into daydream. Siobhan nodded.

"I'll look for him among the dreamers. When I have a location, you can deal with him."

Grave rumbled his assent, but followed it with a slight twitch of an eyebrow.

"What is it?" Siobhan asked.

"Your mother... this *is* what she wants, isn't it? I mean, it's not really normal for me to take orders from someone other than her. Even you, Princess."

Siobhan forced her smile to remain in place. It was easy once you'd had enough practise. "We've been through this. Mother can't be seen to be involved, just in case. But yes, this is absolutely what she wants."

Thomas sat out on the Union's decking, nursing a pint and reflecting that he wasn't nearly as drunk as he probably needed to be for what lay ahead. Though strictly speaking, that might have taken slightly more alcohol than actually existed in the known universe.

Elsewhere in the bar, people were celebrating, despite the early hour. It seemed that finishing exams was having an effect on Wrexford's student body, and on its student bodies, come to that. Thomas momentarily thought about joining in, particularly when a few of the university's netball team showed up, but he could imagine Nicola's reaction to that idea. As girlfriends went, she was a lot of fun, but there were limits.

As if the thought called her into being, she stepped through the doors leading outside from the bar, heading straight for him. She was small and slightly built, with her blonde hair left free around her shoulders, partly covering the slogan for her latest cause that was an inevitable component of any t-shirt she wore. Thomas took his usual moment to appreciate the way her jeans clung to her legs before transferring his gaze to the drink she carried.

"Cranberry juice?"

She smiled, sliding into a chair next to him and giving Thomas the briefest of kisses. "It's full of anti-oxidants. You should try it sometime."

He held up his beer. "It's full of natural plant extracts, well, barley at least. *You* should try it sometime."

Nicola shook her head. "My last exam isn't until later today, remember?"

Actually, Thomas had forgotten. He'd been occupied by other things. Specifically, with how to say what needed to be said next. Thomas needed to explain. Needed to tell her what was happening. He looked into his beer for a moment or two, downed the rest of it, and reached out for Nicola's hand.

"I need to talk to you, Nicci."

Nicola just laughed. "That sound serious." Her lips met his again. "Can it wait until after my exam? I'm at that stage where I've just got revision going round and round in my head until I think it might explode."

"I..." Thomas nodded, knowing it was the only thing to do. "Do you want help studying?"

"I can think of better things for you to do if you want to help me."

Thomas winced as theatrically as he could manage. He could guess what was coming. "What portion of the world needs saving this time?"

"International food aid." Nicola produced a flyer from a pocket. In the fashion of student posters everywhere, it was so fluorescent it was hard to actually make out the words. Then again, maybe he'd just drunk the beer too fast. "It's important, Thomas. There's people out there starving."

"There's a thought. Weren't we supposed to be getting breakfast?"

"Thomas!" Given Nicola's shocked tone, it occurred to Thomas that, what with one thing and another, he probably wasn't at his tactful best. Then again, even his tactful best wasn't always *that* tactful. Nicola pushed the flyer towards him.

"I know you think that this doesn't do any good, but this is important." She said. "I was hoping maybe you'd help hand these out."

"Sure, if you want."

Right then, it seemed like the best way of avoiding trouble. And, truth be told, he didn't have a problem with the latest of Nicola's attempts to save the world. He just doubted that the world's major decision makers would be found in front of the crumbling edifice that was Nether Wrexford's university library, taking leaflets from him. Thomas stretched, and was just contemplating a return to the bar when his phone rang. He took a quick look down at the caller name before sighing and flicking the thing open.

. "Hi, Dad."

His father's baritone voice came back, filled with a cheer that was, to Thomas' ears at least, far too obviously artificial. It was a voice that might have done well in voice-overs. Probably for something big and ambitious that would go horribly wrong just after you bought it.

"Thomas, hey! Just ringing up to congratulate you on finishing. How did you do?"

"Fine, Dad, I did fine." Thomas couldn't keep the flat note from his voice. Maybe it was just the anticipation. For his father to say that he was just ringing up to congratulate him was a bit like a lion telling the antelope that it was just out for a nice walk. You only believed it if you didn't want the chance to run away from what came next.

It didn't take long.

"Look," his father said, "I was thinking, since you're finished, maybe you could come down and stay for a few days. I know Cindy would love to see you again, and it would give you chance to… you know, get things sorted. How about it? A nice break before you have to join the real world."

"Sorry, I can't." Thomas said the words automatically, and his brain raced for a reason. "I'm going to help Nicola…"

"Your girlfriend, right?"

"Yes. Anyway, I'm going to help her study, and then maybe we'll go away for a week, and I'm going to go back and see Mum and Kelly. Maybe we could fix something up for later in the summer."

"That would be good." His father's voice had a different note in it. "You know I don't see much of you…"

"Sorry Dad," Thomas interrupted hurriedly, "that's Nicola now. I've got to go. I'll call you in a couple of days, okay? Bye."

He didn't wait for an answer, but rang off. He wouldn't have thought that it would be possible to sip cranberry juice in a disapproving fashion, but Nicola seemed to manage it.

"What?"

"You're not going to call him back, are you?" Nicola's note of reproach was easy to pick up. Thomas slipped an arm around her.

"What am I supposed to say to him, Nicci? That I don't want to spend time with him and a girlfriend a couple of years older than me? Trust me, you don't know what it was like for my mother when he left."

Nicola leaned into him, resting her head briefly on his shoulder.

"Nice to know there's someone you care about."

"Well, there might be *someone* else." Thomas said it automatically, and hated himself for it even as he said it. After all, he was going to be breaking up with Nicola later, wasn't he? "Look, we really need to talk after your exam."

Nicola nodded. "Sure. You can congratulate me on passing it."

Thomas nodded with more enthusiasm than he felt. "I can't wait."

Chapter Three

The Orchard didn't really deserve the capital letters, Siobhan thought as she wandered through it. Oh, it was impressive enough in its way; row upon row of strange, twisting fruit trees, all bearing the dreams of human dreamers. But what, when you got down to it, was the place but a giant filing system? Would a human say "The Database" with quite that sense of dread? For a tax database, possibly, but not otherwise.

And of course, a simple filing cabinet would have been easier to search. The geography around her mother's castle was always a little uncertain, but still, as far as Siobhan could see in every direction, there was nothing but trees. Billions of dreaming souls, far too many to search by hand.

Idly, Siobhan reached out, plucking something that didn't quite look like an apple from the nearest tree. It was too bulbous, for a start, and no apple was that dead grey. That meant the human wasn't asleep. She could still go in, but it wouldn't be nearly as much fun. Selecting another, brighter, orb instead, Siobhan bit down, tasting the sickly sweet juice of the thing. At once a vision came to her of a handsome young man, engaged in relations with what appeared to be a pair of sisters that would normally have required a visit to a chiropractor afterwards. Young men's dreams could be so... predictable sometimes. Still, Siobhan toyed for a moment with the idea of giving the final push that would have sent her fully into the dreamscape. Perhaps later.

Stowing the rest of the thing away, Siobhan tried to concentrate on the job at hand. There were quicker ways to search if you knew them, and Siobhan did. She knelt, scratching in the earth of The Orchard, tracing neat lines with fingernails that gouged furrows into the soil. The outline of a wing appeared under her touch, then another. A beak followed, leaving something like a child's drawing of a bird in the earth. But it would have been a very strange child indeed who could do what Siobhan did next.

She reached up, only wincing slightly as she plucked out a single red hair, and twisted the thing into the most fragile of loops. Siobhan placed the thing within the outline of her drawing, taking care that it did not stray over one of the lines. A moment later, she spat, the moisture darkening the soil. The whole sat there inert as Siobhan dragged a sharp fingernail over her palm, squeezing out a single drop of blood. As it beaded and fell, she tried to think only of the image that she'd taken from her mother's Huntsman.

The soil shifted. It rose as though some small creature was burrowing through it, but none showed itself. Instead, the earth flowed on its own, forming shapes as Siobhan waited. First legs, then wings, feathers, a beak. Finally a crow stood on the ground, sloughing the last of the soil from its plumage. Around its left leg, a fine band of red stood in contrast to the black of the rest of it. It cawed once, and then took to the air. It circled briefly before setting off in a line over the Orchard.

Siobhan ran to keep up, keeping one eye pinned to the red flash of hair on the crow's leg, while the other kept her from tripping on trailing roots. She flitted deftly through the trees after the bird, trying to guess how far it would take her as she went. There was rarely any real order to the dreams, just a jumbled mess of different things. The ones she wanted could be anywhere.

Anywhere except *there*, that was.

The bird flew towards the edge of the Orchard and on, heading for something Siobhan knew all too well. The cave sat like a carbuncle on an otherwise pristine lawn, looking something like a cross between a burial mound and the entrance to an underground station. A barred gate stood across the entrance, and something spiny and lizard-like slept in front of it. As Siobhan watched, it opened one eye, lazily tracking the progress of her bird.

It had to be a mistake, Siobhan thought. She'd done the spell wrong, or the Hunter had remembered wrong. That had to be it. All the others had been found in the Orchard, with the humans, despite what they were. There was no reason why this one's dreams should be in the place where her mother kept those of the Courts' many inhabitants. Even her mother's dreams were there somewhere, though Siobhan had never looked. She wasn't even sure she'd be allowed to try.

No, this had to be a mistake.

But the bird seemed certain. It flew straight towards the mound, ignoring the lizard-thing as it yawned and stretched, never taking its eyes from the advancing creature. The crow just kept going. Wing beat by wing beat, it headed for the cave, getting closer and…

Slurp!

A tongue like a chameleon's shot out from the lizard thing's mouth, catching the bird in mid-flight. It had time to give a final, forlorn squawk, and then the lizard's jaws closed around it with a crackling, crunching sound. There was only a brief pause before it swallowed the bird, bones and all.

"Fuck," Siobhan swore, even though she'd known it was going to happen. The creature ate trespassers. That was what it did, what it was. Even those times her mother had let her come down here, the thing had looked at her hungrily. Of course, for her mother, it had all but rolled over and played dead. Typical. That wasn't to say that there weren't ways round the beast. If Siobhan had more time, and if she wanted to know that badly, there were definitely ways. They were ways that cost in blood, and sometimes worse, but occasionally that was worth it. Besides, no one said it had to be her blood.

But those ways didn't seem needed, not just yet. For now, it was enough to know where the young man's dreams were kept. If Siobhan was certain of anything, it was that this man was one of them. Whatever he was, with dreams here, of all places, he definitely wasn't human. Grave had done his job well, for once.

⁓⌣⌣⌐

Grave smiled. He had done his job well, even if he did say so himself. Slowly, carefully, he levered the iron jaws apart until they clicked into place. It was the last act of a sequence that he'd followed with all the precision of a watchmaker, though probably no watchmaker had ever produced something with quite so many sharp edges. There were springs and cogwheels, tiny darts and swinging blades, enough to fill most of the interior of the ruined barn that he called his workshop.

Ruined probably wasn't quite the right word for it. Oh, it had lost most of the roof, not to mention a good deal of one wall, but they were things that could easily have been fixed after the War. The real problem was the insubstantiality. Every wall, every board, every bale of hay seemed slightly see-through, and would barely support the weight of anything real. It was enough to keep out rain but not much more. The first owner had given up on the place, but Grave liked it. It gave him a place in which to experiment.

Time to see if his theory worked.

Carefully, Grave extracted an egg and cress sandwich from his pocket. Even more carefully, and it is hard to overestimate the delicacy with which the big man did it, he eased the sandwich onto a patch of floor that looked almost exactly the same as every other patch of floor. The whole procedure might have put an intelligent observer in mind of the caution normally involved with people who handle nuclear triggers for a living. Presumably, therefore, the last thing that observer would attempt, would be to attempt to eat any portion of the sandwich concerned.

Thankfully, Grave thought, the rats probably wouldn't be quite that clever. Probably. Grave edged away from the sandwich, placing his feet in a very specific pattern until he reached the door to the barn. He slipped outside. In the distance, away across fields of green, gold, and other less common colours, Grave could just make out the shape of the Queen's castle. That distance had been one thing Erithnae had insisted on, after a couple of his more interesting accidents. Idly, Grave wondered if they'd ever found all of the servants who'd wandered into his old workshop while Grave had been out. Probably not.

Thoughts of the Queen led almost automatically to thoughts of her daughter though, and that made his hands clench. She was so... *patronising* about his job. Didn't appreciate the fine detail at all. It didn't help that every time Grave talked to her, every time he thought that this time he might say something about the way she spoke to him, Grave found himself clamming up like a teenager with his first crush. Given that he hadn't been a teenager of any sort for considerably longer than most countries had been around, and that the only things he'd ever been known to crush were skulls, it was embarrassing. An annoyed sound escaped from him.

Of course, Grave knew he shouldn't be thinking about royalty if he wanted to relax. That, after all, was what this was about. You had to have a hobby in a job like Grave's, if you wanted to stay sane. At least that was what it had said in a magazine he'd found once in a dentist's surgery. Grave couldn't quite remember why he'd been there, but the faded cover of the magazine was as clear in Grave's mind as when he'd first read it.

"Is YOUR job taking over your life?" the article had asked, in the sort of tone that made it clear that it already knew the answer. After taking a fraction of a second to decide that yes, it probably was, Grave had set to the task of working out what his hobby ought to be. Obviously, it needed to be something that he'd stick with, something that would relax him nicely and that he'd enjoy. It had taken another week and one failed attempt to learn the piano, to decide that hunting was really the only one thing he was interested in, and that he was perfectly happy with that fact. Perhaps if Grave had realised it sooner things wouldn't have ended quite so... violently for the piano tutor. But if you were going to leave him alone around a lot of piano wire, you had to expect a house full of snares and nooses, didn't you?

Grave drummed his fingers as he waited, trying to recall why he'd been in the dentist's. It would bother him all day if he didn't. It hadn't been for the dentist. Grave was sure that he would have remembered that. It was minutes before he finally snapped his fingers.

"The vampire with the root canal!"

Now that had been a fun job. Not like this current nonsense.

His thoughts were interrupted by a very definite *snap!* from inside. Grave grinned and rushed to see the results of his handiwork. There, sure enough, the central steel trap had been sprung. But it was empty! There was no sign of mangled rodent, no prey at all, not even the sandwich!

Grave's eyes darted round the barn, finally settling on a flash of movement in one corner where a very small white rat was dragging what looked very much like the missing sandwich. And it was dragging it through a particularly insubstantial bale of hay.

"Come back here with that!" Grave yelled, and dove forward.

The problem with such leaps of course, is that, should you realise halfway through that they're a really bad idea, they're quite hard to stop.

It's likely that our intelligent observer wouldn't have seen what happened next. Being, after all, an intelligent observer, they would have had the sense not to go back into the barn in the first place. What they would have *heard* therefore is best described as *Snap! Whirr! Slash!* "Aargh!" *Whoosh!* "Come here you little bugger!" *SNAP!*

"Got you!" Grave yelled in triumph, emerging through the doorway to the barn. In one hand he held the soggy remains of the sandwich, while in the other he held the twisting, scrambling form of the rat. That he was a mess of scratches and small cuts, and that there were also the remains of quite a large steel trap attached to his left ankle, appeared to have largely escaped Grave's attention.

Dropping the sandwich, Grave held up the rat by its tail.

"Now, how did you do that?"

Grave was so busy examining it that for a long moment he didn't spot the butterfly flitting around his head. When its frantic motions finally caught his eye, Grave paused, watching the thing's flight as it fluttered closer. It landed, inevitably, on his nose. The words *come to me* sprang unbidden into his brain in Siobhan's voice, along with the obligatory tinkly fairy sound that even the makers of mobile phone ring tones might have found annoying after a while. Grave gave a snort as the butterfly took off, heading towards the Orchard.

"So much for my time off."

Grave gave the rat another long look before shoving it into a spare pocket. He'd have to find time to examine it later.

Grave turned smartly, set off after the butterfly, and promptly fell over.

Forcing himself to his feet, he pulled the trap off his leg with a curse, and set off after the thing again.

Chapter Four

"Siobhan, what are you doing?"

Mothers reserve a special tone of voice for occasions such as this. It's one part assurance that they know what's going on anyway, so you might as well own up, one part drill sergeant, to remind you of the consequences if you don't, and just the tiniest smidgeon of kindness, to lull you into a false sense that you're about to be forgiven, rather than grounded for most of the rest of eternity. At some point, just about every child in existence has been on the receiving end of that tone, and it's nearly guaranteed to produce an overwhelming sense of guilt.

Siobhan didn't even wince. That was partly because she'd been on the receiving end of it so many times it hardly made an impression anymore, and partly because she had some power of her own. Mostly though, it was that Siobhan was the sort of person who could, if necessary, stand quite happily in the middle of a living room reduced to wreckage by a whirling party, wearing nothing but the smudged remains of her makeup and *still* manage to look completely innocent. Compared with that, this was easy.

"Hello Mother."

Siobhan managed her sweetest, most guileless smile as she turned to face her mother's approach. It did a good job of masking her irritation. Erithnae looked perfect as usual, not a dark hair out of place, her velvet gown trailing elegantly behind her as she strolled through the Orchard. She was beautiful in a way that was somehow more refined and graceful than anything Siobhan could be bothered to try. To Siobhan, it was entirely the worst part of virtual immortality that her mother looked like her more beautiful sister, and would for most of the rest of eternity.

Of course, Erithnae, Queen of the Dreaming Court, couldn't just wander around unaccompanied. Six grey, wispy creatures floated alongside her, looking like the world's drabbest ghosts.

"I see you've brought your Figments with you."

Siobhan bobbed in a way that wasn't quite a curtsey. Her mother shrugged.

"You know they only follow me if I try to leave them. Now, don't change the subject. You did something that woke up Jasper..."

Siobhan's eyebrow twitched. "You gave that scaly monstrosity a name?"

"He's sweet," her mother countered, "very affectionate. Now, darling, what have I told you about trying to get into the cave?"

"I'm not a child, mother..."

"What did I tell you, sweetheart?" her mother demanded, and just for a moment, there was a sharper edge to her tone. In that moment, it was the Queen talking, and not just Siobhan's mother.

"That I mustn't go in there without asking."

Siobhan said the words by rote. Her gaze darted over the Figments accompanying her mother. In theory, they were emotionless blanks until changed to play a part, but she could have sworn one of them was struggling not to snigger. Shooting the thing a dark look, she continued quickly.

"I didn't actually go in there, mother. I was bored, so I started to look for dreams, and I was thinking about Grandfather while I did it, so maybe that threw things off..." Siobhan tailed off deliberately. The trick with explanations, she'd learned a long time ago, was to leave just enough gaps for her mother to fill in what she wanted to hear. Mentioning the former king was a good move too. The Dreaming Queen was nothing if not a total daddy's girl.

Sure enough, just the mention of him was enough to soften her expression a touch. "All right then, darling, but I wish you would be more careful." She looked Siobhan up and down. "And I'm sure we talked about you at least trying to dress a little more elegantly. I'll have the servants run up something, if you…" She gave Siobhan a second look, and her eyes narrowed. Siobhan could guess what was coming next. Even so, she waited until her mother sighed and stuck out her hand.

"Hand it over."

Siobhan knew better than to try denial. Instead, she plucked out the dream she'd been saving and set it down in her mother's palm. It was a perfect sphere again, though it still danced with colour. Erithnae studied it carefully for a moment before taking a single, dainty bite. Her nose wrinkled a moment later.

"Really, darling, I'd have thought you'd have more taste."

Siobhan shrugged. "Like I said, mother, I was bored."

"And you never thought for a moment how it might look, my daughter gallivanting around in a human's dreams, especially this sort of dream."

Siobhan didn't answer. There didn't seem to be much point. Besides, there was always the chance that she'd say something that she'd regret, probably right around the time her mother decided to punish her. A mother capable of sending you your worst nightmares was about as good a reason as there was to play by her rules. *Or at least,* Siobhan thought, *not to get caught.*

Her mother didn't seem to mind Siobhan's silence. Instead, she snapped her fingers at one of the floating grey Figments that accompanied her. At once it began to stretch and shift, acquiring form and colour as the grey smokiness of its form flowed inward. It was less than a second before a handsome young man stood in the thing's place.

"If you want to have that sort of fun," Erithnae said, fixing Siobhan with a smile that wasn't entirely motherly, "there are plenty of Figments around, sweetheart. Leave the humans to their dreams. After all, there's the Treaty to think of."

"The War ended years ago, mother," Siobhan found herself

replying.

"But the Treaty did not. Now, are you going to do as you're told for once, darling, or do I need to make sure of it?"

Siobhan forced her hands to keep from clenching and managed to produce a crisp curtsey, bowing her head as she did so. "As you command, my Queen."

She felt the brush of her mother's fingertips on her cheek for the briefest of moments, but didn't look up. Siobhan heard her sigh.

"As you wish, dear. I'll leave the young man. Remember to change him back once you're done playing."

Siobhan waited until the sound of her mother's footsteps receded before she looked up. The transformed Figment was waiting passively.

"Oh, go away," Siobhan snapped, and turned, stalking off.

Grave followed the butterfly as far as the centre of the Maze, trailing a step behind it the whole time. On the way there, it had led him through the gardens, past the roses where he'd disposed of Elizabeth Peter's corpse. The roses had seemed to sway in the wind as he passed, though Grave knew as well as anyone that they were just tracking the warmth of his blood. There wasn't any sign among the flowerbeds that the body had ever been there. But then, you never found small animals there either.

Finally, back by the sundial, the thing alighted on the arm of the bench. It creaked under his weight as Grave sat down, but he didn't feel like standing up to wait. Knowing Siobhan, she'd keep him waiting. She complained the moment he was a minute late, but actually bother turning up on time... Grave stretched out on the bench, settling in for a long wait. As if sharing the thought, the butterfly fluttered its wings, sunning itself.

Luckily though, Grave only had to wait a minute before Siobhan came striding through the arch that led to the Maze's centre.

"Get up. You look like a tramp, laid out on the bench like

that."

Reluctantly, Grave struggled to his feet. While he was doing it, the butterfly drifted over to its mistress, settling on the palm of her outstretched hand. Grave saw her start to close her fingers, but then stop. Bringing the insect up to face level Siobhan blew on it and it took off. It circled her once before settling on the sundial, where it promptly turned into a small banana. Grave saw Siobhan roll her eyes.

"You were supposed to fly away, you stupid thing." She returned Grave's stare evenly. "What? I can like butterflies, can't I?"

Grave shrugged. "As you wish, Princess."

"It was pretty, and it was useful. Neither of which can be said for you at the moment."

"Your mother has always found my efforts sufficient."

The words sounded sulky as they came out. Perhaps he shouldn't have said it, but Grave wasn't in the mood for listening to Siobhan whinge. His leg was still aching from the bite of the steel trap. Even for him, it would take an hour or two to recover. Not, Grave imagined, that Siobhan would wait that long before sending him off on whatever she wanted done next.

"I'm not my mother," Siobhan reminded him, as though he needed reminding. "But I am here on her behalf. You wouldn't want me to tell her that you weren't being helpful, would you?"

Grave thought about that, and about Erithnae's likely reaction. "I wait only to hear your instructions, Princess."

"Of course you do. You remember the half-breed you passed earlier?"

Grave nodded.

"Good. I want you to kill him. He's as much of a threat as the others. I don't have a dream for you on this one, but I'm sure you can track him down. You did well enough with the rest."

"Of course, Princess." Grave felt around in his pockets, succeeding in locating a chewed biro after a few seconds. Another search yielded a worn receipt on which to write. "Do you have a name for me?"

"Not yet, though I suppose… yes, that might work. I just need a good rhyme…"

Siobhan reached inside a fold of her dress, and Grave saw her remove a small hand-mirror. She clouded it with her breath, and an image of the man he was to hunt filled it. Slowly, Siobhan began to speak.

"Mirror, mirror, in my hand, tell me now what I demand. Tell me now this person's name, as you sit within your frame."

There was a brief pause before a high, bright voice filled the air.

"Call that a summoning verse?" it demanded "I mean, yes, the rhymes were there, though even they were pretty predictable, but where's the alliteration, the subtlety, the style?"

Grave saw Siobhan's eyes narrow. "I have a better question," she purred. "Where's a nice solid object I can break you on?"

"You wouldn't dare!" the other voice replied, and by now Grave had guessed its source. "That's seven years bad luck, that is."

"It's worse luck for you."

There was a pause, filled with the silence of a mirror considering its future very carefully indeed. When the voice returned, there was an obsequious edge to it.

"On the other hand," it said, "the customer *is* always right. And the meter was definitely there. Quite a good rhyme between name and frame too, I thought. Sometimes, the old ones are the best, after all."

"The *name*," Siobhan demanded, and even Grave felt like taking a step back.

"What? Oh, yes. Thomas. Thomas Grey, or could that be Greet. Hang on, I can't read my own writing here. No, it's Greene. Definitely Greene."

"Thank you. Now," and with that word Siobhan gave a wicked smile, "tell me; who's the…"

"Please!" The mirror pleaded. "Don't ask me that one. Anything but that one!"

"Who's the fairest of them all?" Siobhan finished. Grave

saw the mirror cloud over.

"You have a mirror and you've asked it *that?*" Grave was surprised that even Siobhan would waste a resource like that. Magic mirrors weren't easy to come by, and if there was one guaranteed way of ruining all but the best of them, that was it. It was practically the first thing the manuals told you not to do, after the long bit explaining how you didn't actually own the mirror in any real sense and that it wasn't their fault if the things a.) didn't work, b.) blew up, or c.) spent their time plotting for your goody two-shoes stepdaughter to overthrow you.

Siobhan just smiled before tossing the thing down next to the banana.

"You know what they're like for blabbing to anyone who asks them a question. This way, it'll spend the next who knows how long trying to calculate the relative attractiveness of everyone in the known Universe. I don't have to break it, so no bad luck. Who knows, maybe eventually it will finish, and I can have it back. Though, honestly, I've been thinking of upgrading."

Grave looked to where the former butterfly sat beside the mirror, as bendy and yellow as the most stringent EU regulation might require. "You won't try to pick it up, will you, Princess?"

Siobhan treated him to a sweet smile. "Oh no, Grave. I'm sure someone will do it for me if I ask. Now, shouldn't you be running along? You've got someone to kill."

Grave looked from Siobhan to the banana, came to his own conclusions about who she planned on ordering to fetch the thing, and made a hurried bow. "At once, Princess."

If popular songs were to be believed, there were at least fifty ways to leave your lover. Probably more. *So why* Thomas asked himself in the courtyard outside the university's student union *can't I think of a single one that will work here?*

He'd been chewing the issue over for hours, ever since meeting Nicola in the bar, and as far as he could see it was still the only real option. Nicola wouldn't want to follow him down to London, and he couldn't afford to give up a chance like the one Murchall and Grey were offering him.

It wouldn't even be fair to ask her, not really. Nicola had her own dreams. They probably involved lobbying, fundraising, and eventual world domination on behalf of cute little animals, but they were dreams nonetheless. She'd probably just say no, but what if see didn't? The idea of her throwing that away just to follow him seemed to Thomas like far too much to be respons- ible for.

Thomas had thought about phoning her, or texting her, or doing any one of the dozen other things that people did to dump one another without having to get close enough to the person be- ing dumped to risk being hit with whatever was close to hand. He'd thought about it most of the morning, and put it off, finally thinking about it some more as he walked to the one place Nicola was guaranteed to be.

A hundred yards away, lecture theatre doors opened to re- lease a spill of students, chattering about how easy the exam had been, or how hard. A few looked worryingly like they'd just woken up from sleeping through most of it, blinking in the sun- light. It wasn't difficult for Thomas to pick Nicola out of the swarm, and she spotted him in almost the same breath. *This is it,* Thomas thought as she rushed forward, *I've just got to tell her straight, that's the...*

"Mmphf" he gasped as Nicola caught him up in a kiss that was all enthusiasm. Well... enthusiasm and about half a tube of "Deep Passion" red lipstick, anyway. When she pulled back, Thomas tried to remember to breathe.

"Guess how I did!" Nicola bubbled before Thomas man- aged to get any coherent words together.

"Haven't a clue. Look... Nicola..."

"It went great, of course!" She had her arm through his be- fore Thomas could say no, half dragging him in the direction of the Union. "I was really worried going into it. I did some final revision last night, and I just couldn't seem to concentrate, but today it just all seemed to come out perfectly."

"That's great." Thomas found himself saying, trying to

work out how to phrase what came next. "Nicola, I've got something..."

"You can tell me while we celebrate. Finally, that's the last exam out of the way. Maybe you and me can..."

"I want to break up."

They jarred to a halt, and Nicola pulled away from him, looking up at Thomas with wide eyes. "What?"

"Well, I don't *want* to break up. Of course I don't. I just think we should."

"You want to what?"

Nicola blinked a few times, her mouth opening and closing with the shock. It was an expression that put Thomas in mind of a stunned goldfish. *A very good-looking one that he obviously cared about a lot*, Thomas added mentally. Taking a breath, he did his best to explain.

"You know it can never work, Nicci. I mean, we're both finishing here, and you'll have your own life, and I've just been offered this job down in London..."

"So you thought you'd just chuck me? For a job?"

There was an edge to Nicola's voice that said that this particular goldfish had just remembered it was at least distantly related to the piranha, and was willing to give things its best shot. Thomas decided it was a good idea to have another go at explaining.

"Not just any job. This is... well, it's important."

"And I'm not?"

Nicola turned away from him and Thomas winced. She was going to cry, as surely as if some poor baby bird had died in front of her. Thomas reached out to comfort her before he remembered two things. Firstly, he was supposed to be breaking up with Nicola, and so probably shouldn't be the one comforting her over the break-up. It was practically a rule, or something.

More importantly, Nicola didn't get tearful when baby birds died. She got angry.

"Ow!"

Thomas' hand flew to his suddenly burning cheek. Nicola was already pulling back for another slap.

"That's for dumping me. And that's for doing it for some poxy job. And this is for telling me straight after my exams have finished."

Somehow, Thomas succeeded in catching hold of her arms. Nicola glared at him before trying to pull free.

"Nicci, stop it!" Thomas didn't really expect the words to have much of an effect, but she went still. Her face seemed utterly slack and empty of emotion. *It's probably the shock of it sinking in,* Thomas thought.

"Look, Nicci, I don't want to fight."

"Okay." Her voice was flat as she answered.

"Okay?"

Nicola nodded, so he let go of her before continuing.

"I know this is all sudden, and I feel totally horrible for doing it, but can't you see it's the right thing to do?"

Nicola nodded again, though her expression didn't change.

"Look, I'm sorry, and I'm really sorry for telling you like this. I'll go away. You just, I don't know, go to the bar and at least *try* to enjoy finishing. I'll ring you later. Ok?"

"Ok."

Thomas nodded before turning away. He was glad that was sorted out, at least.

Chapter Five

Grave found himself at the university for the second time that day, moving through the throng of students and following his nose in search of his new target. Thanks to his nature, humans tended not to notice him, but he had added a little insurance in the form of a broom and rubbish bin, both stolen from a store cupboard where a university porter had started to demand what Grave was doing there before Grave hit him hard enough to send him to sleep for some time to come.

To fit the disguise, Grave started sweeping as he went along. If there was one thing most people would pay even less attention to than someone like Grave, it was a man cleaning up after them. Eyes slipped off of him even quicker than usual, and students stepped round Grave without even thinking about it. When one girl dropped a can on the floor, Grave stared at her until she picked the thing up and threw it in the nearest litterbin. She looked quite puzzled about why she'd done it.

Finally, a whiff of not-quite cinnamon scent carried across the breeze. Grave's head snapped round, trying to track the smell, testing the air like an oversized bloodhound. Locking onto it, Grave followed to the front of the student union building, and then on, around to its rear, where a couple of tree-lined playing fields stretched away towards the sort of misshapen lump of a building that could really only be a leisure centre. A tree-lined path led between them, and at its head sat a cluster of bottle banks.

Grave's eyes found Thomas Greene a second later, and even in the shadow of one of the trees it was impossible to mistake him. He sat leaning against one of the trunks, staring out across the field.

Grave looked the place over with practised casualness, glancing up from behind his broom as he swept. It wasn't the best place to work, too much chance of being spotted, but it would have to do. If Siobhan wanted things done in a hurry, then she'd just have to accept that there wasn't time to do them perfectly. Grave would wait for a moment when no one was walking past, strike, and then try and get the body back through one of the trees before anyone showed up. People *probably* wouldn't notice him, and nobody would believe them even if someone did.

Grave crept forward, past the bottle banks. Absent-mindedly, he took an empty green bottle from one of his pockets and dropped it in as he passed. When a moment's further searching didn't produce a knife, his hands tightened around the broom. He stalked in a wide arc, taking care to keep the tree between him and the target. Thomas Greene had spotted him before, and Grave didn't want to give him a chance to run. Grave hated it when they ran. Strike hard and sure, that was the way. He pressed himself against the next tree along, silently edging round it, trying to ignore the fact that the tree creaked ominously under his weight.

All Grave had to do was pick his moment.

"Of all the moments to pick!" Cranberry juice went flying as Nicola brought her hand down, spilling across the bar like a healthy purple oil slick.

"That will be one pound fifty," the stud-bedecked student working behind the bar said in the flat voice of someone who had just caught the edge of a spray of drink.

"What? Oh, I'm sorry." Nicola handed him the money automatically, as her brain tried to sort through what had happened, staring at the drink as though it could provide her with answers. She'd come out of her exam, and Thomas had been there. He'd broken up with her, and then...

And then she'd come in here for a celebratory drink like nothing had happened. It didn't make sense. In fact, the more she thought about it, the less sense it made, until Nicola could feel the first throbbings of a headache.

Why had she just let Thomas walk away like that? At the very least she should have demanded a better explanation. That or hit him a lot harder. Nicola's hands flexed in anger at the thought, and she caught sight of the bartending student flinching away. Nicola picked up her drink, and was halfway to a table before she realised that she was ignoring what Thomas had done again. Even as she thought it, there was a little voice in the back of her mind telling her that everything would be so much easier if she just forgot the whole thing and got on with her day.

Nicola was used to suggestions like that. She heard enough of them. Between other students ignoring her leaflets, the petitions that languished with just her own name written hopefully at the top, and the days spent planning what turned out to be remarkably undemonstrative demonstrations, Nicola wouldn't have been able to keep going without what she liked to think of as a certain amount of determination. That other people, her parents included, preferred to call it utter bloody mindedness didn't matter.

Pinching the bridge of her nose against the oncoming headache, Nicola tried to concentrate. Silently, she ran through the events of the minutes after her exam again, trying to work out why so much of her still wanted to ignore them. Once Nicola had an answer, she tried the whole thing again, because she couldn't quite believe it. Only once Nicola was certain did she finally allow herself to admit it. Somehow, and she didn't have the faintest idea how, Thomas had done something to her head.

Despite appearances, Nicola wasn't someone who had a lot of time for the supernatural, the paranormal, or even the particularly strange. Oh, she knew she *seemed* like the type. If you happened to be a petite blond woman dressed in fair-trade clothes and trying to save as much of the world as you could reach, then people inevitably seemed to assume that your hobbies included chanting, meditation and trying to harness the universal energy of something faintly unpronounceable. A couple of Nicola's former boyfriends had made exactly that mistake, and one had only given up his attempts to try out alternative therapies on her once Nicola threatened to apply his acupuncture needles in ways they hadn't remotely been intended for.

Instead Nicola tended to think of that sort of thing as rather silly, a distraction from the business of actually helping people. The trouble was, she was also having a hard time coming up with a good answer that didn't involve it. Thomas was persuasive, but this… words like *hypnosis, sublimination* and *suggestibility* all vied for attention in her mind before being replaced by four that seemed infinitely better suited to the occasion.

"That utter, utter bastard."

Nicola finished the remains of her drink in one go, slammed it back down on the table and set off to look for Thomas. How *dare* he do something like that to her? Especially just after dumping her with no warning whatsoever. He was going to be sorry, just as soon as she found him.

There are probably those who wouldn't have thought the sight of Nicola at this moment particularly scary. They would have been wrong. It probably serves as an indicator of Nicola's general mood that when a rugby player twice her size, slightly drunk and trying to get drunker, stepped into her path, he took one look at Nicola's expression and stepped very hastily out of the way.

Now, Nicola thought, *where will he be?* She threw a quick glance towards the library and laughed. There was no chance of that. Thomas had barely gone in before his exams. He might have gone home, of course, but Nicola didn't think it was likely. Instead, she headed the other way, out towards the sports centre. It took only a moment to spot him, sitting underneath one of the trees. Briefly, Nicola's mood lightened at the thought that Thomas only did that when there was something getting to him. It seemed that he hadn't been entirely unaffected after all.

On the other hand, Nicola thought, her expression harden-

ing again, *it didn't stop him from chucking me, or from doing...
whatever it was... to my head.*

There was no one else around, which was good. Telling the
whole world how worthless Thomas was could wait until after
Nicola had had a chance to explain that to him personally.
Without a pause, Nicola strode over towards him, her eyes
drilling into his sitting form. She was so busy working up a
really good furious stare that she didn't even glance at any of the
other trees. Of course, even if Nicola had been scanning each of
the trees in turn, she probably wouldn't have noticed much out of
the ordinary.

She stopped a few feet in front of Thomas, enjoying the
sight of him struggling to scramble to his feet. Thomas' expression alone, somewhere between guilt and a mildly stunned baby
chick, was worth following him for. Nicola took a step forward,
only deciding against hitting Thomas again after deciding that
shouting at him might be more fun, at least to start. She could always try hitting him afterwards, if it didn't work.

"You, Thomas Greene, are a selfish, useless, obnoxious
pig! I don't know what you did to me, but you're going to undo
it *right now!*"

As opening salvoes went, it wasn't bad. Unfortunately, it
didn't get much of an answer, because Grave chose that moment
in which to pounce.

Thomas caught the blur of movement an instant before the crack
of wood against wood came to him. He stepped back, trying to
work out what on earth had happened. It wasn't hard to work
out. A large, hairy, angry man stood by the spot where he'd been
sitting until a moment ago, holding slightly less than half a
splintered broom in one massive hand.

"Now you've gone and done it," the big man grumbled.
"I'll never be able to give this back now."

Even as he spoke the words, a flash of recognition dawned
on Thomas.

"You… you were in that alley yesterday, staring at me."

The big man shrugged. "Might have been."

"What are you, some sort of stalker?"

That drew a grin from the big man, if you could call the sudden flash of teeth somewhere within the beard a grin. "That's me, right enough. Stalking, tracking, hunting. You name it, I've done it. Now, hold still, would you?"

There are only a very small number of situations where it is a good idea to hold still when someone asks you to, and this, Thomas guessed, almost certainly wasn't one of them. He stepped back as the half broken broom slashed through the space where he'd been standing. Thomas circled, trying to find room to run away, but the big man moved with him until Thomas found himself backed up against the tree again.

"Now look," Thomas tried, flashing a smile, "can't we talk about this?"

"No." The other man raised his broom like a spear, and Thomas looked around for somewhere else to dart. There wasn't anywhere.

It was at that point that Nicola stepped between them, staring up at the bigger man and placing a restraining hand on his chest. "Just what do you think you're doing?"

Thomas had heard that voice before, mostly on the verge of throwing away something recyclable. It was the voice of Nicola when she wasn't in a mood to be disagreed with. Even the other man seemed to sense it, because he lowered his impromptu skewer and took a step back.

"I asked you a question," Nicola continued. "Just what do you think you're playing at?"

You should really be shoving her out of the way, the voice of Thomas' conscience pointed out. *Any minute now, this thug is going to realise that all he has to do is stab Nicola first to get at you.* Thomas agreed with the sentiment, but somehow he couldn't bring himself to do it. After all, he could guess what would happen straight after that. *Besides,* he thought, as the big man took another step back, *she's actually got him squirming.*

"S'posed to kill him," Thomas heard him mutter, "'s my

job."

"Well your job can just wait. I was here first." Nicola turned back to Thomas, and suddenly he wasn't quite so grateful that she'd saved him.

"I don't know what that stunt was back outside the Union, but you've got no business telling me to go and get on with my day ten seconds after dumping me."

Thomas started to speak, if only to point out that this probably wasn't the best time to have an argument, and Nicola shoved him back against the tree.

"No," she snapped, "just shut up. It's my turn now. I don't know what that was back there, whether it was some sort of hypnotism, or super-secret pheromone thing, or just you being your *charming* self, but now you're going to keep quiet while I call you every single name I can think of, you total and utter..."

She threw herself forward at Thomas, who tensed, expecting another barrage of blows. It didn't come. Instead, he found her lips mashed against his in the briefest of kisses, before Nicola pulled back. Then she slapped him, and Thomas did his best to ignore the tears clouding Nicola's eyes as she did it.

I've actually made her cry. I didn't think it would be possible.

"I hate you, Thomas Greene." The words came out with conviction, but Nicola still clung to him. Thomas found himself caught between the urge to comfort her, the need to tell her how sorry he was, and the desperate part of his brain pointing out that there was still a very large man standing a few yards away intent on killing him. As if on cue, the big man spoke up.

"Excuse me?" There was a cautious note to the words even then. Nicola's head whipped round. "Are you going to be long? Only I'm kind of in a hurry here. The way you looked, I thought maybe you were going to kill him."

Nicola shook her head.

"Oh, go on," the big man said. "From the sounds of it, he probably deserves it. It would save me a lot of trouble."

"Well I'm not." Thomas was glad to hear those words at least. "So you can just go away."

To Thomas' surprise, the big man shook his head. The mood Nicola was in, if she'd given Thomas the chance to run away, he'd have taken it. Instead, the other man took a few more paces back and hefted his broken broom under one arm like a child playing at being a knight. Of course, children weren't generally eight feet tall and clutching brooms that ended in razor sharp splinters.

"Doesn't work like that. If you're not going to do it, then..."

Thomas saw him start to charge, and some deeply buried, chivalrous corner of his brain took over, probably coughing and choking from all the cobwebs it was disturbing there as it did so. He spun Nicola back towards the tree, trying to shield her with his body since there was no chance to dodge.

What are you doing? The more normal part of his brain demanded. *All it means is that she gets skewered second... hang on, what's happening?*

Somewhere in the confusion, Thomas had squeezed his eyes shut. Despite the evidence to the contrary, the human brain always seems to hang on to the idea that if it can't see things, they might go away. In this case, Thomas suspected that it was probably a lot to ask. Even through closed eyelids though, he could make out a glow. He opened his eyes to find that it wasn't just a trick of the afternoon sunlight. Thomas wondered for a moment if it was that near death business that everyone talked about with the white light, before deciding that would probably only happen after the broom hit. Instead, Thomas realised that the whole tree was surrounded in a corona of golden light, accompanied by the soft sound of tinkling bells.

Thomas had just enough time to think, *well, that's odd*, in the strange, disconnected way of the about to be dead, before his footing went from under him, sending him and Nicola tumbling into the trunk.

Into the trunk, and through it.

Chapter Six

Having decided that shutting them again was definitely better than seeing whatever was happening around him, Thomas was naturally reluctant to open his eyes. The fact that his last sight had let him count tree rings from the inside had a lot to do with it. Even when he'd fallen forward, badly jarring one knee, Thomas had decided against looking. Truthfully, he was just trying to put off the moment when his mind would have to actually start trying to make sense of things, because Thomas suspected it wasn't possible.

It was better to start with the obvious. He wasn't dead. Or at least he didn't think he was dead, and Thomas suspected that being around to have an opinion probably counted for something there. He also didn't seem to have been skewered by half a broom. Those were good things, at least. Of course, there was always the chance that some big, hairy psychopath was creeping up on him while he knelt who knew where with his eyes screwed shut. It probably says a lot about just how great a shock falling through a humble horse chestnut can be that even that thought didn't make Thomas want to look. Besides, if the big man were still there, Nicola would have been haranguing him by...

Actually, come to think of it, shouldn't she have been shouting at *him* by this point? More to the point, since Thomas had been holding onto her, shouldn't he be able to feel her pressed against him? That was enough for Thomas' eyes to snap open, scanning the area around him hastily. Of Nicola, and also of outsize, broom-wielding attackers, there was no sign. They seemed to have been swapped instead for a perfect view over a landscape that *definitely* wasn't Nether Wrexford.

He'd fallen on a heap of stones that stood on top of a hill in a rough pile. If he'd been in any frame of mind to notice, Thomas would probably have realised that was probably what was behind the pain in his knees. Instead, he was too busy looking out over the sort of landscape that most directors would kill for, or at least book a trip to New Zealand over. Lightly forested surrounding hills gave way to fields that mixed the gold of ripe corn with the colour-dotted green of flowering meadows. Streams bubbled here and there, weaving through the rest of it like slightly unsteady old ladies shoving their way through the crowd between them and the buffet table. Further on, Thomas could make out signs of habitation, huddled together in tiny groups that could hardly be called villages. The only thing large enough to call a town sat near the horizon, along with…

Thomas blinked. Castles didn't really look like that. Not in England, at least. He'd been on a school trip to one once, as a child, the sort of thing where you spend a couple of hours on a coach followed by one of those lectures so boring you can't get rid of it no matter how much you try to scrub your brain clean. English castles were squat, tough things, clear lines designed for dividing the world into a nice safe inside and an outside that would do what it was told, if it knew what was good for it. Mostly these days, they sported holes and collapsed walls from moments when someone with gunpowder decided that they'd quite like a turn at being inside.

This castle didn't have holes. It did have turrets though, and odd protrusions, and a strange twist about half way up it. Really, it looked as though it ought to fall over at any moment. The closest things Thomas had seen to it had been on TV, nestled in corners of Eastern Europe with names that would have been worth millions of points if you could have used them when playing Scrabble. And even those castles hadn't looked quite so much like they'd been twisted into a knot.

"Where am I?"

Thomas demanded it of the world in general. Given how weird the whole thing was, he was almost grateful not to get an answer. He stood statue-still for a minute longer, as though hoping that if he just gave it time, the place would fade, leaving him back on the University's sports fields. Of course, if that happened, Thomas would probably find that the thing was a hallucination brought on by being stabbed with half a broom handle. It wasn't a particularly cheery thought, really.

The landscape around him stubbornly persisted in existing, and Thomas knew he had to do something. He couldn't just stand on a hillside forever, even if there was a part of his mind that suggested that was exactly what he should do. Or better yet, if Thomas really wanted something to do, he could have a go at gibbering at the insanity of it all. Yes, that part of his mind continued, a good gibber would do him the world of good, preferably accompanied by a nice long bout of curling up into a ball and staring straight ahead.

Thomas ignored the urge, though he did file it away as a possibility for later. Instead, he looked down the hill, trying to find any sign of someone nearer than one of the villages. Surely someone would tell him what was going on. There was a rocky trail of sorts leading down the hill, the sort of half-formed path that would only really be acknowledged as such by goats or middle-aged hikers determined to assert their right to roam. A few scrubby bushes and young trees lined the edge of it, looking useful for handholds until Thomas noticed the thorns that covered most of them. The trees weren't much, but even so they were enough to mask the path as it curved round the hill's base.

Thomas started to follow the thing, as much on the basis that all paths led somewhere as anything, doing his best to keep his footing as he scrambled down the sloping and uneven surface. Thomas' knees still hurt, but since they were taking his weight, there probably wasn't anything seriously wrong with them. Besides, as he continued looking out to the point where the path disappeared round the hill, Thomas noticed something that was enough to put all thoughts of skinned knees from his mind. A thin trail of smoke rose upwards, presumably from the chimney of a building just out of sight. A building meant just one thing to Thomas. People.

Across the universe, there really aren't that many different types of pub. Whether what's being served behind the bar are glasses holding carefully mixed cocktails, or space-flagons containing flavoured liquid nitrogen, or even, heaven forbid, pints of real ale, the pub itself will tend to conform to one of a few basic types:

There are the big ones, the flashy ones, the ones that say that really they'd like to be a wine bar when they grow up, or maybe a restaurant. Generally they manage to charge so much for a pint that people have to consider re-mortgaging if they want to buy a round.

Then there are the homogenous olde worlde clones of the brewery owned places, where all the staff wear matching t-shirts and what was probably a perfectly pleasant pub once ends up as a mess of exposed beams and horse brasses. They invariably seem to be under new management every couple of months and always resort to karaoke nights just at the moment you most feel like a quiet drink.

And then, here and there, there are the small, badly lit places that don't open the front door even in midsummer, on the basis that someone who isn't a regular might walk in. Often these are in Wales.

It was easier for Thomas to think of the place that confronted him as one of those than as one of the other two. Flashy certainly wasn't the word for it. It would never aspire to be a bar, but might, with a lot of effort, just about manage to be a hovel. Yes, it had exposed timbers, but that was just because it was a wooden shack, and any olde worlde charm it had, it had achieved by the simple expedient of not redecorating since shortly after the dawn of time. The only reason Thomas knew it was a pub at all was because it had a sign saying so. Just that. Just "PUB" in big, scratchy letters that looked like the sign writer had decided to use a broken bit of wood rather than a paintbrush. No sign of a proper name anywhere at all.

Actually, that wasn't the only reason it veered sharply towards type three. There was also the fact that, if Thomas strained to hear really hard, he could just about make out the strains of the sort of folk song people only sang when drunk coming from inside. At least, Thomas hoped they only sang it when drunk. The thought that otherwise honest, hardworking people might be able to sing that sort of thing sober was too much of a stretch.

Yes, Thomas thought, it was definitely one of *those* pubs. Normally, he would have avoided it automatically, because the sort of people who drank in pubs like that seemed to have an inherent antipathy towards students. Actually, most of the time they had a vague antipathy towards everyone, but students were just easier to beat up. On the other hand, Thomas thought, he was lost, he was thirsty, and if there's one thing someone who's just stepped straight through a tree onto a strange hillside needs, it's a stiff drink.

Steeling himself, Thomas stepped inside.

Predictably enough, the music stopped dead. Perhaps in response to some unwritten law of the universe, a single accordion player took a few more notes to realise this than everybody else. He jarred to a halt with a sound like a deflating balloon.

Silences upon walking into a strange pub are natural, even welcoming sometimes, because at least it means everyone else has noticed you. This, though, wasn't that sort of silence. It wasn't even the sort of silence you get when the hero of a western walks into the saloon, that brief moment that the barman has to get behind something solid before everyone starts shooting. No, this was past that, and right into the silence normally reserved for pubs in very small villages where everyone who hasn't lived there thirty years is an incomer. It's the silence where you just *know* that everyone is watching to see if you grow an extra head, or worse, drink out of Old Bert's favourite tankard.

Thomas knew that the thing to do in moments like this was to walk straight up to the bar and loudly order a drink without so much as glancing at all the people staring, so he did just that. Thomas strode forward as confidently as he could manage, taking out his wallet, the words "A pint of your guest beer, please" already lining themselves up for use.

He got as far as "A pint of y..." before looking at the barman. "Aargh!"

The barman shrugged, cleaning a glass. "G'day. Don't think we've got any "y... aargh" mate. Sounds a bit, well... fancy for this place, to be honest. Could do you a pint of lager if you'd like."

"You... you've got a beak!" Thomas took a step back, willing his eyes to see something different. It didn't help. The barman looked completely normal, except for the large multicoloured beak that dominated his features.

"Aargh!"

"I've told you, mate, we haven't got any. I could go with bitter, if you'd prefer. Probably got some cider back here as well, come to think of it."

Thomas spun, staring at the place's other customers, trying desperately to work out how they couldn't notice that their barman looked like he was part toucan. Looking at them wasn't much better. A couple of the dozen or so souls there looked vaguely normal, but even pubs in Norfolk managed better numbers than that.

As for the rest, they seemed to understand "normal" as much as Thomas did particle physics. They might have heard of it, but they hadn't got a clue how to do it. They covered every skin tone from bright gold to a kind of vivid purple, while their sizes ranged between one in a tutu who wouldn't have come up to Thomas' waist and a seven-foot hulk of a man nursing a mug the size of a bucket. One had gossamer wings sprouting from her back, while another seemed to be covered in fur.

"What is this place?" Thomas could barely get the words out. The seven foot man stood up.

"What you staring at?" The biggest of the pub's inhabitants demanded. "You never seen Figments before?"

"What's a Figment?" Thomas asked it automatically, and

winced inwardly as soon as he had. This was the sort of crowd that would probably take "hello, how are you" as an excuse for a fight, and he had to go and ask a question? There was another horrible pause.

It ended with a sudden laugh from the barman.

"Good one, mate. You ease off him, Frankie. Don't make me bar you again. Now, mate, what was it you were drinking?"

Truthfully, Thomas just wanted to run for the door, but he doubted that he'd make it. Besides, maybe if he was lucky, he might get a couple of answers about what was going on along with the drink. *That's right*, Thomas thought, *I'll get answers about why the world doesn't make sense anymore from the nice man with the beak who keeps calling me mate in an accent I could swear is...*

"You're Australian, aren't you?"

The barman shrugged. "More or less, I reckon. Never really thought about it. What are you having?"

"Beer, please."

The beak-faced barman reached under the counter, pulling out a bottle that he quickly poured into the glass he'd been cleaning. "Here you go."

"Thanks, how much do I owe you?"

The barman tilted his head to one side. "What do you mean?"

"How much do I have to pay?" Thomas asked.

The barman gave him another puzzled look. "No, you've lost me there, mate."

Thomas gave up, and sipped the beer slowly. Right then, it was the best thing he'd ever tasted.

"What do they call you, anyway?" Thomas asked the barman, who'd gone back to cleaning glasses.

"Keith."

"Where am I, Keith? I mean, this pub doesn't even have a name."

"Sure it does," Keith replied, misting a glass with his breath. "It's called PUB. It's a good name. Chose it myself."

Thomas looked round in exasperation, downing the rest of

his pint in one long swallow before slamming the glass down on the bar.

"What sort of place is this?" he demanded of the pub in general. "Where the fuck am I? What sort of pub is called PUB and doesn't charge for drinks? Better yet, why do the lot of you look like rejects from a sci-fi convention? Will *someone* tell me what the hell is going on!"

Thomas had finished his outburst by the time he realised just how loudly he was shouting. He wasn't at all surprised when a couple of the inn's patrons rose from their chairs and edged towards him. The big man, Frankie, jabbed a finger roughly into Thomas' chest.

"You ask a lot of questions. Where are you from, anyway?"

"Look," Thomas tried, "I'm sorry, I didn't mean to shout."

"He doesn't want to answer," the tutu wearing patron put in. "Why doesn't he want to answer, Frankie?"

Thomas took a step back, raising his hands.

"I don't want any trouble. If it matters that much, I've come from Nether Wrexford."

Frankie leaned down, which just about brought his eyes level with Thomas'.

"Never heard of it. Know what I think?"

Whatever it is, you probably think it slowly, Thomas thought, but had the sense to keep his mouth shut. Rule one of surviving in strange pubs; never answer rhetorical questions from anyone bigger than you.

"I think," Frankie continued, "that you're one of Her spies, here to find out where we are. Any minute, you'll slope off, and they'll be down on us like a ton of bricks. That's what I think."

"I don't know who *they* are!" Thomas protested. "I certainly don't know who *she* is. I don't know what you're talking about!"

In response, Frankie broke into a grin. "Do you know what we do to… urk…"

Thomas would have been the first to admit that he didn't like fights. More specifically, Thomas didn't like being beaten to a pulp by things twice his size. Unfortunately, there were occasions when it looked more or less inevitable, and a sentence that started "Do you know what we do..." was definitely one of those. That was why, at about that point, he'd grabbed the nearest barstool and hit Frankie squarely across the middle with it, causing him to fold up around it and collapse to his knees.

"Get him!" the tutu-wearing dwarf yelled, but Thomas was already moving. He shoved it out of the way and sprinted for the door while the rest of The PUB's patrons were still trying to decide if they felt like being a lynch mob or not. Judging by the sounds that followed him out onto the hillside, they thought they might be prepared to give it a go.

Now what? Thomas was still looking around, trying to work out which way to run, when a voice came from a nearby bush.

"Psst!" it said. "Over here, quick!"

Thomas didn't have to be asked twice. He dove for the greenery.

The scent of freshly cut grass reached Nicola, and she opened her eyes, scrambling to her feet as she looked round in shock. This definitely wasn't the university. Certainly, grass stretched away under Nicola's feet, but this was a freshly manicured lawn, not a playing field. Flowerbeds surrounded it, containing a range of colours that ran from the merely vivid to the utterly eye-watering, while butterflies and bees darted between them by the dozen.

And as for the structure abutting the garden, the castle twisting impossibly upwards so far that Nicola had to crane her neck to see the top... *No,* Nicola thought, *definitely not the university.*

It was only when Nicola looked down again that she finally noticed a woman in overalls and a sunhat was working on the flowers with a basket and a pair of secateurs. Strands of blonde hair hung loose beneath the hat, as though they couldn't quite be tamed. As Nicola stepped forward, she turned, and Nicola saw that she was good looking, in a girlish, and also rather mud-spattered, sort of way. She gave Nicola a pleasant smile.

"Hello miss. Lovely day, isn't it?"

Despite the oddness of the whole thing, Nicola found herself returning the smile.

"Yes. Could you possibly tell me where I am?"

"Well, you're in the garden, aren't you?"

"But what garden?" Nicola demanded. "How did I get here?"

The other woman just shook her head, before taking off the hat and shaking loose her hair. Nicola couldn't help but notice the mixed green and blonde of it, the two colours fading into each other in waves. *Well,* she thought, *it was hard not to.*

"We're by the castle, of course," the woman said, gently. "You were here when I arrived ten minutes ago, and it seemed like a shame to wake you. Are you all right? You seem a little... confused. If you need help, I could send for a couple of the Queen's Guard."

"No, no, I'm fine." Nicola said it automatically. She didn't know who the Queen's Guard were, but they sounded a little too much like "authorities." A couple of protests had been more than enough to give her a healthy caution around anyone in a uniform.

"Are you sure? If you don't know where you are, maybe you've hit your head or something. I remember reading about that somewhere. It might be better to get it looked at."

"I'm fine, thanks," Nicola replied, trying to be polite. She didn't dare ask more questions. "I was just a little disoriented after waking up. I'll be going." Nicola turned, picking a direction at random. "Lovely meeting you."

"You too, miss. If you're going that way, be careful of the rose patch, won't you? I think someone's been giving them something they shouldn't, poor things."

Nicola promised that she would, and hastily started walking away before the other woman changed her mind about calling for guards. Whatever was going on here, she'd just have to find it out alone.

Chapter Seven

Thomas wasn't alone in the bush, which was quite reassuring when a voice had just come out of it. Voices coming from empty bushes would, he felt, have been one weird thing too many. Of course, if he'd been alone, there wouldn't have been a hand clamped roughly across his mouth, but you couldn't have everything. It was quite a big hand, with long, spindly fingers, but Thomas didn't feel that he was really in a position to appreciate its finer details at the moment.

"Stay quiet."

"Mmmph," Thomas agreed, and the hand left his mouth. He started to look round, but the same hand shoved him down into the dirt.

"Stay still as well."

Thomas didn't argue, and was glad of that when a crowd piled out of the PUB, chattering angrily. The big one, Frankie, was at its head, but most of the others seemed to be there too. Apparently, chasing after suspected spies was a popular activity.

"He can't have gone far." Even with what felt like a shovel-full of earth in one ear, Thomas could hear the anger in the big man's voice. "Split up."

The pub's patrons did so with more angry hubbub, dividing into two groups. Mobs, Thomas corrected himself, definitely mobs. After a certain amount of confusion over who was in which one, the two mobs headed in opposite directions. Thankfully, neither of those directions included the bush where

Thomas lay, trying desperately not to think about what it might be that they did to spies.

Eventually, Thomas found himself hauled to his feet. A man stepped in front of him. He wasn't a big man. He was, if anything, a little shorter than Thomas, slenderly built with cheekbones that seemed to want to break through his dark skin. His clothes consisted of the sort of thing that might have worked as a uniform for castaways; a ragged shirt and Bermuda shorts so brightly patterned Thomas was surprised they hadn't been easier to spot against the green of the bush. For shoes, he had a pair of open toed sandals that looked like they'd been put together from a mixture of driftwood and old string.

While Thomas was still staring, the other man extended a hand. Thomas took it, finding his own hand engulfed in the embrace of the longest fingers he'd ever seen. It was only part way through the shake that Thomas realised each finger had at least one more joint than it should have had.

"Simon Stranded," the other man said, flashing a smile that contained at least one gold tooth.

"Thomas Greene." *Don't mention the fingers, don't mention the fingers, don't mention the...* "That's a pretty... unusual name."

Simon Stranded shook his head, the smile disappearing. "That's where you went wrong in there. You don't ask questions here. You don't ask questions, and you don't pass comments. First rule of the Dreaming Court, that." He appeared to think about it. "No, I tell a lie. The first rule is 'Do whatever her royal majesty says,' obviously. But it's definitely in the top ten. What's wrong with my name, anyway?"

"Nothing, nothing," Thomas said hastily. If there was someone here prepared to help him, someone who, despite the odd clothes and odder fingers, seemed at least fairly normal, he wasn't about to blow it. "It's just that I've never heard Stranded as a last name before."

The other man shrugged. "Not so much a last name as a job description. Some woman starts having dreams about being stranded on an island with her ideal man, and suddenly I, poor

Figment that I am, am like this. Not that I mind. Could be worse, could be a lot worse."

Thomas reviewed what he'd just been told in the privacy of his head. "Someone had a dream, and you're like that because of it? It doesn't make sense. None of this place makes sense. I must be going mad."

Simon Stranded shrugged. "If you like. I wouldn't bother though. It's not really much fun. I had a go at it just after getting off the island. Started talking to this beach ball and... but I'm rambling. You're not from around here, are you?"

"How did you know that?"

"Well, this going on about how strange the place is was one clue. Also," Stranded added, "the way you fell out of the sky was a bit of a giveaway. I saw you arrive up on the hill and fol-lowed you down. I'd have come inside, except that Keith's barred me for the moment. Hang on..." He cocked an ear, listen-ing. "Can't hear them. What about you?"

Thomas tried listening, but when all he could hear was the sound of his own brain trying not to explode from the confusion of it all, there didn't seem to be much point. He said as much and Stranded laughed.

"You're a strange one, right enough. I reckon maybe we should get going before they get back, okay? Maybe once we're away from here we'll have time for a proper chat. You can tell me how you came to be here."

Thomas spread his hands. "I haven't a clue."

"Well," Stranded said, setting off at an angle to the path, "you just think about it while we get away from here. Maybe it'll come back to you. Failing that, just do what I always do when faced with difficult questions."

"What's that?" Thomas asked, loping to keep up. Simon Stranded threw a grin back over his shoulder.

"Make half the answer up."

One of the things Simon Stranded seemed to be making up rather more than half of, at least as far as Thomas could see, was their route. Together, they wove in and out of trees and bushes, darting along a seemingly random trajectory. Well, Simon Stranded darted. Thomas sort of crashed through it all, doing his best to keep up. It wasn't as hard as he'd thought it would be. Despite spending most of his life in towns, within a few minutes he was moving along quickly behind the smaller man.

"You're doing well," Stranded called back to him. "Wish I'd done half as well when I first arrived. I'll tell you, you go your entire existence on a desert island beach with maybe a few palms and coconuts for company, the first deciduous tree you trip over comes as a shock."

Thomas stopped, thrusting out a hand to grab hold of the smaller man.

"Enough! You can't just toss out cryptic comments like that and not explain them. What is this place? How did I get here, and just what is going on?"

"There's no need to shout. Besides, what do you expect me to know? I'm just a Figment. It's not like they tell me anything."

"You're doing it again." Thomas let the other man go roughly. "What's a Figment? And who are *they?* Look," he finished, lowering his voice, "I've had a really rough day. I broke up with my girlfriend, some psycho tried to kill me, and now I'm in some place filled with people who are just... weird. All I want are some answers."

Thomas waited, not very patiently. Simon Stranded glanced around before nodding and settling himself on a fallen log.

"Ok. I guess we're far enough away. No chance of that mob catching up. Fire away, chief."

"What? Oh... right." As with most situations where someone is demanding answers, Thomas wasn't entirely prepared for the possibility that he might actually get them. As such it took him a moment to get his questions into some sort of order. It felt a lot like trying to fit twenty people through a doorway at once: possible, but inevitably involving a lot of pushing. "Ok then. Let's start with the obvious one. Where on Earth am I?"

He caught the slight widening of the castaway's eyes.

"What?"

"Where exactly are you from, Thomas Greene?" There was a cautious note to the words.

"Nether Wrexford. Well, not exactly, but it's where I was before I got into this mess." Thomas watched Simon Stranded's face for any hint of recognition. "It's in England. Come on, you must have heard of England. You're speaking English."

"Not really. It's more like the way you always understand what's being said in dreams." There was a thoughtful look in the other man's eyes. "Is it too late to run away and pretend I've never met you? Yeah, I suppose it is. You're... what? Human? Of course you are. And there was me thinking you'd just jumped in from one of the other Courts."

Thomas was beginning to wonder if he'd ever get a straight answer when Simon Stranded made a grand gesture that took in the wooded scrub around them.

"Welcome to the Dreaming Court then. Which is what this is, incidentally. Well, this is a wood, but you get the idea."

"I've sort of given up on any hope of understanding anything."

Stranded gave a short laugh. "I suppose you would have. Right, how can I put this that you'll understand? You know those magical worlds out of storybooks that you reach by wandering through an old cave, or stepping through the mirror, or not looking where you're going in the second-hand shop, or whatever? Well, this is where they got the idea. Except the bit about second-hand shops. I made that one up."

Thomas took that in for a moment. And then for another moment, since it was such a lot to take in. Finally, he said it out loud, since it was the sort of thing that seemed to demand either that or an awful lot of medication.

"I'm on another world? An actual other planet?"

"More or less. Though, to be honest, it's less of another place in its own right than something tacked on between worlds. All the Courts are."

"There are more places like this?"

"A few, sure. There's the Court of Flowers, of course, and the Court of the Fey, or courts, depending on who's not speaking to whom this week. There's probably a few dozen others, though to be honest, it's pretty hard to keep track most days."

"And this place?" Thomas looked round, fully expecting nice men in white to show up with a straightjacket at any moment. "This is the Court of..."

"Dreams," Stranded supplied. "Technically, I suppose we might be one of the Fey courts, but I wouldn't say that around anyone else. It tends to annoy them. This is where dreams happen. Well, actually they happen in little discrete pockets tacked onto the place because otherwise things would get kind of... messy, but more or less here, certainly."

"Hang on," Thomas interrupted, "dreams happen inside people's heads."

"Sure." The other man shrugged. "But also here. Don't ask me how it works. I'm just a Figment, I don't do multidimensional astrophysics."

Thomas prodded at the nearest tree, at least half expecting his hand to go through it. It felt real enough.

"That word, Figment, what does *that* mean?"

"It's what I am. What a lot of the people around here are. You've got your dreaming folk, who run the place, and then you've got Figments. We do what you might call the actual work; we get different shapes to go with the dreams, obviously. Out here, we're not really supposed to look like this," Stranded waved a hand vaguely at himself. "But trust me, staying in character is a lot more fun than drifting around as a sort of shadow thing with no real personality. If I'd wanted to do that, I'd have become an accountant."

"Ok," Thomas said. He'd hit the point where it was easier to just accept things than try to make sense of them. The last time he'd felt so confused was filling in a student loan application. This was considerably more challenging. "So I'm in this magical world full of fairies or dream... things or whatever, and this is one of loads of magical worlds. Only one question: how did I get here? I'm pretty sure it's something that doesn't happen every day."

"I haven't a clue." Stranded looked uncomfortable. "To be honest, I don't think it should have happened. I mean, we're not really supposed to have any contact with humans these days. Not outside of dreams, anyway. Strictly speaking, you shouldn't be here."

"I'd be only too happy to get out of here, if only someone would tell me how."

"I wish it were that simple." Stranded waved his hands vaguely, as though trying to give an outline to an idea. Or possibly to an invisible elephant, given the general expansiveness of the movements. "These days though, there's a kind of... lock, I guess you could say, on the ways between the Courts. The rulers did it, to keep people in. Only a few people have the keys."

Thomas was still for several seconds. "So I'm stuck here?"

"Hey, don't be so down!" Stranded clapped him on the back. Thomas winced. "With me helping you out, I'm sure we'll think of something."

"You're going to help? Just like that?" Thomas said it carefully, automatically trying to work out what the other man got out of it. Simon Stranded just shrugged.

"Sure. I've got nothing better to do. Besides, it's not like I can go back to the Pub. I'm barred, remember?"

"What for?"

There was another flash of gold as Simon Stranded grinned.

"Keith caught me with his girlfriend. Hardly my fault that she wanted me. Let's just say that it's not just the fingers that are longer, yes?"

Thomas did his best to avoid any thoughts whatsoever about that particular comment. It didn't work. On the other hand, it did bring another thought with it.

"Simon, when you saw me arrive, did a woman arrive too? Only, I think my girlfriend... *ex*-girlfriend, kind of came with me."

"Didn't see her. Doesn't mean she didn't come through, though. Anything weird enough to drop one human here is more than weird enough to split you up. I suppose you want to find her on the way."

Thomas nodded. "I think we'd better. I mean, it's kind of my fault she's here."

Simon Stranded's grin widened. "Fair enough. I'm always happy to meet a good-looking woman. Especially one who's on the rebound. Poor thing's probably in all sorts of trouble by now."

So far, Nicola had done her best to keep away from the castle, wandering through the gardens instead with a mixture of worried bewilderment and surprised delight. The latter was because the place featured a combination of perfectly kept lawns, shady trees and flowers that seemed to come in every conceivable colour, plus a few that didn't seem quite right. Nicola was pretty sure that there shouldn't have been a patch of entirely black lilies growing off to one side.

I wonder how much fertilizer and insecticide they use on this, the watching corner of her mind put in, though the thought was half-hearted. The garden was too pretty to pick at for long. One square of garden *wasn't* beautiful, though. Only a few metres across, it was little more than a patch of faintly blackened earth, left free of grass or any sign of work. Someone had actually fenced it off with wooden posts linked by chain and, as Nicola got closer, she saw that one of the posts had a plaque attached. There was always a part of Nicola that felt uncomfortable about reading that sort of thing. It was a bit like going through someone else's laundry.

This one was simpler even than the usual "In memory of Edith," with just one word, "Remember" etched into the bronze surface. *Remember*, Nicola asked herself, *remember what?* Unconsciously, her fingers reached out to trace the letters, as though touch could perhaps reveal something that sight hadn't. She was quite surprised when it did.

Everything was dark. Nicola tried to look round, only to

realise that concepts like "round" seemed to have vanished, along with her body. It felt like the moment in a theatre when the lights went down just before things started. Though without anyone's mobile phone going off, obviously.

A second later and the garden was back, but there was something different about it. Not the way that she now seemed to be looking at it in some strange disembodied way, or even the way that she didn't seem to *mind* that she was looking at it in some strange, disembodied way, but something else. It took Nicola a moment to realise that the blackened patch of earth wasn't blackened, still less chained off. Instead, it still had the precisely maintained look that said that recently, someone had been round the blades of grass with a tape measure and a pair of nail scissors.

Nicola heard the chatter of voices and would have edged away, had there been any her to do the edging. As it was, she had to watch as a man and a woman came into view, accompanied by a pair of what Nicola could only think of as ghosts – grey things that seemed to drift along with them, flickering occasionally in the breeze. Both the man and the woman were attractive. Quite unnaturally so, Nicola felt. They were also dressed like they had just raided the BBC costume department in the middle of a historical drama. The clothes looked expensive though, even if they wouldn't have been the height of fashion for a few hundred years. Nicola couldn't help a faint sense of... something, about the man.

Nicola heard him laugh at something the woman had said. He leaned down to kiss her before waving a hand vaguely in the direction of the patch of grass. From nowhere, a pink and white checked blanket appeared, along with the sort of picnic hamper that would probably have come with its own ant colony anywhere else. That brought a smile from the woman, who gestured to the two ghostly figures. They flowed and changed as Nicola watched, transforming into a pair of crinoline dressed servants, who proceeded to unpack the hamper while the man and woman danced together on the lawn. With another stolen kiss, she broke away from him and skipped playfully over to the blanket.

Nicola felt it before it happened, in a build up of pressure that managed to make her ears pop despite her not actually being able to locate the ears in question. Nicola tried to yell a warning, but didn't have anything to yell it with. The man seemed to have the same idea, because he turned towards the blanket with a frantic look. It was too late.

Light blossomed first, and heat with it, ferocious, terrible heat. It was the sort of heat that laughed at deserts, that thought ovens were a bit cool, that gently baked suns. Nicola would have screamed if she could have. The light was so intense that she thought for a moment she had gone blind, while the heat felt like someone had taken a welding torch to every atom of her skin at once. Then, as suddenly as it had come, it passed.

It took Nicola a moment see the blackened ground where the blanket and the three figures on it had been, and longer to take it in. One moment, they had been there, the next they were just gone.

The man was very still at one side, staring, just…staring. If the light had been terrible to watch, his face was worse. There was the sort of loss there that the universe might feel on losing stars, except that the universe was not warm and feeling and capable of streaming tears down a face reddened by the blast. The universe was not capable of falling to its knees among the ashes and running them through loving fingers, or of looking up with an expression that made Nicola take an involuntary step back.

The image faded, and Nicola found herself standing back where she had been, on the lawn in front of the plaque. She sucked in a ragged breath, staring at the blackened earth and trying to make some sort of sense of it. What had that been? Was it a real memory? How had she managed to see it? What was this place? Nicola found herself staring down at the plaque again, willing it to give her some sort of answer. As she watched, Nicola saw the word on it fade, to be replaced by neat lines. *The Death of Queen Rae*, it read, *This was how the War began.* They lasted for a few seconds before returning to the original word.

"What War?" Nicola demanded of the thing, but it didn't seem to be about to change again. It looked like the words weren't a real answer, just an epilogue to the images she'd seen. Nicola found the scene replaying in her mind. Not the start, not even the moment of destruction, but the instant when the man, and every instinct Nicola had wanted to call him the King, had looked up.

If that had been the start of a war, Nicola found herself feeling sorry for whoever had been on the other side from him.

Chapter Eight

Grave yanked at the broom, planting his feet against the tree-trunk and putting his not inconsiderable weight into it. Even when the tree started to creak it was no good, the thing just wouldn't come out.

"Well, that's irritating."

Grave snapped the thing off where the handle met the trunk before tossing it aside. After a moment's thought, he picked it up again and stuffed it in the nearest litterbin. Sitting down on the grass, he stared at the tree, daring it to produce the pair it had swallowed. After a moment, a furry head peaked out of one of the pockets of his coat, joining Grave in his staring. It looked around a little longer before trying to scramble free.

"No you don't."

Grave's hand darted out and swept the white rat up by its tail, depositing it back in his pocket. "There's quite enough bits of the Dreaming Court in this world without you joining them." After another moment's thought he searched a few other pockets, finally coming up with a wedge of something that might possibly have been cheese before it got covered with fur from its resting place. Grave dropped it in the pocket after the rat.

"Here, now sit still and let me think."

Grave rested his chin in his hand in a pose that would probably have made Rodin decide against the whole thing if he'd seen it, continuing to stare at the tree. He'd attacked, and there'd been nowhere that Thomas Greene or the other one could go, and then suddenly they managed to go there anyway. Now, assuming that ordinary people hadn't started disappearing into thin air, which even given all the odd things that happened in his job didn't seem very likely, there was really only one explanation.

"Except, of course, that it's impossible," Grave explained to the rat, which chittered in agreement, or in appreciation of the cheese. He wasn't sure which. "Everyone has their borders locked down tight. Without a key, he shouldn't have been able to go anywhere."

But words like "shouldn't" didn't sit well with Grave. Even "impossible" made him twitchy. It was a word for people who sat around working things out. Grave had always been someone who did things first, and worried about whether they were impossible afterwards, like the time he'd caught a hundred pixies in a single afternoon. They'd said that was impossible until he did it, mostly because they hadn't thought to lace bowls of sugar water with enough vodka to…

"Snap out of it," Grave ordered himself, pushing up to his feet. There was an easy way to be sure. He fished inside his shirt, drawing out the necklace that sat there. Grave let it dangle freely from its chain, slowly moving it towards the tree.

Sure enough, it began to glow with the same soft light as it had in the alley. It got stronger the closer he moved to the trunk, until the brightness of it hurt Grave's eyes. Winding it into his fist Grave rapped against the wood like a man checking it for secret passages. In a way, of course, that was exactly what he was doing. Finding the right spot, he watched the doorway blossom in a perfect circle and an annoying tinkle of fairy bells.

The fairy bells weren't a good sign. Still, he could be wrong. It *might* lead somewhere else, and not all the places in the Courts were survivable. After a moment spent looking round to check that there was still no one nearby, Grave retrieved the rat from his pocket and set about searching for a length of string. When he found one, Grave took his time tying it round the thing's middle before tossing it through the hole like a man fishing through a gap in a frozen lake. When he hauled it back a few seconds later, the rat was still there, giving Grave as much of a reproachful look as it was possible for a rodent to manage.

"Finish your cheese," Grave said, pushing it back into a pocket. After a moment's thought he took the rat back out, and then put it back in the pocket that actually had the cheese in it. So, probably not instantly deadly then. It still didn't tell Grave exactly where it led, but Grave had a horrible feeling he could guess. He sighed. There was only one way to find out.

There are probably a lot of ways of describing Grave squeezing his way through the hole in the tree. An elephant trying to squeeze through a normal doorway is one option, while there is also something to be said for the image of someone trying to fit the whole of a Government form into the supposedly handy envelope they've provided. Since neither of these quite captures the thing though, it might be best to simply describe the reality of it. Grave's passage through the portal, therefore, was *exactly* like a very large man trying to squeeze through a hole in the fabric of reality approximately two sizes too small for him.

Grave arrived with the pop of a stuck cork finally coming free from the bottle, and tumbled to his feet with a glare that dared anyone to be watching him. There didn't appear to be. There was nothing but a hillside, a rough cairn of rocks, and a pleasant view out over the lands of the Dreaming Court. At least it wasn't one of the others. Grave hadn't got a clue as to how Thomas Greene had got into the place, but in the Dreaming Court he would be easy enough to track. Grave sniffed the air, trying to catch the scent, but the place was too open to hold it long. With a shrug, he leaned down and tapped on the cairn.

"Wsslg..." the voice came from under the stones, and sounded decidedly raspy. "Can't you see I'm sleeping?"

"There was a man here a little while ago, yes?"

"Might have been."

Grave made an annoyed sound. He hated working with the dreaming dead. They were never exactly at their best when woken up. There was one of them tucked away on Earth somewhere, some king or something, who was so bad in the mornings that they'd labelled him *only to be woken up in times of national peril.* Grave didn't have time for that. He started to move the rocks one by one.

"Hey! What are you doing?"

"If you aren't going to be helpful, I'm going to get angry."

"I never said I wasn't going to be helpful." Even through the stones, Grave could hear the resentfulness. "Who said I wasn't going to be helpful? There was a man, came and knelt on my cairn, he did. Weird, he was, as well. Acted like he'd never seen the place before."

"Did you speak to him?" Grave still had his hand on the next rock, the threat obvious.

"Why would I speak to him? He didn't go round knocking on my cairn, not like some I could mention. Just came, knelt for a bit and went."

"Which way did he go?"

"Do I look like I can see anything through this rock?" Grave chucked another stone down the hillside.

"Ok, ok. I don't know for sure, but he probably headed for the pub. Only thing around here worth waking up for now and again. Now, can I get on with being dead? Only, this dreaming of eternity business doesn't take care of itself."

Grave paused, considering. "What pub?"

Thomas trudged along behind Simon Stranded, trying, and occasionally failing, not to fall over any of the rocks or brambles in their path. As far as he could tell, the Figment was still following the strategy of picking a course at random.

"Why was this place sealed off?" Thomas asked, more for something to say than because he really wanted an answer. There was so much going on that every answer he got from the other man – *the Figment,* he corrected himself – just seemed to generate more questions. But it was that or slog along in silence, and that just meant paying attention to the fact that his feet had started to ache. Simon Stranded spoke without looking back.

"Because of the War, of course. Well... that and the Treaty."

"What war?" Thomas demanded. "What treaty?"

That, at least, earned him a surprised glance.

"You haven't... no, I suppose you wouldn't have heard of them. That's kind of the point, isn't it?"

"I don't know, Simon," Thomas pointed out. "I won't know until you explain."

"Well..." Stranded ducked around a tree, and Thomas hurried to follow, giving only a slight shudder at the memory of walking through one. "You've got to remember that most of this is second hand for me. I mean, technically I probably existed then, but I wasn't really *me* until I got dreamt up, which was only a few years back."

"That's still a few years longer than I have been here."

"Right... well, the Courts, most of them anyway, used to be a lot chummier with your world than they are at the moment. You'll have heard the stories, probably."

Thomas was about to shake his head, but stopped himself. Of course he'd heard them. There were plenty of old stories about local monsters, or magic, or people meeting with spirits and ghosts. A day ago, Thomas would probably have called them children's stories. He shuddered. Fairy tales and myths seemed a lot less nice once you were actually standing in another world.

"Are they all true?" Thomas asked. "I mean, are there really..." he struggled for the words. How exactly did you ask if every monster you thought had been made up around a campfire was real?

Simon Stranded seemed to guess what he wanted, because he cocked his head to one side. "Dragons and fairies and pixies and trolls and all the rest? Sure. I mean, obviously what you run into depends on what Court you're in, and to be honest trolls are a bit on the scarce side anywhere these days, what with all the billy-goats around, but yes, they exist."

Thomas walked a little further as he tried to digest that. Just in time to distract him from some of the things that might be real that he really hoped weren't, another question bobbed up for his attention.

"So what about this war? How did it start?"

"How do any of these things start?" Stranded countered. "Oh, they say that it was with the attacks on half the rulers of the Courts, but that's not really an explanation, is it? You've got all these Courts stepping all over each other's business, and most of them can't stand each other anyway, it gets to the point where they actually *want* a war. After that, the starting point doesn't matter much. The difference was, this wasn't war, this was War."

Thomas thought he could hear the capital letter sliding into place. Not that it made things any clearer. "So what's the difference?"

"The difference is that instead of being some little scrap between a couple of the Fey courts, say, this was everybody. It might have kicked off with the Court of the Damned, but pretty soon every old score out there was being dredged up. From what I hear, it got really bad for a while. Makes me glad I didn't exist, really."

Thomas did his best to imagine what "really bad" might mean, given what seemed to pass for perfectly normal. It wasn't a pleasant thought.

"So why didn't anybody on Earth hear about this?"

"Well, you did, at first. A bit anyway. You got a bunch of would-be prophets seeing it all and declaring that the end of the world was coming, some nasty little intrusions into corners of *your* wars, that sort of thing. Pretty soon though, everyone realised that potentially apocalyptic war wasn't going to do your lot that much good, on the whole. Which is where the Treaty comes in."

"So this was what? Some giant non-aggression thing?"

"It was more a case of completely ignoring you." Stranded waved his hands trying to find the right words. "Or at least not contacting you. No phone calls, no forwarding address, the whole bit. Like a particularly nasty divorce, only we don't owe you any money. All the magic mirrors and special rocks and the rest of it stop reaching us, all the fairies at the bottom of the garden go home. No one goes into your place, no one comes into ours. Everyone seals off their borders so your world doesn't get fried."

Thomas thought about it for a moment, applying what he knew of human nature to the situation. "What was in it for them?"

"Now you're thinking. I mean, it's hardly likely that our illustrious rulers are about to start doing things out of the goodness of their hearts, is it? As far as I can tell, they wanted either to keep your world nice and neutral or save it as a prize for the winners. You see, somehow – and you have to understand that the one time someone tried explaining this to me, everyone involved was drunk – your world affects the Courts. People seem to think that if they could get enough power there, it would help them out here. Now, no one wanted their rivals having that, so they all agreed to leave well enough alone until after the thing finished."

"So this war," Thomas said, "it's still going then?"

Somehow, he had a feeling his luck today might run to dropping him down in the middle of a war-zone. Thankfully, the Figment shook his head.

"Oh no. It finished almost twenty years ago. Now all the Courts, well... the ones that are left, are shifting around like a bunch of cats in neighbouring gardens, watching each other, all waiting for someone else to make the first move towards the big bowl of cream. The thing is, I'm not sure you want to be found here while they're busy doing that. Things would still be pretty dangerous for a human round here, given that your presence could potentially re-start the whole War. As far as I can see, the best thing we can do is get your girlfriend..."

"Ex-girlfriend. I broke up with her just before we came here."

"...Ex-girlfriend, right, and get you both out of here before it causes problems for everyone."

"So you *do* know a way out of here?" Thomas couldn't help but sound sceptical.

"Of course I do. Well... I know where to find someone who'll know. Trust me, we'll soon have you home."

Nicola wanted to go home. She hadn't asked to find herself wandering around the outside of some bizarre castle, experiencing hallucinations and chatting to strange gardeners. She hadn't asked for practically anything that had happened that day. Nicola shook her head. That was just sloppy thinking. Whether she'd asked for it or not, this was where she was. Nicola wasn't going to be one of those soppy, silly girls you found in films, breaking down and crying at the least thing. She was here. The question now was what she was going to do about it.

Nicola kept walking. She wanted to put some distance between herself and the images she'd seen. How anyone could do something that terrible was simply beyond her, particularly in such a beautiful place. Shaking her head, she continued, heading into a small walled rose garden that filled the air with perfume and a pervading sense of peace. Half a dozen shades of pink, yellow and red vied for attention as Nicola took a moment just to pause and look at the place. There was no denying that it was beautiful.

Nicola found herself wondering about the gardening woman's advice to be careful of the roses. These didn't look particularly off colour. If anything, they looked robust, abundantly healthy. Some of them stood proudly on their own, while others wound around canes and arches casually, looking almost wild despite the setting. It took Nicola a second look to realise that there was something odd about one of those arches. Where the others framed views onto the other beds, or bridged the gravel paths, or just framed statues set into niches in the wall, this one opened onto bare brick.

Perhaps it was just that *these* roses didn't need much of a setting. They were among the biggest and most beautiful in the garden, such a dark red that they were almost black, and the sweet scent of them managed to cut through the others, demanding attention in the same way that people with shotguns and ski masks sometimes ask for money. If someone could have captured that scent in a perfume, then, so long as it wasn't tested on animals of course, Nicola would have bought it in a heartbeat. She wandered over to them, taking one of the blooms in her hand and leaning down to get the full scent of the thing.

It is probably instructive at this point to run through Nicola's thoughts. They were, for her, fairly typical thoughts, for the most part at least. *These are beautiful.* She thought, *I wonder how they get them to grow so big? No way is a garden like this organic. They probably coat them all with insecticides and fill them up with chemical fertilizers. Come to think of it, I haven't seen any butterflies or ladybirds on these ones, so that's probably it. Hang on, what's that slithering feeling?*

That last one was a little out of the ordinary, and Nicola snapped out of her thoughts, or tried to. She stared down at her arm. *Oh,* Nicola thought, *there's a rose tendril creeping around my arm, how odd.* She watched the thorny thing progress along her forearm while two others snaked out around her ankles. It was at about that point that Nicola managed to make her mind wake up enough to do something.

"Fuck!" Nicola yanked her arm back, trying to tear away from the thing, but all she got as a reward for the effort was the sharp, sudden pain of thorns tearing into flesh. Nicola cried out as the tendrils snapped tight, dragging her arm and legs out towards the frame of the arch. Another tendril crept down, searching for Nicola's left wrist like the tentacle of some particularly thorny octopus. She squirmed away as best she could, trying to keep the wrist out of reach. At the same time, Nicola gave another wrench, trying to tear free of the plant that held her. It didn't do anything, except to start a trail of warm wetness running down her wrist.

There was nothing else for it. As much as Nicola wanted to avoid attention, as much as she hated the thought of playing the helpless, lost damsel in distress, Nicola knew that there was really only one option.

"Help! Help, I'm in the Rose Garden!"

Nicola repeated herself twice more at the top of her voice before she heard answering footsteps on the gravel and the sound of the gardener's voice.

"Hold on miss, I'm coming."

Nicola slapped at the questing tendril like the hand of an overeager boyfriend, but succeeded only in tearing open her palm. It snaked around her wrist, dragging it out tight as she bit back a cry of pain.

When the gardener appeared at her back, a pair of secateurs in hand, Nicola only just managed to stop tears of relief. Four quick snips later, and Nicola found herself being dragged backwards away from the thing.

"How are you feeling? Silly question. Are you strong enough to stand?"

Nicola tried to stand on her own two feet, but found that her legs didn't like the idea. Gratefully, she leaned against the other woman.

"What *are* they?" she asked in a weak voice. The gardener gave her an odd look.

"You must have lost a lot of blood if you don't remember about the roses. But then, you were pretty confused to begin with. Are you sure you won't let me call for the guards, miss?"

"Nicola," Nicola managed, already shaking her head. "No guards, please." The gardener gave her another long look, then sighed.

"All right, Nicola, as you like. But we will get you inside and have a look at these wounds. No arguments. And I'm Poppy."

Chapter Nine

Grave strode up to the bar, slammed his hand down on it hard enough to crack the wood, and gave the bartender his best baleful glare. Grave knew it was his best because he'd practised it. This was going to be fun.

"Service!"

The bartender half opened his beak to say something, paled visibly, and then forced a smile. Well, as much of a smile as was possible for someone with a beak.

"G'day. I'm Keith. What're you drinking?"

"What do you recommend?"

There was a pause as the beaked Figment looked him up and down. Grave wondered if he'd shout to the others for help. Grave could see them in the edges of his vision, crowding back and whispering to each other. They recognised him, then. Though that wasn't exactly hard. The figment bartender finished his inspection and looked him in the eye again. Either he was braver than he looked, or the bartending had seeped deep into him. Whichever it was, he managed another smile.

"You look like a real ale man to me, mate. Things with names like Herbert's Slightly Unusual, or Speckled Grey Frog. Am I right?"

Grave thought for a moment. "The first one. A pint."

"Coming right up." The pint materialised from under the bar. Despite the name, it didn't look particularly unusual, though it did look like Grave might need a knife and fork to make any sort of impression on it. He took a sip and set it down, leaning on the bar. The wood creaked under his bulk.

"And now," Grave said, "being such an excellent bartender, you will no doubt wish to listen to my troubles."

Grave watched the shocked look come over the Figment's features, only to be replaced a second later by what looked very much like tears of joy.

"You... you'd honestly do that? You'd stand there and tell me your problems? You have no idea what this means to me. I've tried to get the others to do it, tried to be the best bartender I could, but all they seem to want are drinks." He paused, then reached down under the bar, pulling out a glass and a grubby towel. "Sorry about that. I just want to get the full experience, you know? Got to be cleaning a glass with a rag for this, or it just doesn't look right. Anyway, I'm your man. Fire away."

Grave took a moment to give a long, drawn out sigh. After all, if they were going to go through this charade, he might as well get his money's worth.

"Where to start? My boss seems to think I'm an idiot, there's something strange going on with this job, because no half-breed should be able to get into this Court on their own, and to top it all I've run into a bar-full of layabout Figments who've run away from their work. All in all," he finished, taking another sip of the beer, "these have not been a good few days. Particularly since one of your friends is sneaking up behind me right now."

Grave ducked, and a chair slammed into the bar with enough force to shatter into kindling. Beer spilled across the bar, and since it was real ale it was probably going to need a chisel to get it off. Grave slammed his elbow backwards and heard the satisfying sound of someone keeling over behind him. He stood without looking and trailed his finger in the pool of beer, tasting it with all the slow menace of a cat licking blood from its paw. He turned very deliberately.

"That," Grave breathed, "was my *pint*."

The next few seconds were confusing, to say the least. The problem for a dozen people trying to fight one in a confined space is that there are so many more friends than foes. Well, at least until the first time they miss their target and clobber a friend over the head with a bottle.

After about half a second, Grave gave a great roar and picked up Big Frankie from where he'd fallen, throwing him headfirst into the crowd of advancing Figments.

A couple of seconds after that, he was busy bashing two Figments together while treading heavily on a third.

About ten seconds after that, Keith the Bartender came flying out of the PUB through the wall. He gave a soft groan and decided that, on the whole, waking up wasn't worth the effort.

Ten seconds after *that*, Grave strolled casually out of the front door, drinking beer from a bottle. At a sound from inside, he spun and threw the thing, bringing a thud and a scream.

Approximately thirty seconds later, the PUB collapsed.

Grave reached down, lifting the recumbent form of Keith the bartender by the remains of his brightly coloured shirt and hoisting him to eye level. Once there, Grave shook him into something approaching consciousness.

"Now, you were listening to my problems..."

"My... my pub..."

Grave shook him again. "*My* problems, not yours. Though we could talk about your problems if you like. Specifically, we could talk about the problems you're going to have if you don't help me with my problems."

There was a brief pause.

"So," Keith the bartender said with something approaching brightness, "tell me about your problems again."

"My main one is a young man. Dark hair, six feet tall, probably slightly confused."

"What, that bloke we had in earlier? We thought he was spying for your lot, mate."

Grave shook him again, on general principles. "Where did he go?"

Keith the bartender shrugged as best he could while being held approximately a foot off the ground. "He ran off. Didn't want to see what we do to spies."

Grave considered this information. "And what *do* you do?"

"Dunno, never caught one before. Anyway, this bloke legs it, and we can't find him even though we've looked all round here. Personally, I reckon he's had help. Probably that bastard, Stranded. He's been waiting for a way to get even ever since I barred him. Did I mention he was a right bastard?"

"Yes." Grave was thoughtful for a moment. "Tell me about him."

The Figment did it with the lack of hesitation that Grave usually found in people he asked questions of. Once he was done, Grave shrugged and tossed him to the ground.

"Stay here," he ordered. "I'm sure some of the Queen's men will be along eventually."

"So, you're not going to kill me then?"

Grave just set off walking.

It wasn't easy for Nicola to walk, what with the ragged tears to her legs, and she found herself leaning on the gardener, Poppy, more than she would have liked to. The other woman had a scent that was at once clean and faintly earthy. Together, they cut a brisk path through a series of stone lined corridors. At least they'd used a tiny door in the side of the place rather than walking in the front. Until Nicola knew more about wherever she was, she still didn't want to risk attracting too much attention.

Within a few minutes, they'd reached a wooden door that seemed to be an almost perfect circle. Poppy managed to open it with one hand while supporting Nicola with the other. It was impossible not to gape at the room beyond. For a gardener, Nicola had been expecting some pokey little room tucked out of sight somewhere. Or possibly a shed. She might have *believed* a shed.

This wasn't a shed. It was certainly out of the way, but it would never pass for pokey. It stretched maybe thirty metres across, and arched almost as high. The only reason it didn't seem like some vast and open cathedral was the mass of plants that contrived to take up almost every inch of the space. There were almost more plants in that room than there had been in the garden. They swept across a rough workbench, wound around the pillars of a large four-poster bed, and were arranged in neat pots and tubs around a pair of comfortable chairs separated by a small table. It seemed to Nicola that Poppy gave plants the run of her space in the same way that a certain sort of elderly woman ended up with houses full of cats.

"This is..." Nicola tailed off, unable to think of a single word to describe the place. Beside her, Poppy just laughed, and the sound was like sunlight pouring into the room.

"It's a bit much, isn't it? It didn't start like this, but you know how it is. I put a couple of plants in, just to get them started, and then a few more, and pretty soon I could hardly find anything for them. Let's get you into a chair and we'll see about these wounds. I'm a little worried. They don't seem to be closing up like they should."

Nicola frowned, trying to focus on the thorn rips in her wrists. She wasn't an expert, but they seemed to be doing ok. They were bloody and ragged, but at least the bleeding was stopping. Nicola didn't complain though when Poppy lowered her into a chair that was just about the softest she'd ever sat in.

"Now then..." Poppy wandered off among the plants, tossing aside her sun-hat casually to reveal her blonde and mossy green hair. She stopped here and there, picking leaves, examining flowers. All the while she kept up a stream of chatter that seemed almost equally divided between the plants and Nicola.

"Now then, we'll just take a few of your leaves, and maybe a berry, just to be sure... did I remember to warn you about the roses, Nicola? I forget things, sometimes."

"Yes...I just didn't pay enough attention, and I wasn't really expecting it."

"Really?" The other woman's brow crinkled in a frown, before her hand went to her mouth. "Oh, but you were confused in the garden, weren't you? Are you sure you didn't hit your head? Oh I'm sorry, I just assumed that living here you'd know what the roses can be like."

Nicola tried to digest the sudden rush of words, and realised that there might be a way of finding out what was going on.

Before she could speak though, Poppy pressed a mug into her hands. It was warm, and gave off a strange, sweet odour.

"Here, this should help."

The other woman said it with an earnest smile that made Nicola drain the cup in one long swallow. "Uggh! What's in this?"

"Oh, all sorts of stuff. Don't worry about the taste. It doesn't do any good if it doesn't taste horrible. Someone told me that once, I think. Now, how are you feeling?"

To her surprise, Nicola did actually feel a little stronger. "A little better, thanks." She decided that this was probably the best chance she was going to get. "Poppy, you know that I was a little confused before?"

"Yes? Are you still feeling it?"

"A little." That was an understatement. Even so, Nicola felt a little bad about the lie she was about to tell. There was something innocent, almost naïve about the gardener, and she obviously felt guilty about Nicola getting hurt. Still, Nicola needed to know what was going on.

"I think, whatever it is, it's made me confused about a lot of things. I reach for them, but it's like they're not there."

"Oh, that's terrible!" Poppy sat opposite her and reached out, taking Nicola's hand.

"Maybe, if you jogged my memory, things might start to come back to me."

"All right. What would you like to know?"

"Well… where are we?"

Poppy smiled at that. "We're in the castle, silly. Sorry, that didn't help much, did it? This is the castle of Erithnae, the Queen of the Dreaming Court."

"And it's all like…?" Nicola swept a hand round at the waiting plants.

"Oh no, that's just me. I like plants. I make some of them for the dreams. I made the roses down in the garden."

"You made them?"

"They were supposed to protect people." Poppy sounded like she'd had this conversation before. "It's just that things always seem to go wrong."

Nicola decided that it was probably her turn to squeeze the other woman's hand in comfort, and was shocked to find that she could do it without pain. She looked down at her wrist, to find that the wounds had healed to little more than a few pinkish scars.

"That's impossible!"

"What?" Poppy turned her hand over, examining Nicola's wounds for herself. She seemed almost as surprised as Nicola at what she saw.

"But you shouldn't scar. None of us should, unless..."

Nicola didn't wait around for the end of that sentence. Maybe it was whatever Poppy had given her, but she was thinking clearly again. Whatever was going on, the other woman had just worked out that Nicola didn't belong there. Tearing her hand from Poppy's grip, she forced herself to her feet.

"Where are you going? You can't leave! Who are you? What are you doing here? *What* are you?"

"What I am now, is leaving," Nicola said, starting to edge away. "Thank you for helping me."

Poppy bit her lip in confusion for a moment, but then lunged forward, making a grab at Nicola. "Wait, stop! I can't just let you go. Guards!"

With a burst of effort, and feeling slightly sorry for doing it, Nicola shoved Poppy back into the chair. She turned and set off at an almost dead sprint, picking her way between the plants, hurdling one reaching tendril as best she could. As soon as she was at the door Nicola dove through it, slamming it behind her to slow Poppy down. Nicola still didn't understand everything that was going on, but she knew one thing; she had to get out of there.

They'd been walking for a while now, though Thomas was having trouble working out exactly how long. Somewhere in his various falls, brawls and dives into cover, his watch had decided it had had enough. Thomas' stomach was trying to persuade him that however long it had been, it was time to stop and find something to eat.

Sadly, it didn't seem prepared to provide Thomas with any suggestions as to how he should do that. He and Simon Stranded had managed to move clear of the wood, and were making their way carefully along hedgerows now, broken only by the occasional tree, and the odds on them running into a restaurant hidden neatly behind one of them didn't seem high, even in a place this odd.

Of course, Thomas was perfectly aware that it was possible to survive in the harshest of wildernesses. He'd seen the TV programs where assorted Special Forces types managed to survive with nothing more than a length of fishing wire and a bent spoon. They would probably laugh at a lush environment like this one. The trouble was, Thomas was painfully aware that there was no way he was ever going to be mistaken for a member of any kind of Special Forces unit. He certainly hadn't bothered to memorise any of the tips they'd thrown out. He'd usually been too busy microwaving his dinner. Also, he didn't have a spoon, bent or otherwise.

After a few more minutes of trailing after Simon Stranded, Thomas decided that he was being stupid. They were walking past golden fields of wheat, mixed in with trees that seemed to have fruit hanging from their branches. To go hungry while there was that for the taking was little short of idiotic. Yes, it was probably stealing, but Thomas wasn't in the mood to try and explain the legal niceties to his stomach. Instead, the next time they passed a tree, Thomas reached up and plucked the lowest of its fruits.

It was round and smooth, a little larger than an apple and a delicious-looking deep green. Thomas didn't recognise it, but then he didn't recognise much there, and Thomas doubted farmers would leave anything poisonous near to their fields. With the lack of hesitation of someone whose last meal had consisted of mildly furry sausages, he bit down. The juice was sweet and abundant, filling Thomas' mouth the moment his teeth broke through the skin of the thing. It was crunchy and, since he was hungry, would probably have qualified as about the best thing that Thomas had tasted, if he hadn't been concentrating on other things.

Things like the image of a spiral staircase that had just popped unbidden into his brain. Thomas had just enough time to say "what the...?" though it didn't really help.

Blackness, sprinkled with stars in the sort of quantities normally associated with the toppings on ice cream, stretched around him, yet Thomas could see the staircase perfectly. It spiralled up, its white marble apparently stretching into infinity in both directions.

"Excuse me," a voice said, "but are you going to start walking or not?"

Thomas looked round and saw that below him on the staircase there was a rather elderly man, holding a candle and dressed in the sort of old fashioned nightshirt and cap that seemed to Thomas better suited to productions of "Scrooge" than to real life. *But then*, he thought, *if this is real life I've gone completely insane.*

"Oh, sorry. Um... would you mind telling me where we are?"

"Haven't a clue, son, now would you mind getting on with this? I haven't got all night."

Not knowing what else to do, Thomas started walking. For the first couple of minutes, it wasn't so bad, but there didn't seem to be an end to the stairs. Thomas tried taking them two at a time and all that did was to wear him out. Looking up made it clear that he was no closer to the top.

"Tired already?" While he'd been standing and staring the old man had managed to catch up to him. Thomas shrugged.

"There doesn't seem to be much point. I can't see the top."

"Doesn't mean it's not worth climbing."

"But it *does* make you wish there was a lift, right?" Thomas said it with a laugh cut short when he saw the old man looking over Thomas' shoulder, towards the steps immediately above them.

Except, when Thomas turned around, they weren't steps any more. Instead there was a short landing, flanked on the inside by the unmistakable grey box of a lift. It opened as he took a step towards it, and Thomas hopped inside without a second thought. The doors started to close and hastily he pressed the button to hold the lift.

"Are you coming?" he called back to the old man, who, much to Thomas' surprise, shook his head.

"I reckon I'll just keep climbing, if it's all the same. You're obviously in a hurry, but some things are worth the trouble."

He set off, and Thomas let the doors slide shut. Even before he could press another button, the lift started moving, heading up, and up, and...

"Hey, Thomas, wake up!"

Thomas groaned and opened his eyes, feeling more than slightly sick. The fact that Simon Stranded was shaking him didn't really help. Thomas pushed him back and managed to struggle to his feet.

"What happened?" Thomas asked.

"What happened?" There was a panicky edge to the words. "I'll tell you what happened. You found someone's dream lying around and jumped into it. What did you think you were doing?"

"It looked tasty, and I haven't eaten since we got here," Thomas admitted, causing Stranded to roll his eyes in frustration.

"Well, thanks to your hunger pangs, the whole Court knows where we are now."

Something about Stranded's expression told Thomas that it was more than that.

"There's something else, isn't there? What is it?"

"Not only did you jump into the dream, which I seriously doubt you should be able to do, but you also changed it, which you *definitely* shouldn't."

Thomas winced as he tried to get a grip on his rebellious stomach. "Look Simon, can we leave this? I mean it's too late to do anything, and the only person I saw in there was an old man."

"No, you don't understand." Stranded grabbed Thomas,

forcing him to meet his eyes. "It isn't about who saw you in the dream, it's about who felt you there. Normally Figments like me don't get much feedback when someone changes a dream, but I felt it. Maybe that was just because I was close, but the dreaming folk are a lot more sensitive than I am."

"Which means?" Thomas prompted.

"They know where you are now."

Chapter Ten

Grave stomped along the country paths, keeping his eyes carefully peeled for signs that someone had passed that way. He was good at that sort of thing, reading muddy tracks, flattened grass and broken twigs as easily as he might read a map. More easily, in fact, because Grave had never quite got the hang of the idea that maps were better off without a coat pocket's worth of creases in them. Yes, footprints were definitely easier. Between those and the faint there-and-gone-again scent of humanity, Grave knew he was on the right track.

It did mean, however, that it took him a while to notice the butterflies. In fact, it was only when he paused to scan the horizon that Grave realised that a cloud of them was floating along neatly behind him, with rather more purpose than butterflies had any right to. He took a few deliberate steps and the butterflies followed like an overeager puppy. Grave sighed.

"What does she want now?"

As if in answer, the brightly coloured cluster parted a little, revealing that someone had succeeded in attaching a fine thread to each of the fluttering creatures. Between them, they just about managed to support a silk cloth, and in that cloth...

"Clever," Grave grudgingly allowed, "very clever."

He picked up the halved fruit that the butterflies bore, doing his best to snap the threads as he did so. Freed, the butterflies spiralled up and away in a hundred different directions. Only one paused long enough to land on Grave's calloused palm, letting the Princess' words come to him.

Don't just stand there, idiot. Report!

Grave resisted the urge to squash the thing, barely. With an expression of mild annoyance, he trampled a patch of grass into submission, lay down, and took a bite from the fruit. As the dream came, Grave pushed straight into it, knowing that the Princess would be waiting, and knowing that her idea of patience was not demanding that something had been done an hour before she asked for it.

It was a pleasant enough dream, at least. Water swirled and bubbled in a large natural pool, surrounded by trees on three sides and facing a waterfall on the fourth. Bright sunlight poured down onto the place, turning to rainbows as it passed through the sheet of water filling the pool. Siobhan, of course, was floating casually on her back in the thing, dressed in the sort of bikini that might otherwise have provided enough material for a small handkerchief.

A quick glance around the place revealed the dreamer, a young human male, secured to one of the trees with what looked very much to Grave like duct tape.

"I was in a hurry." Siobhan rose from the pool in a manner that would no doubt have inspired artists to paint pictures of god-desses, or at least to take a cold shower. "I'll make it up to him later. Probably. Now though, I'd like to know *what the hell is going on.*"

Grave thought about reminding her that he was doing his best, and that Siobhan was welcome to try herself if she thought she could do any better, but common sense prevailed. Instead he set about explaining as briefly as he could. As he finished, Siobhan looked at him expectantly.

"And the disturbance a few minutes ago?"

"Disturbance, Princess?"

Grave saw Siobhan roll her eyes.

"Yes Grave, disturbance. As in someone messing around with a dream loud enough that half the Court have felt it. Are you really telling me that you didn't feel anything?"

Grave thought for a moment. He'd felt the backwash of

something, but he'd assumed that it was Siobhan. She was usually the only one willing to be that unsubtle in a human's dreams. He just shrugged.

"I don't know why I bother," Siobhan muttered, moving to sit by the side of the pool and kicking her legs in the water. "Are you trying to make this go wrong, Grave?"

That stung. So far, Grave had tracked Thomas Greene down, been berated by a small but violent human woman, run headfirst into a tree, summoned up the sleeping dead, fought a bar full of Figments, and slogged miles across the Dreaming Court. He was, in his humble opinion, doing his best.

"I'll find him, Princess. And then I'll kill him. If he's going around changing dreams, he should be easy enough to find."

He saw Siobhan's expression change for a moment, shifting to something far more thoughtful than it had been. Finally, she nodded. "You're right. With him here, he will be easy enough to find. And easy to capture, too."

"Capture?" The word slipped out before Grave could stop it.

"Oh, don't look so put out, Grave." Siobhan smiled up at him in a way that Grave might have appreciated better if he didn't know she was about to ask him to do something he didn't want to. "Think about it. In his home, he has to die. Here, so long as we can stash him nicely out of the way, none of the other Courts will ever know. Think of it as the… humane option."

Grave thought about it, and had trouble shaking the thought that becoming Siobhan's plaything probably counted as the inhumane option. Even so, he nodded.

"As you wish, Princess."

Siobhan shook her head. "No, Grave, as I *command*. I'll get together some backup and meet you out there. Now go."

She snapped her fingers, and Grave's eyes flicked open, giving him a clear view of the cloudless sky as he came out of the dream. The damp grass brushed his cheek, and he pushed to his feet.

"You know," Grave said to the world in general, "if she weren't the Queen's daughter, I'd probably…" Grave didn't finish it. You never knew who was listening. Instead, he looked around, orienting himself. Sure enough, there were still the faintest shimmerings in the stuff of the Court where someone had changed a dream. Now he was actually looking for them, they were easy to spot. They lay like broken twigs after a storm had blown through. And, like a storm, it was fairly easy to tell which way the wind had been blowing. All Grave had to do was follow it back.

Siobhan woke with a sigh that betrayed her disappointment at having to leave the dream before getting the chance to play with its owner. Sadly, some things were more important. It occurred to Siobhan that, if she'd been feeling kind, she might have cut the tape holding him to the tree. Still, he'd wake up soon enough. Probably. Stretching like a cat, Siobhan opened her eyes, and found the one person she didn't want to see staring down at her.

"Hello mother." Siobhan kept her tone light. It wouldn't do to insult the Queen in front of... she counted... half a dozen Figments, a couple of handmaids and that silly bitch Poppy. Unfortunately, the voice didn't seem to be enough. Her mother reached down, snatching up the last sliver of the fruit Siobhan had eaten.

"I warned you to leave the dreamers alone, didn't I? And you've still gone and done it anyway, making enough noise to wake half the Court. You obviously need a lesson, daughter."

Siobhan cringed despite herself. That the punishments of the Dreaming Court happened in dreams didn't make them any less painful, or, with so many looking on, any less humiliating. And her mother would do it too. Siobhan had no doubts about that. A moment of pure anger cut through the fear, making her want to stand up, look her mother in her oh-so-beautiful face and tell her where to shove her "lesson," but even Siobhan knew she wouldn't get away with that. Which really only left her with the option of lying through her teeth. Siobhan smiled to herself. She was good at that.

"I don't see any reason to smile," her mother snapped, and

Siobhan rose just enough to fall to her knees. It was too much, but then, at times like this it always did to pile it on.

"I am smiling, my Queen, at the thought I might be so clumsy as the one we all felt in dreams."

"Are you claiming it wasn't you?"

"Of course." Siobhan gave the words just a little edge. Play the compliant little daughter too much, and there was no way her mother would believe it. "I heard your command, my Queen, and I obeyed it."

"Then what were you doing in this dream?"

Though the words were laid down with the care of a prosecutor pointing out to a bank robber that fifty people had seen them do it, Siobhan jumped for joy inside. That her mother had even stopped to ask was all the opening she needed. It was time to wind the Queen of the Dreaming Court around her little finger.

Siobhan looked down, carefully composing the expression that would do the job. One part hurt, one part fear, and all innocence, it would probably have made her a fortune if it hadn't already been perfected by small children everywhere.

"I was just trying to help, mother. I felt someone playing with dreams, and I wanted to see who it was. I... I just wanted to be useful."

"And did you find them?"

Siobhan shook her head. She couldn't afford to let on what she knew about Thomas Greene. Not now. "I thought they were in this dream, but I must have been wrong. Please don't be angry, mother."

A moment later, Siobhan felt the touch of her mother's hand against her cheek. Just a brush, but enough to make Siobhan breathe an unheard sigh of relief.

"Of course I'm not angry, darling. But perhaps next time you should leave these things to others. What if they had been there, what then? I wouldn't want to see you hurt."

Unless it's you doing it, Siobhan thought, remembering that only a minute ago there had been the threat of a punishment. Wisely, she didn't reply, letting her mother continue.

"But we have other problems now. Poppy informs me that

there is someone loose in the palace."

"Is she certain? Not that I doubt her," Siobhan said in a voice that made it perfectly clear that she did, "but Poppy isn't usually... very clear headed."

Both her mother and the gardener nodded at the same time, giving the impression, to Siobhan at least, of a weird pair of dolls being operated together.

"In this case, it seems she is certain. There is an intruder. A young woman."

Siobhan's interest faded as soon as the last words were out of her mother's mouth. She'd been half hoping that Thomas Greene had saved her the trouble of looking for him. But it occurred to Siobhan that perhaps this new development could be used to her advantage. Quickly, she plastered the most earnest expression she could manage over her features.

"Let me help, mother, please?"

"I don't know darling..."

"I won't get in the way. I fact, I'll look somewhere no one else does. I'll check outside, just in case this woman has made a run for it. Please mother, I want to make up for troubling you like this."

"Darling," her mother swept her up onto her feet, "you have nothing to make up. But if you really want to help..."

"Oh, I do."

"Well then, you're right. No one else would have thought to search the area around here. But you're not doing this alone. We don't know yet what sort of threat this woman is. For all we know, she could be from one of the other Courts, sent here to hurt us."

Siobhan sighed. The last thing she needed was a bunch of her mother's servants tagging along to "protect" her, making her search that much harder. Not to mention how hard it might be to keep them quiet afterwards once they saw that Siobhan wasn't looking for who she was supposed to.

"Mother, I'm sure I'll be fine. There's really no need..."

Erithnae, Queen of the Dreaming Court, held up a hand for silence. "This isn't open to question, Siobhan. You can search, but I want you to have help. I'm lending you... the Nightmare Hunt."

There was a brief pause, as though she were waiting for a sudden crash of lightning, or at least an appreciative "oooh!" from the audience of courtiers. Instead, Siobhan winced.

"Why do *I* have to put up with that bunch of idiots?"

Thomas snuck along the hedgerows around the tiny hamlet, trying to get a good view of the place without being seen. It probably counts as a pretty good demonstration of just how worried he was that he was doing so even though Simon Stranded was strolling along and whistling loudly.

"I thought you said we had to be careful," Thomas hissed. "You know, something about people knowing where we are?"

"I am being careful," the Figment replied. "And they know where you *were*, not where we are. We're well away by now."

That, at least, was true. In the half an hour or so since Thomas had woken up, they'd managed to cover a lot of ground. More, in fact, than Thomas would normally have thought possible. When he'd mentioned that to his travelling companion, Simon had bobbed his head in agreement.

"It can be like that round here. You've never had a dream where you suddenly went from one place to another? It's not as bad as that outside the dreams, but time and space are still pretty messed up. I hear they tried to get someone to map the whole Court once. Drove the poor bloke mad. Spent his days doing origami down in the castle cellars, trying to get it right."

Thomas sucked in a breath, and tried to wrap his head around yet another thing that he wouldn't have believed just a few hours before. The really worrying thing was that it did actually make a kind of sense. If this... place really did run like dreams, moving around at odd rates was about the least weird of the things that could be happening.

"That still doesn't explain why you're strutting around in full view." He tugged Stranded's sleeve to try and get him down out of sight. The Figment pulled away.

"What do you think is going to attract more notice? Me walking around nice and normally, or you skulking around like you're practising to be a cat burglar?"

Thomas thought about it for a moment, and then, reddening slightly, stood up.

Stranded nodded. "That's better. The way I see it, no one this far out will know about us. They might even help us if we ask. They're just ordinary dreaming folk, nothing to do with the Queen."

Sure enough, when Thomas took a better look at the place, it looked more or less normal. Well... if normal ran to buildings and clothes that looked a few hundred years out of date, not to mention inhabitants who mostly seemed a lot better looking than average. It was as though the BBC had run short of extras for a costume drama, and decided to populate it with the contents of the nearest modelling agency.

All in all, it looked perfectly safe. Despite his fears, Thomas started to relax. Maybe, if they were lucky, the pair of them might be able to talk the people there into letting them clean up a little, or even into feeding them. Just the prospect of it was enough to set him climbing over the hedge. He was about half way across when something in the distance caught his eye. From where Thomas was, it was just possible to make out a crowd of figures progressing towards the village in a rough mass. He strained to see closer.

"What on Earth...?"

Siobhan let the great black nightmare horse carry her along, spurts of flame coming from its nostrils, and tried desperately not to look around too much. It was simply too embarrassing. That was why she'd kept arguing with her mother until they were almost out of the castle, not that it had done any good. But the Nightmare Hunt? If this was all her mother thought of her...

Other Courts had proper hunts. The wild hunts of the Fey

before the War, the tearing raptors of the Court of Air, even the great mossy, shambling things that the Flower Court could boast, more compost heap than anything and able to overcome whole regiments just with the smell. *Of course* the Dreaming Court had had to get its own. And then some bright spark had suggested that it should be put together from humans' worst nightmares brought to life. It was the sort of idea that sounded great, absolutely terrifying. At least until you remembered that humans were capable of having some seriously weird nightmares.

Siobhan couldn't stop herself from looking round any longer. She immediately wished she hadn't. A boot the size of a man hopped along beside her, a broad smile of teeth set into the toe, the mouth occasionally opening to allow a huge tongue to loll randomly. A surprisingly scary looking armchair rolled along on castors at Siobhan's other flank. Further off, a trio of badly made up clowns juggled and tossed custard pies at each other while unicycling as quickly as they could. A man with no face blundered into things whenever he lost his grip on the arm of a hag so old that she seemed to exist mostly as wrinkles and cardigans.

Oh, there were a few scarier things. A mass of tentacles floated improbably above them, while a couple of large black dogs with glowing eyes kept pace at a trot. The trouble was, even these seemed to have been affected by the rest of them. The tentacled thing had some sort of green and blue striped goblin on top, pulling various devices from a bag and fiddling with them with a screwdriver until they stopped working, while the black dogs yipped and scampered round the heels of a small girl in a pink dress. The only frightening thing about her was a stare that could have cut through teak.

Siobhan tried to imagine the effect of being chased by this mob, and decided that on the whole the prey was more likely to die from laughing than being torn to shreds. Still, at least they were all too stupid to report back to her mother that Siobhan had taken them this far from the castle. She looked over to where the village clung to the hillside like a particularly stubborn limpet, and decided that it was as good a place as any to ask after

Thomas Greene. Who knew, maybe after being stared at, covered in custard, and occasionally licked, they might be inclined to be helpful.

Failing that, Siobhan would just order the things to spread out and search. After all, how much damage could they do? Or, at least, how much did she really care?

Chapter Eleven

When faced with a shambling (not to mention hopping, unicycling, and skipping along daintily) horde of nightmare creatures, there are really only so many things that qualify as sensible responses. Screaming is a perennial favourite, as is passing out from the horror of it all. Running away is generally recommended by the experts, where an expert can be defined as "someone who didn't get eaten while they were busy screaming or passing out." Afterwards Thomas wasn't quite sure why, perhaps it was the influence of being around Nicola so long, but he decided to do none of them. Instead, Thomas got off the hedge and started for the village. Or he would have done, if Simon Stranded hadn't grabbed his arm.

"What are you doing?" Stranded demanded.

"Look!"

Thomas pointed to where the villagers were happily going about their business, apparently unconcerned by the horde that was gibbering – and sadly honking big red noses, in the case of the clowns – as it bore down on them. "They haven't seen it. We should warn them."

"Or we could run," the Figment suggested. "Running sounds good. We might just get away if we run."

Thomas looked from the village to the fields and track ways behind him, trying to work out how much time they had. "Maybe we could just shout a warning."

Stranded raised an eyebrow. "From here? They'll hear you,

but I doubt they'll have a clue what you're on about. They'll probably be so busy looking this way that they won't see what's coming. When you think about it, they'll actually be better off if we don't shout."

Thomas considered it for a moment longer.

"What if..." he began, but Stranded cut him off.

"You're about to ask, 'what if we go closer?' aren't you? Well, look at it this way: how do you feel about trying to outrun that horse? Not to mention those dogs. Now, I'm all for helping people. I mean, I'm helping you aren't I? But there's helping people and then there's hurting yourself, you know?"

Thomas thought about it. The annoying thing was that he did know, just as he knew that Stranded was right. They couldn't afford to get any closer, and shouting would just attract the wrong sort of attention. "I suppose... well, they're after us, aren't they? So it's not like they'll hurt anybody else. The best thing we can do is not to be there."

"Whatever you say. Just so long as you start running now."

Thomas gave the place one last look. In the time he'd spent making up his mind, the horde had managed to arrive at the outskirts of the village. Thomas saw a man walk from his cottage, just in time to catch a custard pie full in the face. He was about to mention this to Simon Stranded when he saw the figure on horseback pause, look out towards them, and point.

"Run!" Thomas yelled, and set off at a dead sprint in the other direction.

"That's more like it."

They ran. More than that, they barrelled along, barely caring where they were running; tripping, scrambling upright again and continuing again, all at the sort of speeds that normally meant the chases in a silent movie were being played on too fast a projector. They ran like the worst things imaginable were bounding (and hopping, and unicycling, and...) just behind them.

Which of course they were, Thomas reminded himself as an ear splitting howl sounded only a little way back. But that was all right. All he had to do was keep running. So long as he could keep them as far behind himself as possible, Thomas would be happy.

Of course, the minor difficulty in concentrating on what you're running away *from* is that occasionally you forget about what you might be running *towards.*

Grave had been enjoying a scone and a nice sit down in the long grass when he heard the hunt begin. Grave didn't see much reason to hurry. He'd done his hurrying, running to catch up like a great bear that'd just been told someone was giving away free honey. Or possibly marmalade sandwiches, though Grave wasn't sure where that thought had come from. You picked up all sorts of things in dreams.

Regardless, Grave had done the hard part. He'd loped to where the disturbance in the dream had occurred, and then hurried to track Thomas Greene from there. If this was going to be his only break today, Grave didn't see much point in rushing things. Besides, judging by the sound the Nightmare Hunt was making, he was in the perfect spot. Grave liked being in the perfect spot.

The general rightness of his positioning was confirmed by the sound of approaching feet, along with breath being gulped in ragged gasps. *That's the problem with people today,* Grave thought, *no stamina. It's like they don't expect this sort of thing to come up,* though he also found time to think something fairly unpleasant about people who didn't let other people finish their lunch. Scowling, Grave settled for stuffing the last of the scone in his mouth before creeping silently a little further into the grass. It wouldn't do to be seen. He waited until the footsteps were almost on him, thundering along almost beside him, before he jumped out.

Grave was good at jumping out. He felt the thud of someone slamming into him, and felt them bounce off. People usually did. He looked down and smiled, because he'd chosen his moment well. Thomas Greene lay sprawled on the rough track in front of him, looking up with something close to terror.

"Look, I don't know what this is about, just... let me go, all right?"

Grave felt the push that came with the words, pressing on his mind and urging him to do what Greene wanted. Idly, he squashed the urge, wondering as he did so if the young man knew that he was doing it. Probably not, Grave decided, because then he'd know it didn't work on most of the things from the Courts. Casually, Grave drew himself up to his full height. It took some time.

"Mmmphf..." he began, and then remembered to swallow the scone, "sorry, where was I? Oh yes... I've got you now, you little bugger."

Grave reached down and lifted him with one meaty hand. When Thomas Greene began to struggle, punching Grave as best he could, Grave just held him out at arm's length and shook him a little. It wasn't like the blows hurt, but there was the look of the thing to consider. Besides, Grave was still more than a little annoyed about running into a tree. He gave the task of shaking Thomas Greene into submission a bit more attention. Grave gave it so much attention, in fact, that he didn't even notice the second figure, who dodged into the long grass and lay there quivering.

Simon Stranded hunched closer to the ground, willing the grass to arc over him and shield him from view. He could taste the dirt, he was that close to it, while damp grass soaked through his shirt and twigs dug into his legs. It was almost certainly better than what would happen if someone spotted him. It was at times like this that Simon suspected he should have stayed in his dream. After all, what was so bad about living a life on the island, occasionally wandering out of the trees to bring a little pleasure to some sleeping beauty?

Sooner or later the thing would have been shut down, Simon reminded himself, *and what then? Changed back to some floating thing? I'd look awful in grey.*

Not that he'd have much choice if they found him. They'd render him down to a blank form the moment they caught him. That, or they'd kill him outright. Not that there was really much to choose between the two. Losing everything that made him... *him* sounded an awful lot like death from where Simon Stranded was standing. Sorry, lying. Compared to either option, staying very still in some nice, concealing grass was by far the better choice.

Of course, there was the minor difficulty that lying there doing nothing made him feel like a complete heel. By rights, Simon knew that he ought to be jumping up and helping Thomas, regardless of the personal danger. The trouble was that the danger in question was so dangerous. The big guy who held Thomas looked worryingly like the Queen's Huntsman, and everyone knew the stories about him. Actually, Simon didn't, but he knew that everyone else knew the stories about him, and he suspected that they weren't remotely pleasant ones. Leaping out to try and fight him didn't seem like the way to a long and happy life.

Even as Simon watched, the big man stopped shaking Thomas, sighed, then brought one hand round in a blow that might have seemed almost delicate, until you saw that after it Thomas was slumped unconscious. The sound of hoof beats drew Simon's attention away from the scene in front of him, making him squirm a little further back from the path. There would be nothing like being trampled by a horse to brighten his day.

Unless, of course, it was being stamped on by a giant boot.

That landed approximately where Simon had just been, flattening the grass in a way that suggested it wouldn't have been the only thing flattened if Simon had still been lying there. Despite the boot's apparent lack of eyes, he nevertheless got the distinct feeling that it was staring straight at him. Now, Simon Stranded's time in his dream and afterwards had prepared him for a lot of things; lying to women about how beautiful they were, creating a cosy love nest out of the materials provided by a few palm trees and some sand, even surviving Keith's attempts

to hold a happy hour in a place that didn't charge for drinks anyway. What it hadn't done was tell him what to do when an out-
sized article of footwear was giving him a funny look.

In the end he settled for remaining very, very still.

Over the top of the thing, Simon could just make out the
woman arriving on horseback. Now there, Simon was prepared
to admit, was one woman whose arrival on his little island he
would have welcomed. Not that it made him want to give away
his hiding place any quicker. He'd heard descriptions of Princess
Siobhan before, and they'd invariably been accompanied by a
warning to keep well away from her. Although those warnings
hadn't included any advice about what you did if she currently
had her horse only a few yards away. Perhaps you weren't supposed to let it happen.

"You haven't killed him, have you?" Siobhan demanded it
of the waiting thug in a voice that Simon was almost certain
would have earned almost anyone else instant death. Instead, the
huge man just shook his head and shifted uncomfortably.

"Should just be knocked out, Princess," Simon heard him
mutter. "I *am* a professional."

"A professional what?"

The big man looked hurt by that, and Simon saw the Princess roll her eyes.

"Oh, very well. If he's in one piece I suppose you've done
well. Good job, Grave. There, is that what you wanted to hear?
Good, now get him up on the horse. I'll take him on ahead."

Simon wondered where she was planning on taking
Thomas. More to the point, he wondered if he was about to be
left in a field full of Nightmares. It didn't seem like a particularly
pleasant prospect. Obviously the big man had the same idea, because he called after the Princess as she turned her horse,
Thomas slung in front of her like a sack.

"What should I do with this lot?"

"I don't know, use your imagination." The Princess paused
for a moment, obviously considering the sort of things that the
Huntsman's imagination might conjure up. "Actually, I have an
idea. I'm supposed to be using these to hunt down some woman

near the castle. Take them back there and look for her. It will be less suspicious that way."

She didn't wait for an answer, but galloped off. Simon heard the big man sigh.

"Right, you lot. You heard. Back to the castle with you." There was a brief pause. "That means you too, Boot. Get moving."

Simon held his breath, knowing that this was the moment when things might go horribly wrong. If the boot chose this moment to attack or sound the alarm, he was dead. Even if it stayed still, someone would come over to see what was wrong. Simon stayed there, pressing himself so tightly to the ground that anyone passing might have thought that he'd heard the gravity was about to be turned off and was determined not to go anywhere. A heartbeat passed, then another.

With the hugest, pinkest tongue Simon Stranded had ever seen, the boot licked him once before bounding off.

Siobhan drove the great black horse to a gallop, its strides eating up the distance despite the added burden to its back. She'd taken the time to tie him over the saddle. After all, Siobhan didn't want the half-breed falling off the thing. She'd blindfolded him too, in case he should wake up. With luck though, that would only happen when they were close. Her mother's idiot had hit him quite hard.

It took time to reach the castle, even at the speed the horse was moving. Siobhan spent most of it guessing at how she might be able to convince this one to be useful. She doubted it would take much. He'd run simply at the sight of the pack of freaks her mother called a Hunt. A little fear then, and he'd probably do as he was told. That was good. It wasn't as though she *liked* having to hurt people. It was just that they so rarely seemed to do exactly what Siobhan told them otherwise.

Thinking about it, Siobhan decided that Thomas Greene should really be grateful. Well, not for the being hunted down and tied over the back of a horse part, obviously, but certainly for the not being killed part. He was going to be kept nice and safe until Siobhan found a use for him, which was more than might have happened without her involvement.

Actually, since he was quite good looking for something so human, Siobhan could already think of several uses for him. Unfortunately, Siobhan imagined he'd be more interested in cursing her and begging for his freedom. People were, in his position. Couldn't they see that some things were for the greater good? Or Siobhan's good, anyway, which to Siobhan amounted to much the same thing.

Eventually, they arrived, and Siobhan headed straight for the gardens, hopping lightly from the horse before considering how best to get her prisoner down. In the end Siobhan settled for simply pushing him, giving a slight smile at the "oof!" that came with him hitting the ground.

"You're awake then? Good, I thought I was going to have to carry you. Just hang on a moment, and don't try anything silly like calling for help. Trust me, most of what would come is worse than me."

Siobhan patted the nose of the nightmare horse as she said it, feeding the thing a sugar lump. It nuzzled her hand affectionately, which would have been a lot more pleasant without the sudden jet of flame as the thing whinnied.

"Ouch! Stupid thing!" Siobhan shook her burned hand. "Get out of here. Go on. Back to Grave and the others. Next time I'll find a bloody unicorn."

The horse hung its head, but trotted off anyway. That was one advantage of working with something out of nightmares; there wasn't any need for grooms or stables afterwards. Siobhan returned her attention to the half-breed, who seemed to be trying to inch away. She sighed and half-dragged him up to his feet.

"If you mess me around, I'll only have to hurt you, Thomas, so don't."

"How do you know my name?"

Siobhan gave a soft laugh. "It wasn't easy, but this is neither the time nor the place for a question and answer session.

Now, come along… or do you want me to give you back to Grave?"

That was enough to get him moving. They walked arm in arm through the rose garden, which struck Siobhan as nicely Jane Austen, though possibly no such scene from a costume drama has had the hero tied and blindfolded. At least not in the versions sold over the counter. As soon as she saw that there was no sign of anyone else, especially not that stupid bitch Poppy, Siobhan led Thomas over to the rose arch she wanted.

The roses hissed and swirled threateningly. Siobhan gave them a vicious stare.

"Less of that. Now, wall, open up!"

Siobhan watched, because no matter how many times she saw it happen, she was still proud of this bit. The roses slunk back onto their arch, sulking as much as plants ever could, while the bricks behind them seemed to fold away, revealing the sort of tunnel that in a certain kind of children's book would have almost certainly led to a smugglers' cave. To Siobhan's mind, what it actually led to was even better.

It had taken a lot of effort to tack a dream pocket onto the garden like this, particularly without her mother noticing, but Siobhan had decided that some things were worth a little extra work. The room that the short tunnel led to was the size of a small banqueting hall, complete with a chequerboard floor, the most ornate throne Siobhan's mind had been able to conjure, and a bed that could easily have slept a dozen people, though unfortunately she hadn't had the chance to test that thought out yet.

About the only thing that didn't fit with the décor was the black barred cage that filled one corner of the place, a good ten feet tall and more than that on a side. It held a small bed, a table, and the sort of bucket that could only ever have one use. On the whole, it didn't fit with the rest of the room, but then, what did go with a cage, really? Well, prisoners, obviously. The woman who laid sleeping on the bed looked up as Siobhan approached, the usual mixture of fear and hopelessness etched into her features.

"No time to talk, Melissa dear." Siobhan opened the cage

door. "Untie this one, would you? I'm a bit busy right now."
With a heave, she shoved Thomas inside.

Erithnae, Queen of the Dreaming Court, Ruler of Dreams and Nightmares, Commander of Figments, Lady of Daydreams, and about a dozen other titles she really wished she'd never let the heralds come up with, because she never seemed to hear the end of them, was taking a brief walk outside. What with the crowds of Figments, servants and guards searching the castle for a possible intruder, it seemed best to get out of the way.

Not that Erithnae was actually alone, of course. One of the first lessons any ruler had to learn was how to put up with an entourage determined to avoid even the slightest risk of said ruler doing even the simplest things for themselves. By her usual standards though, the pair of Figments who drifted along behind Erithnae hardly amounted to much at all. Figments were so useful, like one of those knives that armies seemed so fond of, able to transform into just the right tool for a particular circumstance. And once you'd done with them, of course, it was easy to change them back.

Erithnae was so busy thinking of new things to turn Figments into that she almost didn't notice her daughter emerging from the rose gardens. Almost, but not quite. If there's one thing a mother is guaranteed to spot, it's her child not doing what they've been asked to. That applies equally whether the child in question is six or six hundred.

"I thought you were searching with the Nightmares, darling."

It was hard not to give the words an edge. As much as Erithnae loved her, Siobhan never seemed to see things through. The girl was too easily distracted. Mostly by pretty faces, not to mention other assorted body parts. There was just the slightest of pauses before the reply.

"I'm still looking, mother. I just thought that Grave might be able to get more out of the Hunt than I could."

That, at least, was true, even if the rest was almost certainly a lie. Just what her daughter thought she was doing giving command of the Hunt to someone else though was anyone's guess. *She's probably gotten bored and decided not to play any more*, Erithnae thought, but decided to let it go. There were days when Erithnae wished she could give up responsibility for an hour or two. "Well, keep at it, sweetheart. I have the business of state to attend to. One of our patrols found a group of Figments in a partially collapsed building. Some were dead, but there are still a few that need rendering back to their real form. Unless you'd rather do it?"

Predictably, her daughter seemed to shrink from the idea. Then again, it *was* roughly the equivalent of suggesting that she might like to do the washing up for a change.

"I think I'll just keep looking, mother."

"Yes, I thought you would."

Chapter Twelve

Conversations, as a rule, have certain predictable elements. This is particularly the case when one of the participants is tied up.

"Um... could you untie me, please?" Thomas asked.

"I'm trying." The voice was female and surprisingly pleasant. "Hold still. I can't get the knots if you squirm. Hmm... this is going to be tricky. Let me get the blindfold first."

A second later and bright light stung Thomas' eyes, giving him a good view of the woman doing the talking. It was a nice view. She couldn't have been much more than his age, with slender, high-cheek-boned features and hair that managed to make a mousy sort of brown seem like something beautiful, even when it was hacked brutally short. Her eyes were a deep hazel that bored into his, even as she shifted her attention back to his hands. On second thought, Thomas replaced "slender" with "clearly underfed." Her clothes looked like they'd been worn for a while.

She got the first question out. "You're human, aren't you? Not a Figment, or one of *them*."

Thomas nodded. "I'm Thomas."

"Melissa." She swore as she picked at the knots, but Thomas felt them loosen. "There. It seems Siobhan would make a good Girl Guide."

"Siobhan?"

"She brought you here. Was she the one who grabbed you too?"

Thomas shook his head, then winced when his head threatened to explode at the movement. To his surprise, Melissa put a cool hand to his forehead.

"Are you all right?" She gave a brief laugh and looked pointedly round the cage that held them. "I mean, besides all this?"

"The... thing that grabbed me knocked me out. I suppose I should be grateful. It's an improvement on trying to kill me, anyway."

"A big man with an ugly old overcoat?"

Thomas nodded.

"That will be Grave. Siobhan told me about him, once, when I wasn't doing what she wanted. She said I was lucky to be here, that after me, she just sent him to kill people. Lucky."

Thomas saw the first hints of tears in her eyes, but Melissa brushed them away.

"Sorry."

"Don't be."

They stayed silent like that for a while. Thomas didn't know how long. Eventually though, he couldn't help the urge to talk. After all, what else were they going to do?

"Whereabouts are you from, Melissa?"

He saw her start at the sudden words, but she answered, at least.

"Colchester. Well, a small island just off it. What about you?"

Thomas shrugged. "That's a difficult one. My mother moved down to Devon after the divorce. My dad went for Canterbury. Neither really counts as home. I was up in Nether Wrexford at university when this happened. So, have you been here long?"

"Under other circumstances, that might sound like a variation on 'do you come here often'." Melissa laughed again and stood, but the humour in her expression didn't last. "I don't know. Months, maybe. It's hard to tell when this place never changes. Siobhan comes in to feed me, but it's not regular enough to count as days. Besides, who knows how time runs in this place?"

"I know the distance doesn't work quite right."

Thomas paused, trying to think of a good way to ask what he really wanted to. *The hell with it,* he thought, and ploughed in. "Melissa, what are we doing here? If you've been here for so long, surely you must have some idea by now. Who is this Siobhan? What does she want us for?"

Thomas watched Melissa move to the edge of the bed, sitting down. He could almost see her getting her thoughts into some sort of usable order.

"The easy question there is who Siobhan is," Melissa answered. "She's a bitch. Sadly, she's also the daughter of Erithnae, the Queen of this place, so no one dares tell her that to her face."

"So what does she want with us?" Thomas asked. Melissa stared at him for a while.

"What is it?"

"Thomas, have you ever done anything that you couldn't quite explain?"

Thomas started to shake his head, but stopped himself. "A few things."

"What sort of things?"

In the end, it was easier just to tell her everything, from what had happened with Nicola, to falling through into the Court, to what had happened in the old man's dream. Telling it to Melissa was easier than he'd hoped. In the end, she nodded.

"With me it's plants," Melissa said. "Sometimes, I can get them to do things. And I can talk to them."

Thomas tried to take that in. "Doesn't everyone talk to their plants?"

"Not everyone gets answers. I had a geranium that started telling me what my cat had been doing all day. And most people can't make flowers bloom just by touching them, can they?"

Thomas had to admit that he'd never heard of that one.

"So what," he asked, "we've been kidnapped for our special talents? Have I wandered into an episode of the X-Men by mistake?"

"You're in the middle of the Dreaming Court after falling through a rift in the fabric of reality," Melissa pointed out. "You've been inside someone's dream, and you've met things that aren't even close to human. It's a little late to start denying that this is happening."

"Sorry..." Thomas pinched his brow, wishing that the headache would go away. How did you know if you were concussed? Weren't you supposed to check for double vision or something? Thomas tried waving a hand vaguely in front of his face, but since he wasn't sure if it worked if you did it yourself, he gave up.

"All right then," he said, "we're both prisoners in a magical world. Fair enough. It's because we can both do odd things. Fair enough again, I can see why someone might think that was useful. What I don't get is *why can we do them?*"

"Ah..." Melissa looked away for a moment, and Thomas knew he wasn't going to like what she had to say next. "You know I asked if you were human? Well, strictly speaking, I'm not. And, um... neither are you."

There were times when Thomas hated being right.

Literature, particularly that of the sort where the hero wanders round carrying a sword approximately the same size as himself, traditionally says that those trying to sneak through a castle while avoiding searchers should find themselves pressed into niches, climbing up above doors, ducking behind statues, and a dozen other things that suggest the writer is extremely glad to be sitting in a nice, comfy chair.

What it doesn't mention is just how easy it is to get lost while doing all of this. Castles are large, complicated places, especially when they don't appear to have to obey the normal laws of physics. Combine that fact with trying to avoid being spotted, and you have a recipe for getting hopelessly confused.

Not that Nicola had to do anything particularly dramatic to stay out of sight. Once she'd worked out that half the searchers didn't have a clue who they were looking for, and that the other half could be avoided simply by ducking into the nearest room, it was fairly easy to keep from being captured. Finding an exit was another matter entirely.

After more than an hour of wandering aimlessly, the only thing Nicola had been able to find was a huge, vaulted room that appeared to be a space for showing off statues. Mostly they seemed to be of people long dead. Not one of them seemed to be less than cover-model beautiful. After what had happened in the garden, Nicola was very careful not to touch any of them. Other than the statues, the room contained just the door she'd entered by and a rather larger door in the opposite wall.

A door that was slowly swinging open.

Nicola swore to herself and started for the original door, only to find that it was opening as well. Left without too many other options, she decided that it was a good moment to give the traditional brand of statue hugging castle-guard-avoidance a go. Picking a specimen as far from the doors as she could manage, Nicola pressed herself up behind it. It was of a man who had clearly gone in for body building in a big way, or who had at least had a particularly generous sculptor, so there was plenty of room to hide. By curving her body round almost painfully, Nicola just about managed to see under the thing's armpit.

She quickly wished she couldn't.

Through the door that she'd entered by, Nicola watched the arrival of a woman whose resemblance to the people she'd seen in the garden was so great she couldn't be anything other than royalty. Also the crown was a clue, not to mention the pair of floating... things that flanked her like bodyguards.

There were more guards with the group that entered through the larger door. Real this time, or at least looking it. Actually, Nicola thought, they looked like the sort of pike-carrying, livery-wearing soldiers whose main role in life was to be photographed by tourists. Except of course, their major role as far as Nicola could see was to use the pikes to herd forward a crowd of the strangest looking people she'd ever seen.

Some were tall, some were tiny. One was bright purple,

while another, who had the misfortune to be at the front of the group, had what Nicola could only describe as a beak protruding from his face. The guards forced them roughly to their knees and Nicola bit back an angry outburst. They might be criminals, but there was no need to be like that. People, even those with beaks, deserved better. As she was thinking that, the woman who had arrived through the other door started to speak.

"I'm disappointed in you, Figments. You are needed in your dreams, or in others, and yet you've still run away like this. You let yourselves get caught up." Nicola heard her sigh. "Well, we can fix that."

She pointed at the one with the beak, and a pair of guards pulled him to his feet.

"What do you call yourself?"

"Keith, your majesty. G'day. Um...we didn't mean any harm."

"I know you didn't." There was something approaching gentleness in the words, and for a moment Nicola was hopeful. "But can't you see what has happened? You've been this... *this* for too long. As your Queen, I'm asking you now to change back. No, I am commanding you to do it."

The beak-faced man shook his head, and there was a set to his eyes that might have been called stubborn if there hadn't been such a large helping of abject terror getting in the way. Nicola heard the woman, the Queen, sigh.

"Then this will hurt."

She pointed at him again, and there was the sort of ear splitting scream normally associated with the actresses in bad horror movies. It took Nicola a second to believe that the sound could possibly be coming from the beak-faced man. By that time, the sound had dropped an octave. It kept going, and Nicola could just about make out the poor thing's last words.

"Aaarrgohshiiii...."

As last words went, they probably weren't up to much, but they were still better than the sound that followed. Later Nicola thought of the sound as that of every cell of a body changing into grey mist all at once. It seemed more impressive that way. At the time though, it just sounded like *"pfft!"*

Another of the floating things hung where the man had stood. As she watched, pressing closer and closer to the statue each moment, he floated over to those beside the Queen, who smiled like a mother who was happy that her child's injections were done with since it meant they might finally stop crying.

"There, that wasn't so hard, was it? And I'm sure his next shape will be better than that thing. So, who's next?"

Funnily enough, there didn't seem to be any volunteers.

"Or you could just turn back on your own. It really wouldn't hurt, that way."

There didn't seem to be any volunteers for that either. Nicola saw her point again, and the guards started forward.

"Stop it! Just stop this!"

The words were out of her mouth before she could halt them, and Nicola found herself storming out from behind the statue to place herself, hands on hips, between the Queen and the crowd of frightened creatures. It was only at that point that she remembered that this also placed her roughly in the middle of a semi-circle of pike-wielding guards.

"Oh… um… hello."

"This is a joke, right?"

Melissa shook her head and reached out, but Thomas moved back, despite the pain the movement brought.

"No, don't. You're wrong. You have to be."

"Thomas," she said, "I only know what Siobhan told me, and what she said is that I'm some sort of half-breed. Part human, part one of… them."

"So maybe she lied." Thomas clung to the hope with the tenacity of a climber above a thousand foot drop. "You said yourself she wasn't exactly nice. Or maybe it's just you. I mean, I know my mum and dad, and for all their weirder moments, I'm pretty sure they're both human."

"Then how did you manage to do all the things you have?"

Thomas didn't have an answer for that one, but if three years of university had taught him anything, it was that not having an answer wasn't any sort of reason to stop arguing.

"I don't know, maybe I'm psychic, or maybe I've gone mad. Maybe this whole thing is some sort of elaborate nightmare brought on by breaking up with my girlfriend on a full stomach."

"What sort of explanation is that?" Melissa gave a smile that managed to be both very kind and gently mocking at the same time.

Thomas threw up his hands in exasperation. "A better one than 'by the way, you're not human' at least." He winced at another stab of pain shooting through his skull. It was enough to make him glad he didn't normally get hangovers, though right then he could certainly have done with a drink.

"It still hurts?" Melissa asked, and put her hand to his head again before Thomas could pull back. "Hold still. This only works sometimes."

Warmth seemed to spread from her hand, feeling a lot like a summer breeze that had somehow managed to find its way inside Thomas' skull. It passed as quickly as it had come, and the pain seemed to melt away with it.

"That's a handy trick," Thomas managed.

Melissa shrugged. "Siobhan doesn't seem to think so. She keeps threatening to get rid of me if I don't come up with a more useful talent. She'll probably try the same thing with you, which is why you've got to start dealing with this."

"I am dealing with this."

"You're ignoring it. It's not the same thing."

It was Thomas' turn to shrug, mostly because it was better than trying to come up with a coherent answer.

"I didn't ask for any of this."

"And you think *I* did?" Melissa turned away, and Thomas saw her fragile-looking hands ball into fists. Given that he'd been attacked about five times already today, Thomas winced.

Thankfully, Melissa kept talking. "How do you think it feels to be grabbed off the street, dragged to a castle and locked up in a cage? To be told that everything you thought was true isn't, and that you aren't even human? How do you think it makes me feel that my mother cheated on my father with something from this place?"

"Probably about the same as it makes me feel."

Thomas left the words hanging as he tried to think. Well, he didn't *try* to think. If anything, he tried to stop the torrent of thoughts. But they slipped around his mental guard as easily as stacks of paper slip through the hands of people trying to stop the contents of their office desk becoming the contents of their office floor. And, like the filing system afterwards, putting things back together wasn't going to be easy.

"My mother wouldn't have…" Thomas started, and tailed off. "I mean, she left my dad for doing exactly that."

"Are you adopted?" Melissa asked.

"Well… no."

"Then how else do you explain it?"

Thomas couldn't. He simply couldn't. Everything that had happened to him in the past day or so said that what Melissa had told him was true, whether Thomas believed it or not. There was the stuff with the strange things that he'd managed to do, and then there was the way this "Grave" had come after him. If Thomas were as truly human as he wanted, desperately wanted, to believe, would that have happened?

"Ok," Thomas admitted at last, "I'm not human. I'm just like you. Are you happy now?"

To Thomas' surprise, Melissa wrapped her arms around him. "Not really. But you needed to know."

As much as Thomas appreciated the sentiment, not to mention the sensation of Melissa pressed to him, he pulled back after a second or two. He looked around the largely empty cage, and then at the room beyond, before finally taking a seat on the edge of the table.

"So," he said, "what happens now?"

Melissa's gaze swept around after his, as if to emphasise the emptiness of the place. "Not a lot."

Chapter Thirteen

Sure enough, not a lot happened. It continued not to happen. It was followed by a brief period of nothing, and then a longer period of complete boredom. Thomas had never been very good with boredom. The idea of just doing nothing for hours on end, while appealing in theory to his student mind, in practice tended to produce an urge to go out, get away, find something to do. Not, Thomas tapped the bars of the cage, that going out was really an option here.

For a while, he and Melissa passed the time by talking. The trouble was, even apparently innocent details tended to produce awkward moments of silence as the both thought about what they'd been taken away from. It didn't help that something seemed to be weighing on Melissa's mind, even though when Thomas asked, she denied that there was anything. When he asked if she was sure, she snapped back that anyone would be tense after living for a few months in a cage, and Thomas let it drop.

It meant that when footsteps sounded along the tunnel leading from the place, he roused himself immediately in anticipation. Behind him, Melissa lay casually on the bed, barely opening an eye at the sound. "There's no point in being eager, Thomas. It's just Siobhan. It's always Siobhan. Besides, it makes you look like one of those meerkats poking their heads out of the den."

Thomas ignored her, and as a result was treated to the sight

of Siobhan arriving bearing a laden tea tray with the obvious distaste of someone who normally had servants for that sort of
thing. Treated was the right word, because Siobhan moved in a
way that oozed attraction, while perfectly fitting the sort of dress
that only qualified as such because nobody would let it be a belt.
Frankly, Thomas was too angry to notice.

"What's going on?" he demanded. "Why have you locked
me up like this? Let us out right now!"

He heard Melissa start forward behind him, but Siobhan
just laughed. "Oh, it's all right, Melissa dear. No need to worry
about him just yet. It's understandable that he will be angry until
he learns his place. Just like you did."

Thomas thought about another outburst, but the touch of
Melissa's hand on his arm was enough to stop him. Or at least to
make him lower his voice a little. "What is it you want from
me?"

That earned another laugh, this one lighter and accompanied by an appraising look. "Oh, lots of things. But that's all for
later. Right now, my 'dear' mother wants me. I just thought I'd
show you a little kindness now, so that later you won't think I'm
not capable of it. Besides, I'm sure Melissa will tell you
everything. After all, the poor thing has to have *some* use. Now
though, I must be going." Siobhan set down the tea tray next to
the bars and started to turn, but stopped in a movement Thomas
was almost sure she'd practised to blow a kiss in their direction.
"Such a tiny cage. Do a good job of explaining this time, won't
you Melissa?"

With that she stalked away, leaving Thomas poring over
the food she'd brought. It wasn't much of a selection, consisting
mostly of bread, a few vegetables, and some cheese, but it was
far better than nothing. Reaching through the bars, he managed
to fish back most of it. "What would you like?" Thomas called
back to Melissa, but got no answer. When he turned to ask again,
he saw her sitting, shivering and pale, on the bed. "Melissa?
What's wrong?"

Melissa just stared ahead. Abandoning the food temporar-
ily, Thomas moved to sit beside her. When he reached out to

touch her shoulder, she started, almost as though noticing him there for the first time.

"It's all right, Melissa. No one's going to hurt you."

"She is! You heard her."

"All I heard was her being unpleasant. That and telling you to explain something to me. But you already did that, right?"

To his surprise, Melissa shook her head. "Not all of it." She went silent, and Thomas thought that might be it, but after a few seconds Melissa spoke again. When she did, her voice was barely on the edge of hearing. "I didn't do what she wanted, at first. She hurt me for it, and starved me, and all the while I didn't seem to matter at all to her. All that matters to Siobhan is what she wants."

Thomas gulped. He'd thought that being locked up was about the worst thing that could happen. Obviously he was wrong. But Melissa wasn't done. "The worst part is that Siobhan will turn round and be the kindest, gentlest person sometimes," she said. "She comes down here just to talk sometimes, and then she treats me like I'm some long lost friend. She hates her mother, you know. She talks about that a lot..." There was another pause. "Siobhan's going to kill me, Thomas."

That was a jump, and Thomas barely knew what to say to it.

"What? I mean... why would she?"

"You heard her, Thomas. This cage is only big enough for one of us. I haven't been able to give her what she wants, so you're here to replace me. It might not be today, but it *will* happen. And the worst part is that when she's got what she wants, Siobhan will probably kill you too. After all, it's not like she can afford to leave evidence that she's been involved with our world."

Thomas looked Melissa in the eyes, trying to work out if she meant it. The trouble was, he was fairly certain that she did. And if Melissa was right, then it didn't leave a lot of options.

"We've got to get out of here."

For her part, Nicola had given up any hope of escaping about an hour before, shortly after she'd run through every trick of escapology she'd ever heard about. Both of them. Of course, Nicola had always known that this sort of thing was a possibility, at least in theory. Being grabbed by the agents of a heartless regime was almost a compliment, the sort of thing that meant you were doing exactly the sort of good *They* didn't want you to.

Nicola was a big believer in *Them,* though exactly who *They* were tended to vary depending on what she was doing. At various points it had included her parents, the government, big business, and even the manager of her local supermarket, who hadn't been pleased to be told in the middle of the frozen goods section that he was almost single-handedly responsible for world hunger. What Nicola hadn't believed was that she'd ever be enough of an annoyance to someone that they would want to grab her. Well, except for the supermarket man, and that mostly because she'd stamped on his foot after a particularly heated exchange.

This grabbing had been remarkably efficient. The strange guards with the pikes had whisked Nicola off her feet and away in a matter of seconds, dragging her bodily to this place, wherever it was, without so much as a word. From what little Nicola could see, it wasn't much more than a stone walled box. That part worried Nicola a little. She'd heard about the sort of things they, no…, *They* did to people in rooms like this. Nicola could just imagine the sort of things that might be stacked behind her, waiting to be used in inventively nasty ways. She really, really wished she couldn't.

Nicola had to imagine them because of the chair they'd bundled her into. It was the sort of high-backed, beautifully carved thing that somewhere else might have promised a nice sit down in the kind of old fashioned library that had heard of ergonomic furniture and decided it couldn't be bothered. The only things spoiling the effect were the straps pinning her to the thing at wrist, throat and ankle. They promised something considerably less pleasant than an afternoon with an old book.

On the other hand, after the first hour or so, Nicola would have been happy for just about anything to happen, so long as it didn't involve staring at the same patch of wall for much longer. Funnily enough, it wasn't a feeling that lasted very long. Specifically, it didn't last beyond the point where the door in the far wall of the place started to swing open, promising that whatever was going to happen would finally be happening. Nicola did her best to force herself not to show any fear. She suspected she probably wasn't doing a very good job.

The Queen, Erithnae, stepped into the cell. She'd changed out of the formal robes and crown, and into an elegant cream dress edged with what appeared to be living flowers. There didn't seem to be anyone with her. She took one look at Nicola and made an annoyed sound, starting forward. Nicola did her best not to flinch.

"What?" the other woman gave Nicola a long look. "You don't think I mean to hurt you, child? I'd hardly have worn this dress if I were going to, would I? Even with magic, bloodstains never really seem to come out." She paused to give a brief laugh. "I'm Erithnae, the Queen of this Court. You must be Nicola. Poppy has told me all about you. Well, as much as she could remember, anyway."

She moved next to Nicola and knelt, using the gentlest of touches to bring Nicola's gaze to hers. Nicola couldn't help the feeling of falling into those eyes, and falling, and...

"Human, just as she said." Erithnae said, and touched the nearest of the straps holding Nicola. They all seemed to melt away. "I don't think we need all this, do we?"

"How...?"

"Most of this castle is made out of the dream stuff. Most of this Court. I'm the Queen, so it does as it's told. Shall we take this somewhere more comfortable?" She held out a hand, and Nicola put hers in it without thinking. The grip was light, but with an underlying sense that it could crush bone if it had to. Nicola had more sense than to believe that she would be able to run this time.

Erithnae led her out from the cell and on through a bewildering array of corridors, staircases and rooms. All Nicola could tell was that they seemed to be heading upwards. As they walked, the Dreaming Queen asked questions. There was something about her voice that demanded answers without really consulting the conscious part of Nicola's mind.

"How did you come to be here, Nicola?"

"It was Thomas," she said before she could stop herself. "We were being attacked by this man, and then..."

"Which man would this be? And why was he attacking you? Tell me everything, please, from the beginning."

It seemed entirely natural to Nicola that she should do so, so she did. She explained every detail as they walked hand in hand up a long staircase. It was only at the top that she realised what had to be happening, and by that point she'd told Erithnae everything, about Thomas, about their arrival there, and about what had happened afterwards.

"You're doing something to my mind, aren't you? Like Thomas did."

The other woman nodded gently. "Nothing that will hurt you, I promise. It sounds like you've had a rough enough day as it is. You're sure that this 'Thomas' can do what I'm doing?"

Nicola nodded, despite herself. A few more steps brought them to a landing, on which there was a single door. It opened at Erithnae's touch to reveal a comfortably furnished room beyond.

"What's this?" Nicola asked.

The Queen's smile faded a little. "For now, it's your prison. I think you're an innocent in all of this, Nicola, but I also have to think about my people. If certain others found out you were here, it could mean war."

Nicola started to turn and demand a better explanation, but a soft push on her back sent her stumbling into the room.

"I'll be back soon," Erithnae said, "and I'm sure Poppy will want to visit. She seems to like you. But for now, I need to go and find out more about your boyfriend."

"Ex-boyfriend!" Nicola managed, just in time to see the

door shut in her face. When she tried it, it wouldn't open.

When Thomas put his shoulder to the door, the only thing that happened was some light bruising.

"Ow!"

"It was built by someone who's stronger than the average human." Melissa pointed out, watching the attempt and finishing the last of her share of the food. "Of course it's going to be solid."

Thomas didn't give up. As motivations went, the thought of being kept caged and then killed once Siobhan found someone better was a pretty good one. He tried kicking the door, only giving in when his foot started to ache in a way that he was pretty sure wasn't normal. After that, Thomas switched to trying to pull the bars apart like some circus strongman. Needless to say, he couldn't budge them an inch.

"You could help."

Melissa just sat on the bed, watching. "What good would it do? I'm not any stronger than you are. Face it, we're stuck here. It's hopeless."

Thomas shook his head, amazed that Melissa could just give up like that. Then again, he had no way of knowing what she'd been through. Months in somewhere like this would probably sap his hope too, even without whatever Siobhan had done to her.

"There has to be a way out. This door doesn't even have a lock."

"It doesn't need one," Melissa sighed. "It's magical. The whole cage is. Siobhan just has to touch it to get it to open."

Thomas looked at the cage again. There weren't even any welds where the bars joined, not that he'd have the strength to force them open even if there were. With a sigh of his own, he went back to sit beside Melissa.

"How did she even get this in here?" Thomas asked. "It couldn't have fit down that tunnel."

"She didn't have to. Siobhan just waved her hand and it sort of grew up from the floor. She said something about this whole place being a pocket of dream stuff. She can do what she wants here." Melissa shut her eyes, and Thomas thought he saw the trickle of a tear from the corner of one of them. "She can do what she wants with us, too. There's no one to stop her."

Thomas found himself brushing the tear away. "It will be all right."

Even to himself, the words didn't sound very convincing. Melissa gave a little snort, but seemed to make the effort anyway.

"Of course it will. We should probably get some rest. There won't be time when she gets back. Is it all right if I take the bed?"

Thomas nodded. In the state Melissa was in it would have been cruel to do anything else. Besides, he doubted he'd be able to sleep, on the floor or not. Even so, Thomas lay down, willing to give it a chance. After all, sleep might come, in much the same way that a door-to-door salesman might sell you something. Thomas must have been more tired than he thought, because almost immediately he started to feel his eyes growing heavy.

"Off to dreamland we go," he muttered bitterly. A second later Thomas sat up sharply, only narrowly avoiding hitting his head on the bars. "Melissa, wake up!"

"'m not asleep," the drowsy words came back. Thomas reached out, shaking her into something approaching full consciousness. She stared up at him. "What?"

"You said this place was made out of 'dream-stuff' right?"

"You woke me up to ask that?"

"I think it might be important."

Melissa sat up, and Thomas watched her wipe the last of the sleep from her eyes. "Yes. She said it was a pocket of it. Why is that important?"

"Earlier, I went into a dream by accident. I changed it. Maybe I can change this too."

Suddenly, there was hope in Melissa's expression. "That

might just work. Do you remember how you did it?"

"Um… not exactly."

"Oh." The hope faded a little.

"But how hard can it be?" Thomas made his way over to the door. "Maybe if I just sort of… concentrate?"

"When I'm working with flowers, I have to be touching them." Melissa supplied. "I sometimes shut my eyes."

Thomas did both things. He concentrated on the door, on the feel of it beneath his fingers. He tried to imagine some sort of power flowing through him and into the thing, which was harder than it sounded, considering that he didn't have the faintest idea what that power should feel like or how exactly it should be flowing through him. Thomas decided to think of it as being like someone pouring golden syrup through him. He wasn't entirely sure why.

And then he knew exactly what it felt like, because it was happening in a rush. It felt like someone had indeed managed to inject him with molten golden syrup, while at the same time plugging him straight into a power socket, but, and this was the amazing part, *in a good way.*

"Thomas!"

"Is it working?" Thomas asked it without daring to open his eyes. He could still feel the door under his fingers, and it didn't seem any different.

"You could say that. Look!"

Thomas dared to lift one eyelid, then the other. He was prepared to see the door hanging open. There was even a part of him that half-hoped the thing had been torn from its hinges, mostly because that would impress Melissa. As to exactly why he wanted to impress her so soon after meeting her, Thomas didn't feel up to examining his feelings on the matter. By that point, he'd opened his eyes, and had other things to think about.

The door was still there, and in exactly the same place. As for the rest of the cage, there wasn't any sign of it, but there *was* a patch of gloopy stuff that covered a large portion of the floor. It looked suspiciously golden.

"Syrup…" Thomas breathed, and a laugh escaped "…I actually got syrup." He laughed again, the sort of laugh that, once it starts, doesn't stop until either someone slaps you or the nice people in white coats come to take you somewhere with lovely soft walls. Thankfully, Melissa did the former.

"Ow! That bloody hurt!"

"Never mind that." Melissa shook some feeling back into her hand. "Let's get out of here."

Chapter Fourteen

Get out of there they did, as rapidly as they could run along the corridor leading out of the place. It came to an abrupt halt in a brick wall, but when Thomas touched it, the thing just peeled back like an umbrella closing up, only without all that irritating business of shaking the water off it and trying to work out how it had managed to get twisted inside out.

The roses on the other side of it were another matter. They sprang into violent life the moment the doorway opened up, whipping back and forth across the entrance like the tendrils of some monstrous jellyfish. Thomas gulped, and reached out to touch them. Presumably if Siobhan could get past them, he could too.

Or not, he thought as a tendril snaked around his wrist, biting down sharply enough for the thorns to draw blood.

Thomas lashed out at the thing, striking wood, but it did nothing. Thorns raked across Thomas' chest and face, making him bite back a cry of pain. Maybe trying to touch the things hadn't been such a good idea. He struggled as the thorn-edged tendrils started to wrap around him, cocooning him like the prey of some giant spider.

"Wait, stop!"

Thomas was about to point out to Melissa that he didn't really have much choice in the matter when he realised that she wasn't talking to him.

"Please. Just wait a minute." She said it gently, and

Thomas saw her reach out to stroke one of the rose's thorny creepers. To his surprise, it didn't make a grab for her. Instead, the whole thing made a rustling sound that reminded Thomas of nothing quite so much as a cat purring.

"You like that?" Melissa asked. "Of course you do. She doesn't do this? No, well she wouldn't."

It occurred to Thomas that while hearing only one side of a conversation with a plant was bad enough, hearing it while entangled and bleeding was even worse. "Um... could you hurry up please, Melissa?"

"Shh! We're talking."

She went back to stroking the plant, and the plant went back to making pleased sounds. Finally, just when Thomas was starting to be convinced that he'd be stuck there until the thing had sucked him dry...

"Could you maybe let my friend go, please?" Melissa seemed to listen for a moment. "I know he did, but he was frightened. Yes, I know. All right, I'll tell him."

"What have you got to tell me?" Thomas asked, expectantly.

"Apparently, it wants you to say sorry."

"What for?"

"For hitting it. It says it hurt."

"*That* hurt?" Thomas looked around pointedly at the thorns pressed to his skin. "This doesn't exactly tickle. Tell it to get stuffed."

Maybe it was just a response to the tone of his voice, but Thomas was certain he felt the thorns tighten around him a little. "On the other hand... I'm sorry. There I said it. Is this thing satisfied?"

He saw Melissa lean a little closer to it, as though listening carefully. "It doesn't think you mean it."

"I do. Anything if it will stop squeezing."

"He does mean it." Melissa whispered to the thing. "Yes, he really does. Please, he's my friend. Yes, of course you can be my friend too. Thank you."

Abruptly, the creepers unravelled themselves from around

Thomas leaving him trying to staunch the flow from the worst of the cuts. A touch from Melissa was enough to stop the bleeding, at least, but the scratches remained.

"That's the best I can do," she said. "Like I said, it can be a bit hit and miss."

"Thanks. Can you talk this thing into letting us out now?"

Thomas watched while she tried, admiring the gentle way Melissa spoke to the thing, as though it was little more than a child. "Yes," she said, "I know you're supposed to stop anyone who isn't with her. Of course I wouldn't want to get you into trouble, but she wouldn't blame you, surely? Oh, I'd say that we came up with a special magic way of doing it. No, I'm sure she wouldn't be angry. Please?"

At that, the creepers pulled back out of the way. Thomas darted through, still not quite trusting the thing, while Melissa came through slower, touching her fingers to one of the flowers as she passed. The plant seemed to shiver in pleasure.

"Can we get out of here now?" Thomas asked, and Melissa nodded. Behind them, a thorn-covered tendril gave what Thomas could only think of as a cherry little wave. They got out of the rose garden as quickly as they could, and tried to get their bearings. Thomas took a long look up at the castle above them, and found Melissa doing the same. They shook their heads at exactly the same moment.

"No, absolutely not."

"I'm not going in there," Melissa agreed.

"We've only just got out of one cage."

"And Siobhan will be in there somewhere."

There was a pause, in which they both continued to stare at the thing. Thomas spoke first. "On the other hand… we do need to find a way out of here."

"And maybe no one but Siobhan knows about us."

"They might even help."

"Where else is there?"

They nodded, unable to synchronise the thing this time, but no less certain of it for that. They still hadn't taken a step towards the place, but they scanned it, looking for a way in that

134

wouldn't be too obvious. What they saw instead was a bush that seemed to be shaking and fighting with itself.

"Is that you?" Thomas asked.

Melissa shook her head. "I haven't been near it."

"Then what's going on?"

"How should I know?"

The bush shook a little more, and it occurred to Thomas that it wasn't actually a plant fighting with itself. Instead, it was more a case of a man struggling to extricate himself from a plant he had almost certainly fallen into the middle of. A moment after that, it occurred to Thomas that he only knew one man who made a habit of hiding in bushes.

"Thomas," Simon Stranded called. "Am I glad to see you again! Here, you couldn't give me a hand getting out of this thing, could you?"

Erithnae had to wait while Poppy knocked on the door to the human woman's room. Partly that was because she was Queen, and queens didn't knock on their own doors. Mostly, it was because Erithnae was holding a tray full of tea things. Technically, of course, queens didn't carry their own trays either, but for once the servants had left at a look from her. Poppy had been a late addition to the visit. It seemed like a good idea to bring along one of the few friendly faces the girl had come across in the Court, and Poppy seemed eager to see her again.

When there wasn't any reply from inside, Erithnae flicked a finger at the door. It opened silently.

Poppy gave her a questioning look. "Your Majesty, shouldn't we wait?"

"It's my castle, Poppy, even if she is sulking. Besides, the tea will get cold."

They stepped inside to find Nicola ensconced on a small couch, staring pointedly out of the room's window. The bed in the corner was rumpled, which suggested that she'd at least tried to get some sleep. The couch had a couple of chairs across from it, separated by a low table. It was on this that Erithnae put the tray she carried. "Hello, Nicola."

"I have nothing else to tell you."

Erithnae dismissed the harsh tone. It was too much to expect that the girl would enjoy being locked up like this.

"Poppy wanted to make sure you were all right."

"Hello again... Nicola."

That, at least, drew the ghost of a smile from her. "Hello Poppy."

"We thought you might like something to eat," Poppy explained. "Well, her majesty did, and she said it might be nice if I came along too. Oh, I almost forgot."

Erithnae watched Poppy search for the flower she'd brought before finally finding it on the tray, just where she'd left it. The human girl allowed herself a full smile this time. Erithnae decided to take advantage of it while she could. "May we sit down, Nicola?"

"Can I stop you?"

"If you want me to do so, I'll leave, but I'd like to stay. I'm not your enemy."

"No, just my jailor."

Erithnae sat down anyway, leaning forward to look at Nicola more closely. "Do you know about the War?" she demanded, and saw Nicola shrug in reply.

"I saw the... illusion, or hologram, or whatever it was, outside."

A flash of pain touched Erithnae then, but she managed not to let it show. Another thing that queens weren't allowed to do.

Poppy took the silence as her cue to speak. "It was horrible. Queen Rae, dead, just like that. And then the War. So many people, until the King..." She'd obviously caught a glimpse of Erithnae's expression, because she paused. "I'm sorry, Your Majesty."

Erithnae sighed. "No, don't be, Poppy. It's no more than the truth." To Nicola she continued. "I lost everyone except my daughter in that war, Nicola. My mother at the start. My father at the end, and before it. He walked off halfway through, leaving me to try and run the Court in the middle of the greatest War we've seen. And then he came back just in time to throw himself into a suicidal charge."

"It won the War," Poppy said.

Erithnae nodded, even though she wanted to say that it hadn't felt much like a victory to her. Losing her father, first to the bleak madness that had followed his wife's death, and then to the sort of battles where you could only tell you'd won because you saw what happened to the losers, just made her feel empty.

"But now, of course, we're expected to hold the peace together," Erithnae said, with a lightness she didn't feel. "Dinners with people I frankly can't stand, where we reassure each other that we're all best friends. Envoys lying to me about how their rulers just want to be nice and aren't interested in their own advantage at all, even if that's all they have been interested in for the last thousand years. Trying not to do anything that might upset anyone, even though some of them are far too prickly for anyone's good."

"How does any of this mean I've got to stay here?" Nicola demanded.

Erithnae did her best to explain. She explained about the Treaty, and about what that meant for Nicola's presence. She didn't explain what else it might have meant, but the girl seemed to grasp it anyway.

"So why didn't you just kill me?"

Poppy spluttered over the crumbs of a biscuit she'd obviously managed to snatch from the plate on the way up.

"Her Majesty doesn't do things like that," Poppy insisted. "She's kind, and good, and..."

Erithnae held up a hand and Poppy stopped. "Now, Poppy, we both know I'm none of those things."

"You always have been to me. Even when I do silly things like making a Tulip that will sound the alarm."

"Well, you weren't to know that it would go off constantly, and it was all right once we put them in a sound-proofed chamber... all right, maybe I am kind to you, but not to everyone. I'm a ruler. I can't always afford to be."

"The greater good?" The human girl said the words in a way that made them sound like something dirty.

"You don't like the idea?"

"I've seen what too many people do for 'the greater good.' They always seem to use it as a way of excusing whatever they wanted to do anyway."

"Except, of course," Erithnae countered, "that I don't *want* to keep you here like this." She waved a hand vaguely at the surrounding room. "Please believe me, Nicola. If it wouldn't hurt a great many people, I'd send you straight home. As it is, this is the best I can do."

There was a brief silence, and Erithnae pushed back her chair. "And now I've completely spoiled the mood. I'll leave you and Poppy to it."

To Erithnae's surprise, Nicola reached out to stop her with a light touch of her hand. "You don't need to go. I'd like to hear more about this place, if you'll tell me. Besides, I don't imagine that a queen gets much time off."

"Not much."

Erithnae paused, considering it, and then reached down for the teapot. "All right then. I'll pour, shall I?"

Thomas lifted Simon out of the bush by the collar of his ragged shirt, hoisting him into the air. He hardly seemed to weigh anything.

"Thanks," the Figment said. "Um… Thomas? You can put me down now."

If anything Thomas hoisted him a little higher.

"What's going on, Thomas?" Melissa asked. "Who is this?"

"This is Simon Stranded," Thomas replied, tightening his grip, "the Figment who abandoned me the moment I got into trouble."

"Thomas, Thomas, mate… I couldn't do anything… too many of them… think about… all the help I gave you before…"

"Thomas! Let him down before you hurt him!"

The horrified note in Melissa's voice was enough for Thomas to do it, letting Stranded fall on the grass. The Figment struggled to his feet, rubbing his throat.

"That's quite a temper you've got there. I guess I deserved it, but what else could I do? Those Nightmares are nasty. I mean, that little girl, she just keeps *staring*."

"What's so bad about staring?" Melissa asked, and Stranded stopped his explanation to flash her a smile that was probably intended to be roguish and interesting. To Thomas, it just looked lascivious.

"Thomas, you must introduce me to this vision of loveliness. Is she, perhaps, the delectable ex-girlfriend, Nicola?"

"No. This is Melissa."

"May I say, Melissa, that I have rarely had chance to meet such a beautiful lady in the course of an escape attempt?"

Thomas was starting to wish he hadn't stopped choking him. Melissa just rolled her eyes. The really annoying part was that, despite Stranded's antics, Thomas suspected that the pair of them would need his help if they were going to get out of there.

"Talking of escapes, do you think you could maybe help us out with this one?"

"Of course. I said I'd help you, didn't I? And you, dear Melissa, I would cross continents to help. Well, principalities at least. There's a little path over that way…" he gestured in a way that could have indicated any one of half a dozen directions, "… somewhere. Anyway, wherever it is, it leads down to the village."

"There's a village?" Melissa asked.

"Of course. There's always a village. Can't have a castle without a village. What would be the point of something like this…" Stranded nodded towards the impossible spires and turrets, "without a village full of mildly subdued but essentially happy yokels?"

"I don't know," Thomas put in. "We were just trying to find a way inside when you arrived. It looks more likely to have answers."

"It looks more likely to have guards, dungeons and sharp pointy edges to me," Stranded shot back. "You go in there, how far are you going to get? On the other hand, I think I might know someone in the village who can help. Got to be better than getting yourself killed. Besides, the place has a good pub. One I haven't been thrown out of," he added hastily.

Thomas looked over to Melissa, who nodded.

"All right then."

"All right then," Grave grumbled. "That was ten pints of ale, one saucer of it for the boot, a packet of crisps for the gremlin and an orange juice for the little girl."

One by one they nodded. Well, those that had heads. Grave stood up and headed for the bar. *The Missing Spoke* was a good place, catering mostly to the villagers and a few of the staff from the castle. The landlord was a friendly sort, who didn't seem to mind that the Nightmare Hunt had taken over one corner of his pub. A few of the dreaming folk patrons gave them worried glances, but Grave thought the Hunt deserved the treat.

He brought the drinks back from the bar and handed the gremlin its crisps.

"You know what I don't like?" Grave said after a minute. The various members of the Hunt considered it.

"Audits?"

"Giant Hairy Things With Teeth?"

"Spiders?"

Grave shook his head.

"I don't like that they didn't even tell us we should stop looking. There we were, slogging through fields searching for this girl, and some farmer has to tell us that they've caught her."

The little girl just stared back. Then she stared at her orange juice. Then she drank it. Her voice, when it came, was deeper than her tiny frame might have suggested.

"Why are you surprised? 'S not like we're important. 'S just the job."

"They're the ringmasters," one of the clowns offered, honking his nose sadly, "and we're just the acts."

"But it would be nice if once in a while they'd tell us something," Grave continued. "Now the last King, he was always very courteous, very considerate. He'd always ask me how I was doing, even if he was there to send me off to hunt someone. That was class, that was. Now, the Queen, she's all right too, but that daughter of hers? I'll tell you, these days it's like she can't even make up her mind if she wants someone dead. One of these days, I'm going to say something I'll regret to that little madam."

Grave sat back and waited for the sympathy he was sure was his due. Instead, the gremlin piped up, in a voice so squeaky as to be almost beyond hearing.

"Your mouse has gotten out again. It's eating my bloody crisps!"

Grave reached out to snatch the thing back, stowing it in a pocket again.

"I like mice," the little girl said. "They're cute."

She stared pointedly at her drink. But then, she stared pointedly at everything.

"Same again?"

"Yes, please, Mr Grave."

This was what he was reduced to, Grave fumed silently. Just one more freak for the Hunt, sent out at the beck and call of the Queen and her daughter. And being the only one of the dreaming folk among the crowd of Figments just meant that he got to pay the bar bill while they sat around with nothing to do between jobs but wait. He deserved better than this.

Two of the clowns got up to play darts.

Chapter Fifteen

Nicola was enjoying herself despite her reservations. The idea of having tea with royalty could have been awkward. It was a level of privilege that would normally have raised Nicola's hackles as surely as people not recycling their papers. When you threw in her current status as a prisoner, the whole thing should have been full of suspicion and awkward silences. Kind of like dinner with her parents, only with the added disadvantage that Nicola was already in her room, and so couldn't retreat to it.

In the end, though, it was hard to maintain much wariness with Poppy chattering away on whatever topic came into her head. Usually before she'd finished thinking about it.

"Do you still use horses to get around? I used to like horses. They had whole herds of them the last time I was in your world."

"They have cars now, Poppy," Erithnae supplied gently.

"How did you know that?" Nicola asked. "You said you weren't supposed to contact our world, right? And that's been true for hundreds of years?"

"You're right, of course," Erithnae replied. "But this *is* the Court of Dreams. Those of us who spend a lot of time around human dreams see all sorts of things. Poppy is just a little... different."

"Stupid, you mean." Poppy said it with a laugh, but there was a false note to it.

"You know that's not what I mean at all, and I'm sure Nicola knows it too."

Nicola nodded. Poppy wasn't exactly stupid, she just seemed very easily distracted from everything except flowers. Her attention seemed to flit from one thing to another without ever really settling.

The Dreaming Queen was a lot harder to read.

"Um... Your Majesty..." Nicola began, but the other woman stopped her with a shake of her head.

"Nicola, please just call me Erithnae. I've got a whole Court full of people who won't use the name. Even my daughter uses my title when she's trying to be difficult."

"You have a daughter? How old?"

"You know, I've lost track. Is it three hundred and five, or three hundred and four?" She paused for a moment, apparently trying to work it out, then gave up with a shrug. "Still, she'll always be my baby. Now if only she wouldn't act like it sometimes."

"Now that's something that could take some getting used to," Nicola said. "You hardly look old enough to have children at all, and... how old are you?"

"A little over a thousand. I like to think it doesn't show."

"Trust me, it doesn't. Don't you get bored, living so long?"

Nicola waited while Erithnae took a sip from her cup.

"Some of us do. Mostly, though, the universe is far too interesting for that. Humans in particular."

Nicola stalled by taking a bite from a muffin, and tried to think of anything in her life that would possibly be interesting enough to keep someone entertained. It must have shown on her face, because Poppy reached out for her hand.

"Nicola, humans are fascinating. So fragile, so brief, but so varied. It's like with plants. In the Courts, we're like seeds grown from single plants. We're all part of our Court in some way. You know what you're getting. You humans are more like seeds plucked from the wind and planted. You could turn into anything."

Nicola wasn't entirely sure about the compliment. She tried to turn the conversation back towards the other two.

"So," she asked, "what's it like being Queen?"

Erithnae gave her a long look while she considered it.

"The hours are long, the pay is awful, and your every decision seems to mean life or death. You wouldn't want the job. I know I didn't."

"Why not?"

"I never thought I'd be Queen. My people live, if not forever, at least in a happy suburb on the outskirts of it. I thought I would be a princess forever. When my mother died and my father… left, it was only duty that made me take the job."

Another silence followed in the wake of that, and Erithnae stood.

"Talking of which… I have work to do. I trust you won't object if I come back again?"

Nicola smiled. It seemed like the right thing to do.

"Of course not."

Erithnae wasn't surprised to find her daughter waiting outside. She had, after all, invited Siobhan to join them. She wasn't even surprised that Siobhan had stood outside rather than come in. Nothing much about her daughter surprised Erithnae anymore.

"Have you been out here long, darling?"

"Long enough." The reply was accompanied by a toss of auburn hair.

"And that means?"

"I heard you admiring your new pet. Now if only you'd occasionally lavish that attention elsewhere occasionally."

Erithnae didn't take the bait. They both knew that she indulged Siobhan more than anyone. At least, Erithnae knew it, and she thought her daughter ought to, and should be grateful for it. Sadly, there were days when Siobhan seemed to be stuck as a teenager. When the next question was about business, it almost caught her off guard.

"So, what do you plan on doing with her?"

"She's safe enough where she is."

"Why not just kill her?" Siobhan demanded. "It would save a lot of effort."

Erithnae shook her head. It was enough to bring a frown from Siobhan.

"*Why* won't you let me do it, mother? Are you just going to keep her around forever, or until one of the other Courts gets word of her?"

"You wouldn't feel the same if you'd go in and talk to her, Siobhan. You'd like her. I'm sure the two of you would be good friends in no time."

Siobhan paused, leaning against the doorway. After a second or two she licked her lips with deliberate slowness.

"Hmm, good friends has possibilities."

Erithnae cursed herself for being so careless in her choice of words.

"No, Siobhan." She levelled a finger at her daughter. "No. I'll not have you making Nicola into one of your playthings. She's deserves better."

"She might enjoy it."

"But it is not what I desire, Siobhan, and she is under my protection. Nicola is going to stay here, and she is going to be perfectly safe. Isn't she?"

Erithnae watched the change in her daughter's face. She probably thought she was doing a good job of hiding the anger.

"Isn't she?" Erithnae repeated.

"Yes, mother."

There are a great many places in the world that are villages in name only. They only stay villages because someone from the planning committee of the next town happens to live in them, meaning that they won't be swallowed up at least until the house prices go up a bit. Even so, their post offices have long since closed, their schools are heading towards it, and their houses have mostly been sold off as weekend cottages for people who will never really understand what it means to be knee deep in slurry at three AM on a wet morning. Apparently, it counts as progress.

The village that Thomas found Simon Stranded leading them down to wasn't like that at all.

True, it didn't have a post office, but that was mostly because they clung to the rural tradition of shoving letters into the hands of anyone who was heading in the right direction, when they didn't have enough magic to send messages that way. It didn't have a school, either, but that was only because the rare children there got their lessons up at the castle. And as for the slurry… well, that was nobody else's business, really.

To Thomas, the place looked like the sort of village designed to produce pitchfork-wielding mobs for monster movies: all pretty thatched cottages and carefully tended gardens, full of just the sort of people who sit around waiting for the creature to pass, and who give strangers looks that wonder if they'll fit into the wicker man they've been working on in their shed. Then again, that was probably just Thomas' nerves talking. The place certainly seemed happy enough. If anything, it had the feel of the sort of village where the worst thing that was likely to happen was somebody cornering you long enough to sing folk music, though to Thomas that seemed bad enough.

Simon Stranded was surprisingly blasé about the whole place. When Thomas and Melissa started to glance around nervously, looking for signs that they'd been noticed, he just shook his head.

"Calm down, both of you. No one here knows who you are, and you'll fit in well enough. One advantage of the Dreaming Court, they're used to people looking a bit strange. Just enjoy it."

That was easier said than done, so soon after the escape. Thomas couldn't help but think that at any moment hordes of guards might descend on the place looking for them, and he didn't want to be around when they did. Even so, he did his best to at least look confident as they strolled through what passed for a village square. Melissa did a better job of it, even stopping at the line of shops that filled one side of the rough patch of cobbles. When Stranded went over with her, chatting and flirting, Thomas found himself following along. Melissa seemed to appreciate that, taking his hand and pointing out some of the stranger things in the shop windows.

The bakery featured cakes in its window that matched the castle for gravity-warping designs. One particularly baroque arrangement was surrounded by butterfly buns that winged their way around the thing as they watched. The milliner's next door, on the other hand, seemed to specialise in hats that things could be pulled from. Rabbits, of course, but also ribbons, flags, and even snakes. Those flowed from a turban in a slow trickle, falling into waiting buckets. A hastily written sign advertised the benefits of pythons as pets.

There was a tiny clothing shop next to that, and Simon Stranded gave the pair of them an appraising look.

"You know, the two of you would stand out less with some proper clothes."

"A pity we can't afford them," Thomas tried, mostly because he'd seen the knee britches and stockings that passed for fashionable men's-wear there. When Stranded's expression widened into a grin, Thomas winced. Sure enough, the Figment produced a small money pouch from somewhere within the mess of rags that constituted his own clothes.

"I've got enough for this."

Thomas thought about asking how a castaway like Stranded had managed to get hold of money, but then it occurred to him that he almost certainly didn't want to know. Backed into a corner, or at least into the doorway, Thomas stepped inside the shop. Twenty minutes later, he stepped out again, having been measured, fitted, poked and prodded by a dreaming-folk woman who barely came past his waist. She had to stand on a stepladder to take most of his measurements, all the while peering through inch-thick spectacles at him.

The results were every bit as bad as Thomas had feared. Dark knee britches covered cream stockings, while his upper body found itself contained by a shirt, outer jacket, and the sort of waistcoat that would have been dismissed by even most snooker players as too gaudy. Thomas' feet had to cope with the replacement of perfectly good trainers by a pair of fancy buckled shoes. As soon as they'd got him into this get up, Simon Stranded had sent Thomas out of the shop with a few coins and directions to the pub, declaring that Melissa should have privacy to try things on. Not that Simon had made any move to leave with him. Thomas considered arguing, but eventually decided that his outfit might look better after a drink.

At least *this* pub looked fairly normal. More than that, *The Missing Spoke* seemed almost welcoming as Thomas made his way across the square to it, contemplating what sort of beer might lie within. The pub continued to look that way for at least another couple of seconds, right up to the point where a bulky shadow filled the doorway.

A spark of the same recognition that lets arachnophobes spot the tiniest of spiders across a room sent Thomas scrambling for cover. He pressed himself flat against the pub's wall, holding his breath. Seconds passed. From the corner of his eye he could make out Grave standing in the doorway, stretching in the manner of everyone who's ever sat too long while some particularly slow drinker has finished their pint.

Thomas looked around, trying to find a way to get out of there. There wasn't any cover in the square, and Thomas couldn't work out a way of getting even a couple of yards without being spotted. Worse, in a moment, the big man was going to step outside. A moment after that, he would almost certainly spot Thomas. Thomas didn't want to think about what he'd probably do a moment after *that*, because it would probably involve quite a lot of pain.

Still from the corner of his eye, Thomas caught a glimpse of a small form tugging at Grave's coat, and a voice that seemed to be that of a young girl came to his ears.

"Mr Grave, Mr Grave. One of the clowns has thrown a custard pie at the dartboard, Mr Grave."

Thomas heard the big man sigh before turning back inside. It was nothing compared to his own sigh of relief. He all but sprinted for the clothes shop.

Simon Stranded met him at the door to the place, putting an arm across it to stop Thomas from running in.

"I thought we agreed that you'd head over to the pub and get the beers in."

Thomas sucked in air, and as he did so noticed that the Figment was still in the same clothes he'd been wearing all along.

"Why do you get to keep your old clothes?" Thomas demanded.

"I'd hardly be much of a castaway without them, would I? There's such a thing as maintaining an image, you know."

Thomas was about to ask exactly what sort of image when Melissa's voice came to them from within the shop.

"I'm ready. Come and look."

They did, testing the limits of the doorframe in an effort to squeeze into the shop first. Thomas was just about to point out that they should be worrying more about the fact that Grave was in the pub than about what Melissa was wearing when he caught sight of her. The shopkeeper had outfitted her in what she'd probably imagined was a simple combination of a cream dress and overskirt, topped with a short coat a few shades darker. It should have been simple, but it managed to be a lot more than that on her.

"You look…" Thomas started, and stopped, lost for words. "…wonderful."

"Thank you." Melissa gave him a brief hug before moving back to examine herself in a long mirror. "And thank you, Simon, for all this."

"Guys," Thomas said, reminding himself that he'd only just broken up with his girlfriend, and probably shouldn't be staring. "I think we might have trouble. At the pub there was…"

He trailed off as Stranded put a finger to his lips, glancing pointedly at the shopkeeper. Thomas responded by taking both of their hands and hustling them outside.

"The big guy, Grave, is in there," Thomas finished. "I

don't think he saw me, but it was close. We need to get out of here."

Simon just looked at him for a moment, and it occurred to Thomas that he still had hold of his hand. He let go hurriedly. Thomas let go of Melissa's hand more reluctantly.

"You said you knew people here, Simon," Melissa put in. "Will they help us?"

"I hope so. We've just got to get there. Are you sure he's in the pub, Thomas?"

Thomas shrugged.

"He was two minutes ago."

"Then we'll have to risk it. My friend lives on the outskirts anyway, so it shouldn't be a problem. Just try to act naturally."

Those words, Thomas thought, were the combination in the English language most guaranteed to ensure that someone draws attention to themselves. Combined with the strange feeling of unusual new clothes, not to mention the fact that they were with someone who would never fit in anywhere lacking in palm trees and sand, and he was quickly convinced that almost every eye in the village was on them as they made their way to the house they wanted.

It was a bungalow, thatch-roofed and stone-walled, with a tiny garden in front and a picket fence around that. To Thomas, it looked like the sort of place someone might find in the woods in a fairy tale, possibly just before they managed to get turned into something. There was obviously someone there, because there was smoke coming from the chimney. That it was bright purple didn't seem to bother Simon, who strode up to the front door and knocked. The door swung open.

"Come in, all of you," a woman's voice called from inside. It sounded papery and cracked. Actually, to Thomas, it sounded like a voice that might break into cackling at any moment. It was the first truly old voice Thomas could remember hearing since he'd arrived.

It matched its owner. She sat on one of half a dozen chairs, almost tiny in a room overrun with knick-knacks, straight backed, white haired and wrinkled. The black dress and matching shawl she wore looked ragged, but also looked like they'd started life that way. A stick lay across her knees, and something about her gaze said that it was mostly for hitting people who annoyed her.

"Hello Simon," the old woman said. "Back so soon?"

"Freli, how could I keep away from you?"

"Quite easily, with such a pretty young thing in tow."

"But then, I've always had a thing for older women."

"For any woman with a pulse, more like." She cackled at her own joke, and some part of Thomas' mind came up with the words *I told you so*. "Now, come and sit down, all of you, and tell old Freli what you need a witch for."

Thomas replayed the last sentence in his mind, and found himself focussing on the crucial word. Then he found himself staring at some of the "knick-knacks" that decorated the room. Sure enough, there was a crystal ball propped up on the mantelpiece. There were also at least three sets of tarot cards scattered around the place, along with about a crateful of stones and pendants marked with symbols Thomas didn't think he wanted to be able to read. And, oh yes, there was the skull of some large creature, looking remarkably annoyed that someone had pinned it to the wall and run off with its body.

Thomas was still looking when he realised that Simon was explaining their problem to the woman, who sat and listened for a while before standing and making her way to a battered looking iron kettle. Thomas half expected to hear creaks with every movement.

"I don't know about you, but I always find that a problem like this needs a nice cup of tea."

Thomas saw Melissa start to rise, but Freli waved her back.

"I'll do this, dear. I'm not completely useless yet."

She started to boil the thing, and hunted among the clutter for cups and a brightly patterned box of tealeaves. The old witch made the tea with the crisp movements of someone half her age. Or possibly a hundredth, given how old she looked. Once the tea was ready, she passed Thomas a cup.

"Look," Thomas said, taking the thing, "this is nice, but

there's probably someone pretty unpleasant looking for us. Can you help us or not?"

"Drink your tea first dear. Afterwards, we'll talk."

Both Simon and Melissa treated him to looks that said as plainly as if they'd spoken, *humour her. She probably just wants the company for a bit.* Both did it while pointedly sipping from their own cups. With a sigh, Thomas drank his down with almost indecent haste.

About ten seconds later he really wished he hadn't. Thomas clutched at his throat, which felt like it was on fire, while his eyes were suddenly convinced that the room was a lot larger than it had been, and was instead the size of a small aircraft hangar, albeit one full of everything an old woman had collected over the years. A quick glance over at Melissa and Simon Stranded showed them slumped in their chairs, their cups lying where they'd fallen.

"Just remember," Freli said, her expression not nearly so nice now, "if some idiot wants you to step into the light, tell them to get stuffed."

Thomas tried to reply, but by that point he was too busy falling backwards into infinity to bother.

Chapter Sixteen

At least there weren't any staircases this time, just a small park filled with people Thomas didn't know. Or did he? There, beneath one of the shadier trees, sat a woman who seemed vaguely familiar. She was dark haired and good looking, in a studious sort of way, her glasses perched well forward on her nose as she read a well-thumbed copy of *Pride and Prejudice*, her light dress apparently her only concession to the sunny day. Thomas tried calling out to her, and she looked up, but not at him.

Instead, her gaze tracked the progress of the man who walked past Thomas without so much as a glance. He was dark-haired, male-model handsome, and again, faintly familiar. There was a sadness about his eyes that seemed to fade a little just from looking at the woman. Thomas wished he could remember where he'd seen her before.

They sat, and presumably they talked, because Thomas could see their mouths open and close, but it appeared that someone had left the volume control on the dream turned down. Thomas found himself wishing he could hear what they were saying. Almost as soon as he did so, the words faded in.

"...to go, Gwen. I see now that they need me."

There was a pause, and in that pause Thomas' brain had plenty of time to take that name and face, add a few wrinkles, a few years, and come up with the conclusion that the woman was unmistakably his mother, and that Thomas should feel very stupid for not having realised it immediately. And that incidentally, he should visit her more often as well. Thomas ignored his brain, and tried to concentrate on the conversation.

"*I* need you."

Yes, Thomas thought, that was definitely his mother's voice. But he'd never seen her looking like this, except in photos. As for the man, he didn't think he'd ever seen him before, though there was still *something* about the lines of his face.

"I love you, Gwen, but I can't stay."

He leaned in to kiss her, and Thomas looked away as the kiss deepened. There are some things that no one wants to watch their mother doing. By the time he looked back, the man had already stood up.

"Don't go," Thomas heard his mother say, and there was another pause as she wrung the next words out of herself. "I'm... pregnant."

"I know." The man moved back to her side. "That's why I have to go. I don't want our son born into a universe where there is still... *this* going on. It has to stop. For him. For you, Gwen."

"How do you know it won't be a girl?" His mother asked, obviously trying to force a smile. The man looked round, and just for a moment Thomas had the uncomfortable sensation of eyes drilling into his. There was kindness there, and pride, but also a terrible knowledge. They were eyes that had seen far, far too much.

"Trust me, Gwen. It will be a boy. And he'll make," he looked Thomas up and down, "a fine young man."

"Then stay and see it." She caught his hand, but the man gently pried her free. What happened next was impossible, but Thomas had got used to that sort of thing. The man made a few movements of his hands, during which they almost seemed to pass through one another. A circle of golden light opened, apparently in thin air.

"I love you Gwen," he said, and stepped through.

The dream faded into blackness, but it felt more like an interval than a conclusion. A drumming sounded, like the low thrum of a heartbeat, pulsing through Thomas with every note. Thomas didn't care. He was too busy feeling a bit cheated that this vision seemed to have stolen its dialogue from a soap opera somewhere, while at the same time trying to make sense of the things he'd just seen.

Questions milled around in his head. Had that been his... father? Had it really been his *mother?* She'd looked so young, so happy, so sad, all at once. Was he going to have to sit through a whole season's worth of episodes before he woke up? *Why hadn't she told him?* The words lined themselves up in his con- sciousness like lead weights, until they were all he could think about. Thomas was still thinking it when something beside him cleared its throat.

"Excuse me?"

Pushing the questions away for a moment, Thomas turned to see a huge, hairy creature that managed to look like some un- holy combination of a lion and a rabbit, floppy eared and button nosed, but with lion's paws, and very definitely lion's teeth. It looked like the sort of thing that might evolve if the carrots star- ted fighting back.

"What is it?" Thomas demanded.

"Well, I was wondering if we could get on with this?"

"Get on with what?"

"Well, it's your basic shamanic type dream vision, isn't it?" the beast thing explained. "First you have your vision, and then you undergo a sort of rebirth thing."

"And how does that work?" Thomas asked cautiously.

"Well, you see, first we're supposed to have this big fight, all symbolic of the struggle of man against his darker nature, like. Then I eat you, strip off all your skin and spit out your bones."

"To symbolise getting rid of the old life?" Thomas guessed.

"Well, that too, but mostly 'cause I like it. And after that you're reborn." The thing twitched its nose. "So, are you ready?"

Thomas looked up at the thing where it waited patiently, hunger evident in every movement of its slavering jaws. Less so in the floppy ears, but definitely in the slavering.

"Let me just get this straight. I've just had a dream vision of what I assume is my biological father leaving my mother pregnant with me, and you're asking if I'm ready to be eaten by... what are you, anyway?"

"They call me the Eater. Look, are you ready or not?"

Thomas looked around at the blackness again.

"No."

"Well tough."

The thing's muscles bunched, getting ready to pounce. Its claws extended, its mouth opened hungrily. Without even thinking about it, Thomas waved a hand at the Eater. There was a loud pop as the space where the beast had been came to be occupied by a perfectly normal sized hamster. It paused for a moment, before running over and trying to nibble on his shoe. Thomas ignored it.

There were no hamsters in Nicola's dreams. No clowns, no old ladies, not even a strange little girl with a tendency to stare too much. For the moment, at least, there was nothing but blackness.

Nicola knew she was asleep. She could remember talking to Poppy until the effort of keeping up with the sudden leaps in the fairy woman's chatter had tired her right out. Nicola could remember seeing her out and deciding to get some sleep. She could even remember the moment her head hit the pillow, which she didn't think you were supposed to be able to do in dreams.

What Nicola didn't seem to be able to do was wake up.

The darkness gave way to the sense of a cold stone floor beneath her back, and in the same moment Nicola realised that she was chained down. There was the sight of someone, an indistinct shape, staring at her. Nicola didn't know what was going on, but she fought to keep from shaking.

"Now," the figure said, in a female and surprisingly pleasant voice, "what first?"

As soon as she said the words, Nicola felt the insects. There were thousands of them, tens of thousands. Flies and beetles and other things crawling and landing and biting all over her. Nicola wanted to open her mouth to cry out, but she knew that would just let the things into her. Instead she squeezed her mouth and eyes tightly shut, hoping it would stop soon.

"No? Then we'll just have to try something else."

The crawling web of insects was gone as soon as the words were out, but what replaced them was worse. Points of light floated just above her, some a soft blue, some red and angry. They hovered as though taunting Nicola, daring her to guess what would happen when they touched her.

And then she didn't have to guess, because one of the blue ones darted down and *into* her, fading through Nicola's skin like it wasn't even there.

It isn't there, Nicola told herself, *it's a dream. Just a dream.*

It was harder to remind herself of that when the cold erupted in her stomach. It was so intense that it felt like someone had compressed the entire arctic into a space approximately an inch across.

Before Nicola could even scream at the agony of it, one of the red ones descended into her foot. This one felt like a miniature sun, burning hotter than anything Nicola could have imagined.

"It's… only… a… dream," Nicola forced out, and the indistinct figure laughed.

"But that won't make it hurt any less. Then again, pain isn't quite what I want."

The dream changed, and then changed again. One moment Nicola was hanging above a thousand foot drop, the next she was running for her life from some faceless killer. After that, she started to lose track. Nightmare followed nightmare until Nicola started to feel more dizzy than scared. With a snap, she was back in the concrete-floored room. The figure she couldn't quite make out was back, and tutting as she ran through ideas.

"No, I've tried the flies. The dogs are out. I don't suppose you're scared of clowns, are you?"

Nicola managed to shake her head.

"I find them more sad than anything."

"I know. But still, you must be afraid of something. What do you *really* fear, Nicola?"

Nicola clamped her mouth shut as the thought rose up through her like a traitor, determined that she wouldn't give it to this woman. It didn't help. She plucked the fear from Nicola as easily as she might have picked up a small rock and sent it skimming across a lake.

"Ah, of course."

Blackness closed in with all the pressure of an ocean made from emptiness, crushing the air from Nicola's lungs, making it impossible to even breathe. She didn't die from it, the blackness wouldn't let her, but the pain of needing air screamed through Nicola's lungs. There was no air to carry the sound, but even if there had been, Nicola got the feeling that it wouldn't have carried. This was the sort of blackness that swallowed everything; sight, sound, even the sensation of being there.

Worse, in the darkness, somewhere that she couldn't see, the sound of screams came to Nicola. There were hundreds of them, all just out of sight, and all accompanied by a single thought; *you can't help them.* Helpless in the darkness, all Nicola could do was listen as the cries of agony got worse. Each scream came with the knowledge, the kind of absolute certainty that you could only have in dreams, that Nicola hadn't managed to save them, and that they hated her for it.

Nicola opened her mouth, and now she could scream. Her cries joined the others in a sort of counterpoint, rising and rising and...

Nicola woke, sweat soaked, on the bed of her room. For a second, she didn't even realise it. The room was too dark, and the blind panic of the dream too great. She sat up, the sudden silence of reality almost too great, trying to catch hold of her breathing long enough to still it.

There's a special sort of confusion that goes with waking up in a strange room at some hour of the morning you'd rather not acknowledge the existence of. Almost inevitably, any scramble for a light switch is going to involve skinned knees or a fall over some table that wouldn't have been there if the world had done the sensible thing and arranged all bedrooms the same way as your own.

Nicola knew that, but still scrabbled for some means of making a light. Was there a dressing table next to the bed? Nicola couldn't remember until her questing fingers found it. They searched it, and somehow managed to brush across a tiny glass globe that warmed a fraction with Nicola's touch, giving off a gentle glow. With that little bit of light, she was able to take a few deep, calming breaths at last, lying back as the last of the nightmare subsided.

"It was just a dream." Nicola reassured herself, grateful as much for the sound as the light. She repeated it again, more confidently.

Even so, she didn't turn off the light.

The warm glow of dawn light welcomed Thomas back to consciousness. It was a better sight than the face of the old hag, just inches from his own.

"Did you have a nice sleep, boy?"

"You… you drugged us."

Freli just shrugged, before moving over to the hearth. Thomas could see now that over the fire was a big iron… he struggled to avoid the word cauldron, and failed. He could only guess at its contents.

"It's porridge," Freli supplied. "Want some?"

Thomas' stomach grumbled an agreement, and he wolfed down the bowl she handed him. Thomas was about halfway through it when the foolishness of accepting food from someone who'd already poisoned him once occurred to him. By that point, of course, there wasn't much else to do but finish the porridge.

Finally, Thomas felt in a fit state to ask questions, and to check on the other two. Simon was nowhere to be seen, but Melissa still slept peacefully in her chair.

"Why isn't she waking up?"

"Probably just needs the rest more, poor thing," Freli

answered. "Don't worry, she'll come round in a minute. As for your Figment friend, I've sent him out to fetch me a few things. Always helpful, Simon, at least if you keep an eye on him."

"What did you do to us?" Thomas asked, rising to his feet. "I wanted a way out of here, not some weird dream where a hamster tries to eat me."

The old woman seemed to ignore this, fussing around the cauldron instead. Thomas went over to her, taking her by the shoulder.

"I said, what did you do to us?"

"I heard what you said, boy. Now sit down, I'm fixing breakfast for the girl. I'll explain, but I'm only doing it once. Didn't anyone ever teach you to be respectful to your elders?"

Thomas might have answered back to that, but a kind of horrified fascination settled on him instead.

"Just how old are you?"

"Five thousand, one hundred and twenty seven years old." Freli answered promptly, still stirring the porridge. "Though that's not why I look like this. Most of them look like cover models all their lives. Me, I've been a hag almost from the start."

"That's terrible."

Thomas said it mostly because it seemed to be the only appropriate response. Eternal youth was hard enough for him to get his head around, but eternal old age?

"Oh, it's not so bad. After all, it's not like I get too many aches and pains with it, just the wrinkles really. And it's a big help with the business. No one seems to want a young dream oracle. Still, it would be nice occasionally to see a birthday that had more cake than candle. Incidentally, your friend is waking up."

Thomas looked round to Melissa and, sure enough, her eyes flickered open. She gave him a sleepy smile.

"Hello Thomas. Did I fall asleep?"

"Just for a while. Are you all right?"

"Mmm... yes. I had the nicest dream."

Melissa thanked Freli as the old woman handed her a plate of porridge, eating it with the gusto of someone who'd given up on the concept of regular meals a while ago. Somewhere in the middle of it, Simon returned, passing a basket of assorted groceries over to Freli.

"Such a strong young man."

She said it with an inflection that made Thomas shut down his imagination hurriedly, for fear of what it might come up with. Stranded interrupted it just in time.

"I've got news," he said, but Freli shushed him.

"Afterwards. The girl is still eating. Still, now we're all here and awake, I suppose it's time for explanations."

"You put something in the tea, didn't you?" Melissa asked, though not as reproachfully as Thomas had. Freli nodded an answer.

"A little something to make you sleep. You looked like you could do with it. And the boy, of course, got a little extra ingredient in order to get the dream quest going."

Thomas waved a hand at all the paraphernalia cluttering the place.

"Couldn't you just have used some of this?" he asked. "Why did I have to go round fighting off magic beasts and turning them into hamsters? Why did I have to..."

"Why did you have to see what you did?" Freli finished for him. Thomas nodded silently. "Well, three reasons really. Firstly, it was your question, it seemed right that it was up to you to go and get the answer. All nicely mythic and balanced and so forth. Secondly, you seemed like a young man with more questions than just the one you were asking. Now, I don't know what you saw, but I reckon it probably showed you something you *needed* to see, not just what you wanted to know, yes?"

Thomas didn't answer that. After a second, Melissa broke the silence.

"What was the third thing?" she asked. "You said there were three reasons."

Freli gave them a slightly embarrassed look.

"Well, the third reason is that most of these things don't work. They're fakes. What with the dream visions, I've never really needed them. Besides, do you have any idea what a good crystal ball costs these days?"

Thomas didn't, but he might have been prepared to pay it for some straight answers.

"What about my question?" he demanded. "We were after a way of getting home, and all I got was… well, it wasn't that."

Freli raised one white haired eyebrow.

"Are you sure? Usually someone who goes through the whole thing gets an answer, even if they don't know it. Think, boy. Maybe you missed it at the time."

Thomas thought. Mostly, what he thought was that the old woman was extremely irritating. He was sure he hadn't seen anything useful, had he? Maybe it had gone wrong when he'd refused to be eaten, or maybe he hadn't been paying attention at the crucial moment. But then, what could he possibly learn from the parting that he'd…

"I've got it!" he said. "In the vision, I saw a… portal or something being opened. If I copied how it was done, would it work do you think?"

"Possibly." Freli shrugged as she answered. "Try it."

Thomas did, struggling to remember what the man in his vision – Thomas refused to think of him as his father until he'd had rather more time to think about it – had done. He'd moved his hands like *this* and then like *this*, and then they'd crossed like *this*.

A pop like someone opening a thousand soft drinks cans all at once filled the room, followed closely by the sound of tiny bells. In a sudden glare of light, a hole appeared in the nearest wall. Thomas stared at it, before finally sticking his head through, into a landscape Thomas had never seen before, full of sand, baked red stone, and heat. Something huge and lizard-like slithered nearby, and Thomas pulled his head back hurriedly.

"That's not my home," Thomas said. Almost as soon as the words were out, the hole closed up.

"Well, no," Freli said. "But it's interesting that you can do it at all. Next time, try concentrating on where you want it to open. And don't stick your head through. You should be able to make the thing transparent enough if you try, and it's a lot better than getting your head bitten off by anything that's passing."

Thomas gulped, thinking of the lizard, and resolved to be more careful.

"All right, I'll try again."

He was just about to start the gestures again when Simon put a hand on his arm.

"Before you do that, I've got something you're going to want to hear."

"What?"

"I think I know where your ex is."

Chapter Seventeen

At a touch on her arm, Siobhan pulled herself out of the dream and stood. She looked levelly at Grave until he took his hand away, then threw the last of the dream fruit out across the orchard. Even in the dawn light, it flared like a meteorite before vanishing in a puff of golden dust.

"Will your mother be happy at you being here, Princess?" Grave asked her, in a tone of voice that knew exactly how happy she would be. Siobhan raised an eyebrow.

"And how would my mother find out?"

She saw the big lunk shuffle a little at that. It was amusing in its way to watch him caught between the pair of them like this.

"I am still her Huntsman," Grave tried to remind her, but there wasn't any real menace in it. Particularly not when Siobhan stretched just *so*, in a way guaranteed to draw the eye. It seemed he wasn't made of stone, after all. Good.

"You haven't thought, have you Grave?" Siobhan took a moment to arrange herself lazily against the tree. "I'm still acting in my mother's interests."

"Even though she has the girl as her prisoner?"

"Because of that, you idiot." Siobhan watched him redden. "Oh, don't be angry. I know you can't possibly understand. My mother wants to be seen to be fair and just, correct?"

"Well… yes, Princess."

"So she can't be seen to take in a stray one moment and have her killed the next. Maybe if she did something stupid, but even with a human we can't count on it happening quickly enough."

Grave's eyebrows drew together, reminding Siobhan of nothing so much as a draught excluder glued above his eyes. She sighed.

"Look, it's really very simple. Firstly, this bitch is human, and so shouldn't be here anyway. Secondly, everything points to her being the one who came through with Thomas Greene, which means she can tell too many people too much about what is going on."

There was a brief silence, in which Siobhan realised she was going to have to do the rest of the work as well. There was no doubt Grave was good at hunting, but really, would a *little* understanding of the politics of the thing hurt so much? Actually, she considered, it might. It might hurt her at any rate. It was a very special blend of deadliness and utter naivety that made Grave so useful.

"We can't kill her, because then mother would have to appear angry. But if I terrify her close to madness, she'll not be in a position to talk, you see?"

Grave nodded slowly, and Siobhan relaxed. For a while there, she'd begun to suspect that he wasn't going to believe her excuse. Of course they didn't need to drive this human mad. Her mother would make certain none of what Nicola knew got out, even if she believed it. But Siobhan couldn't afford to let Grave know that the night's work had been about little more than jealousy, pique and the desire to take what her mother said and do exactly the opposite, could she? That would just make Siobhan look... petty.

"Why did you come here, Grave?" Siobhan asked. "Shouldn't you be out completing our little list?"

"I thought you might have orders for me, Princess. About Thomas Greene."

"Why would I?"

The shuffling, looking-at-his-own-shoes pause was just a little too long.

"What's happened?" Siobhan demanded.

"I thought you'd know, Princess," Grave replied in the unhappy voice of a man who'd just realised he was going to be the first to break the bad news. He went back to not quite looking her in the eye. Ordinarily, Siobhan might have enjoyed the ability to reduce the Courts' foremost hunter to something so uncomfortable, but impatience got the better of her.

"Look, can we get on with this? What... has... happened?"

"I think he might have... escaped. A bit."

Siobhan put aside thoughts of how exactly you escaped "a bit." Maybe you popped out for lunch and then broke back into your cell afterwards for a nice lie down.

"And how exactly do you know he's gone?"

"The door in the rose garden. I thought you might be there, so I'd gone down to check, and it was just open when I got there. So I came here."

Siobhan resisted the urge to hit something, which surprised her. Normally she didn't bother resisting urges like that. Then again, the nearest thing to hit was her mother's Huntsman, and that would probably just result in a broken hand.

"Show me," she snapped instead, following as Grave led her. Not that Siobhan needed him to show her where her own hidey-hole for prisoners was. It just made sure that there would be someone to shout at once they got there. The door was indeed open. Siobhan, in a display of restraint even greater than her last one, actually waited until she'd been inside, until she'd seen the gloopy and suspiciously yellowish pool that had been her holding cage before she exploded.

"Damn it! Stupid..." Siobhan stormed up the tunnel leading outside, pausing to glare at the roses around the entrance. "And what did *you* think you were doing? Are you torn from some mighty contest? Are you burned to a crisp where they've used magic on you? No! You just let them out as meek as mice, didn't you? Useless things."

In as much as it was possible for plant life to look sheepish, the roses did so.

"I should have you uprooted and replaced with daisies, for all the good you are. Grave, why are you still standing here?

Find them."

"And when I find them, Princess?"

Siobhan got a grip on herself.

"I'd still like them alive, Grave. They're too useful to just discard."

"Even after all this?"

Especially after all this, Siobhan thought, but didn't say it. Yes, she'd need to replace the cage with something a little stronger, but Thomas Greene could be just what she needed. Grave didn't need to hear that.

"Just do as you're told. And find someone to clean up this syrup."

"Are you sure?" Thomas asked. Simon took a bite out of an apple.

"It's kind of hard to be sure when she's shut up in the castle. I wasn't going to break in and look. Do you know what they do to people like me in there?"

"No, what?"

"Trust me, you don't want to know."

"What they do," Freli interrupted, looking up from a bizarre arrangement of herbs and spices, "is to take Figments like Simon and make them assume the form they were created with. I think our castaway doesn't fancy being grey mist."

"I said he didn't want to know," Stranded snapped back. "I certainly didn't."

Freli continued fiddling with the ingredients that Simon had brought her. Melissa stood with her, apparently looking for something to help with. For his part, Thomas was busy trying to make sense of what he'd been told.

"It has to be her, doesn't it?" Thomas mused out loud. "I mean, how many other humans can there be around here?"

"That's what I thought," Simon Stranded confirmed. "But if it is, I think we can forget about rescuing her."

"Simon!" That came from Melissa, who only seemed to

realise how loudly she'd said it once the word was out. More quietly, she continued. "I've been their prisoner. We can't just leave her there."

Thomas was surprised at the quiet determination of her tone. After what she'd been through, he didn't think Melissa would want to head back to the castle. Thomas knew *he* didn't want to, and he hadn't even been there a full night.

"Just how impregnable is this place?" he asked. By way of answer, Simon just pointed out of the nearest window, to where the castle towered over the village like a school bully demanding lunch money.

"But won't there be, I don't know, secret passages and things?" Thomas asked. "Ways for people to slip out if they're attacked?"

"What good would that be?" Stranded asked him. "The whole point of your basic castle is to divide the world into inside and outside, then to say to everyone outside 'you're not coming in.' Sort of like a bouncer, but stonier. Well, marginally."

"So there's no way in except through the front?"

Thomas didn't know whether to be disappointed or relieved. On the one hand, of course he wanted to rescue Nicola. He'd got her into this, after all, and he owed it to her to get her out. Besides, it seemed a bit much to abandon her in some alternate world as well as dumping her. By any standard, that probably counted as a bad break-up. On the other hand, Thomas strongly suspected that wandering into a heavily protected castle would be only just short of a suicide mission, and Thomas was pretty sure he had an allergy to those.

Naturally, Freli chose that moment to speak.

"Actually, there *are* a couple of extra ways in. After all, if your main enemies can drop into your world where they like, walls are mostly for show. And you've got to have some way for servants and deliveries to come in without getting in the way of the fancy folk ruling the place."

"And, let me guess, you know exactly where they are." Thomas heard the depressed note that had managed to creep into his voice. The others didn't seem to notice.

168

"Of course. I used to go up to the castle that way quite regularly. Let's just say that one of the butlers had a bit of a thing for the... more mature woman."

I will not imagine it, Thomas repeated to himself, *I will not imagine it, I will not...*

"That's great," Melissa said hopefully. "At least we've got a way in now. We'll sneak in, find her, and Thomas can zap us all out of there."

Simon was less enthusiastic.

"Sure. All you've got to do is sneak up there without being spotted, dodge past whoever's guarding this entrance, assuming it isn't locked, which it will be, avoid being seen while you search the whole castle, break his ex-girlfriend out of whatever prison they've got her in, and then escape by using a piece of magic Thomas didn't know he could do five minutes ago. What could possibly go wrong?"

"Does this mean you won't be coming?" Melissa asked.

"I didn't say that. I probably *should* have said that, but I didn't."

Thomas was beginning to wish *he* could say that, but suspected he didn't get to opt out of the rescue attempt. Besides, Thomas reminded himself, cursing himself for having to remind himself at all, he owed Nicola more than that. While he was thinking that, Freli continued with whatever she was doing, mixing ingredients seemingly at random. Simon seemed to be taking a particular interest in it.

"Please tell me that's some special potion that will get us into the castle. At the rate we're going, we'll need to be either invisible or able to move through solid walls."

"Now Simon," the old woman replied, "you know my potions don't do that sort of thing. Anyway, this isn't a potion. This is something better than that."

"What could be better than that?"

"I'm baking a pie."

The Figment formerly known as Keith the Barman was quite en-joying being a guard. Not that he could remember being any-thing else, of course. Everyone knew that Figments didn't retain memories from their last forms while they were being something new. It interfered with their ability to get into the role, or some-thing. No, as far as the guard on the southern basement entrance was concerned, he had never spent any time as a stereotypically Australian barkeeper. Particularly not one called Keith.

He didn't actually have a name yet, since the Queen hadn't given him one when she'd told him who to be this time. The job of guarding an entrance was a happily undemanding one, which was why a Figment got it rather than one of *them*. The dreaming-folk guards probably thought it was boring to guard a gate hardly anyone used. The as-yet-unnamed guard didn't get armour. He didn't get much of anything except a halberd and instructions to watch over the little doorway until further notice. Perhaps, if he hadn't been so busy getting used to the idea of existing, he might have thought to ask when that was likely to be.

Not that he minded. Standing in front of a gate, whistling tunes to himself and waiting for the next person to show up wanting entrance seemed like a happy enough lot in life. He would probably have been quite surprised if someone had poin-ted out that the tune he was currently whistling was *Waltzing Matilda*.

He was so caught up in this that he almost missed the ar-rival of a surprisingly lovely figure, accompanied by the scent of the sort of baking a single man could normally only dream of once he'd left home. Or at least, the guardsman who had been Keith assumed that was the sort of thing they dreamed of. He hadn't really had a chance to find out.

"G'day." He began, and then shook himself. That wasn't the greeting that a good guard should be giving, now was it? "I mean… halt, who goes there?"

"Do we have to bother with names?" The woman asked with a smile that made the guard think of things other than pastry. Her brown eyes met his as she spoke, and she actually winked. "I just thought I'd bring our brave boys this pie as a token of our appreciation down in the village."

"That's really kind of you." The guard said, surprised that she might go to such trouble. "I'll definitely see that everyone gets some of it, if you'll leave it with me."

She wrinkled her nose in a way that was prettier than he could have thought.

"I was sort of hoping that I might be able to give this to them myself, maybe get a chance to let them know that I'm very, *very* grateful, you know?"

Since the ex-bartender had only a few hours' worth of memories, he didn't know, but he could guess.

"Well… um, really… I shouldn't let you past, you see. I'm not allowed to."

He found himself treated to another heart-melting smile.

"Now that's a silly rule, isn't it? How am I supposed to deliver this pie now?" She seemed to think for a moment, before moving closer to him in a way that made the Figment think that there might be more interesting things than guarding out there after all.

"How about," she suggested, "if you just let me sort of slip through? After all, it's only me, and I'm sure no one would know."

"I really can't. I'm sorry."

She pouted, actually pouted, at that.

"Well, how about if you show me the way? No one can say then that you let me in unguarded."

"I'm not allowed to leave my post."

"Oh. Well, I wouldn't want to get you into any trouble. Here, you might as well take this." She pressed the pie into his hands, at which point the guard discovered that attempting to juggle both a halberd and a large pie dish was something that ideally required at least one more hand than he actually had.

Trying to control both, he took a step back, just in time for a pair of men to throw themselves at the spot where he'd just been standing. The shock of that was enough to send the pie clattering to the ground, but it did at least mean he had both hands free to use the halberd. He levelled it in what he hoped was a threatening manner.

"Halt!"

The two men didn't halt. They did pick themselves up from the patch of ground where they'd fallen. One looked like he'd scoured the place for rags to wear, while the other was dressed more normally. It was the second one who spoke.

"Look, we're sorry about trying to ambush you like that, but we really *do* need to get inside. Can't you see this is important?"

"All I can see is that you've ruined a perfectly good pie." The guard retorted. "This young lady has laboured long and hard to produce something nice, and you two have gone and ruined it. Get out of here, both of you. Go on!" He prodded vaguely forward with the halberd, and it looked like the better dressed one might be about to try something, but the other put a hand on his arm. They stalked off together. The guard looked down to the ruins of the pie, fruit juice flowing from it like blood from a critical wound, and then up to the young woman, who seemed to be staring at him as though unsure what to do next.

"I'm sorry about your pie, miss," he tried. "I'm sure it would have been lovely. Perhaps you could bake another?"

Her reply wasn't quite what he'd expected. It had rather more swearwords in it, for a start. The woman turned on her heel and set off in the direction that the other two had taken. The guardsman searched his pitifully short memory, trying to find the right words for a situation like this. Only three came to mind, and he said them even though he couldn't quite remember what they meant.

"Strewth. Bloody sheilas."

Chapter Eighteen

"Well, that didn't go according to plan."

Thomas didn't comment. The two of them stood by the side of the path that led to the village, waiting for Melissa to catch up. Thomas used the time to brush off the worst of the mud from his clothes.

"Maybe if you'd timed your jump a bit better..."

"Me? What about you? You missed him too."

"You both missed him," Melissa chimed in, looking surprisingly annoyed as she arrived. "And I don't know why."

"Perhaps we were distracted by your loveliness," Simon ventured.

Thomas rolled his eyes.

"Knock it off, Simon. And Melissa, wasn't that whole sex kitten routine a bit... over the top?"

That comment earned him the sort of glare that might have melted steel, at least for the first half second or so. After that, it faded a little.

"All right," Melissa admitted, "maybe I did overdo it a bit, but remember I've spent the last couple of months hanging around Siobhan. Something was bound to rub off. Maybe *you'd* like to be the distraction next time."

"Next time?" Stranded interrupted. "Are you mad?"

Thomas was inclined to agree with the sentiment, but not with the tone of voice. Particularly not when the words made Melissa fold up like a piece of badly constructed origami. Despite the confidence she'd shown with the guard, it seemed that being caged up for so long had done its damage.

"Simon," he said, "do me a favour would you?"

"What?"

"Shut up." He put an arm around Melissa, feeling oddly protective all of a sudden. She stiffened for a moment, but then relaxed into the touch.

"Maybe I am mad," Melissa murmured. "But I think we should try again."

"I don't think you're mad," Thomas assured her. "I'm pretty sure you'd be going on about the invisible purple people telling you to do it if you were."

"Oh well," Melissa managed a smile, "that's probably all right then."

"I'm just not sure what we could do that might work."

He started them walking back towards the village. Simon Stranded, happy to be headed away from the castle, took the lead. Melissa was more reluctant.

"There has to be something. Come on, Thomas, she's *your* girlfriend."

"Ex-girlfriend." It occurred to Thomas that that probably didn't count as a good reason. "Seriously, Melissa, what can we do? I want to save her, of course I do, but I'm not going to get us killed trying. That won't help her or us."

Thomas watched Melissa think a little. It took them a few strides closer to the village.

"We could try to sneak in."

"Didn't we just try that? And if we can't avoid one fairly stupid guard, I don't fancy our chances of getting past a whole castle full."

"We could pretend to be, I don't know, laundresses and sneak past in disguise."

"I expect the castle does its own laundry," Simon Stranded supplied from in front. "Besides, I am *not* wearing a dress. I have a reputation to consider. Not that I'm going back."

Thomas wanted to agree. Certainly with the dress part, and probably with the rest of it too. At least they were still heading away from the castle. After a bit more thought, Melissa spoke up again.

"How about if we pretend to take Simon in as our prisoner; say that we've captured a dangerous Figment and that we need to take him to the cells? She's bound to be there."

"You stole that one from Star Wars," Thomas said.

"So? It's a good plan."

"What if they realise who we are? Or if they decide to kill Simon straight away? Or if Nicola isn't in their cells? Or if they take him from us at the gate?"

"Also," Stranded added, "did you hear the bit where I said I'm not going back there?"

They walked on in silence a little way. Thomas found that Melissa was sort of slumped against him now, as though the effort of arguing had taken up the little energy that she had. Maybe it had. After all, one good meal was hardly likely to undo the work of weeks of hardly being fed.

"You both sound like you're just... giving up," she managed after a while.

"I am giving up," Simon Stranded responded. "I'm good at giving up. I got here by giving up and running out of my dream. Giving up is practically my main skill in life. I don't see any reason to give up on giving up now."

Thomas shook his head.

"If I were giving up, I'd just zap the pair of us out of here and straight home. We'll go back to Freli's house and see if she has any better ideas than baking a pie. You look like you could do with the rest anyway."

"If she had any better ideas," Stranded said, "wouldn't she have told us them by now? You might as well just cut your losses and get out of here while you can."

Thomas gave the Figment a hard look.

"What's wrong, Simon? You want to see the back of us?"

"Let's just say that I'm beginning to wish I hadn't dragged you into that bush. I've trekked over miles of the Court, been chased by the Queen's Huntsman, been licked by a boot, and nearly been skewered by a suspiciously Australian guard. Helping is one thing, but this is ridiculous." He stopped, and gave a sort of shrug. "Besides, by now they'll know you've escaped. I wouldn't want to hang around to be found if I were you."

Thomas felt Melissa shudder against him at that, and he drew her out to arm's length, looking her carefully in the eye.

"We can go if you like," Thomas offered, doing his best to disguise the note of hope. "Or I could send you back. At least, I'm pretty sure I could send you back."

Melissa shook her head.

"No, I'll go back when you do. I'll be fine. We'll go back to the village, find another way of rescuing…"

"…Nicola." Thomas supplied.

"…and leave together. I'm sure they won't be onto us yet."

This time, there was a scent that Grave could track, at least. Not the cinnamon trace of Dreaming Folk that he could pick up in their world, because that would be like trying to sniff out an un-washed leather vest at a heavy metal concert. Instead, he focused on the scent of human. Since there weren't supposed to be any humans in the Court, *that* was simple.

Grave had been a bit surprised when the scent in question started to lead back towards the village. After all, he'd been there off and on through the last day or so. Surely he'd have noticed a couple of half-breeds wandering around. Then again, it was hard to notice much of anything when you were busy trying to scrape custard off a dartboard and checking that the gremlin didn't take anything important apart.

No, Grave was definitely better off working alone. Alone, Grave could hunt as he wanted to. Alone, he could track and run and wait exactly as he wished. Well, not *exactly* as he wished, because there was still the Princess' instruction to bring them in alive to consider, but Grave felt he could work around that. He generally could.

They knew him in the village, so Grave didn't bother trying to skulk around. Trying to skulk when you were his size tended to defeat the object anyway, at least when there wasn't human suggestibility backing it up. Small children tended to turn to watch and ask their parents what that fat man was doing tiptoeing around everywhere. Occasionally, they started to tell him what they wanted for Christmas. It was far more trouble than it was worth.

Instead Grave strode briskly into the place, sniffing and changing direction as the scent led him. After about fifteen minutes of that sort of thing, Grave came to rest before the door to the cottage belonging to village's soothsayer and witch. Grave knocked on the door, which is to say that he pounded his knuckles on it hard enough to make the thing burst open, the lock in tatters.

"You might as well come in, if you're going to be like that," a woman's voice said. "Mind you take your boots off."

Feeling extremely silly about it, but slightly embarrassed about the door, Grave did just that. The removal of his boots revealed thick woollen socks that appeared to contain about a sheep's worth of wool each. He strode into the living room, doing his best to look menacing. Somehow, it didn't work quite so well without his boots.

"Where are they?" Grave demanded. The old seer just held out a cup and saucer.

"I'm sure they'll be back soon, dear. Now, won't you have a nice cup of tea?"

Grave took it and sniffed it.

"What have you put in it?" he demanded. "Some poison so I won't be able to hunt? Some strange witch's brew?"

"Well," Freli admitted, "I probably overdid things on the sugar a bit, but other than that, it's just tea. Sometimes that's really all you need. Now, be a good boy and sit down where I can see you."

It had been a long time since anyone had called Grave a boy, but the woman certainly looked old enough for it. He sat down and took a reluctant sip from the cup. There were, indeed, no strange poisons in it. Grave felt slightly cheated, but drank the rest anyway.

"You know what they are?" Grave demanded, in between slurps.

"A Figment and two children of the Courts. Of course I know. I'm a seer, aren't I? The question, oh great and powerful Hunter of this Court, is whether you know that you're being used."

Grave's massive hand started to tighten on the cup.

"If you break it," the seer snapped at him, "you can sit on your hands so you don't touch anything else."

"Sorry."

Grave put the cup down with a delicate clink. That just drew a sigh from the woman.

"There was a time when you wouldn't have been so easily cowed, Grave."

"It's called being polite."

Grave growled it in a way designed to make it clear that being impolite was also an option. It didn't seem to have any effect.

"You're so cowed I can practically hear you mooing. There was a time when your name was feared all over the Courts. Now, you're running round doing the bidding of a silly girl who should know better."

Grave drew himself up to his full height, or would have done if the beams for the ceiling hadn't been too low.

"Do you *dare* speak about our Queen like that?"

"I'm not talking about the Queen, and you know it. Now sit back down." Grave did it automatically. "I'm supposed to be a seer, so here's a prophecy for you, Huntsman. One day, not far from now, you'll take a look at some of the things you've been doing without thinking, and you'll realise that, if you had thought, you probably wouldn't have done them."

"And I suppose I'll meet a tall, beautiful woman who'll take me in her arms and tell me that she loves me?" Grave jibed, but his heart wasn't in it. Particularly not when Freli the seer closed her eyes. After a second, she voiced what might have been a mystic note, but sounded rather more like someone trying to stifle a laugh.

"Amazing. Against all the odds, not to mention the state of that beard, that's almost exactly what *will* happen. I never knew you had the gift, Grave."

"Now you're making fun of me."

"Oh no. I never joke about what I see. Still, you won't believe it until it happens, so who am I to interfere?" She paused just long enough to shoot Grave a look that was far too smug. "Incidentally, to return for a moment to the topic of our three young scamps, they're currently running rather quickly away from my front door. I'd wish you luck catching them, but I wouldn't mean it."

It took Grave a moment to take the words in. As soon as he did, several things happened. First, he swore quite loudly. Then he surged to his feet. Then he swore again, because hitting your head on a low ceiling is never comfortable. Finally, he sprinted through the doorway, pausing only to grab his boots on the way out.

Thomas ran with Melissa alongside him, Simon Stranded sprinting ahead. Thomas dared a look back, and was just in time to spot Grave emerging from Freli's house, a boot in either hand and a murderous expression on his face. The boots had been the clue. There were some signs that just said "run for it" as surely as if it had been painted on a sign. After all, what elderly woman was ever going to wear working boots in a size somewhere between "gigantic" and "canoe"? Of course, the door ripped nearly off its hinges had been a bit of a giveaway too.

"Faster!" Thomas urged Melissa, who managed to put on a burst of speed in response. They left the cottage behind them as quickly as humanly possible. Quicker, in Simon's case. As for where they were heading, Thomas wasn't sure. He was leaving that to Simon. Frankly, anywhere that didn't contain eight foot tall men intent on his death was fine with Thomas.

When they emerged after a few seconds in the village's

main square, Thomas began to suspect that paying more attention might have been a good thing. They skidded to a halt. Since there was no sign that they'd lost the oversized thug behind them, this didn't strike Thomas as a particularly good thing either.

"What are you doing, Simon?" he demanded, only for the Figment to point breathlessly to the other side of the square, where half a dozen guards seemed to be engaged in the sort of activities that are almost traditional pursuits for royal guards across the universe, which is to say that they were loitering, dicing, and passing a suspicious looking mug between them.

"What are you doing bringing us here then?" Thomas asked.

"Me? I thought you might come up with a plan. I've just been running."

"So have I!"

"Boys!" Melissa's voice cut through the start of the argument. "We don't have time for this." She gave a pointed look over her shoulder. There wasn't any sign of Grave yet, but Thomas knew it would only be a matter of seconds. He winced.

"We'll have to bluff it out." He started to stride across towards the waiting guardsmen. "Just try to act casual."

That was easier said than done. It's hard to be casual when you are all too conscious that a killer is hot on your heels. The more you think about it, the harder it is to walk at anything approaching a normal speed. For Thomas, Melissa and Simon Stranded, the net result was that odd, stiff, far too fast walk familiar to anyone who has ever hurried to catch a train without wanting to actually run. The effects of doing that in front of a group of slightly bored guards were fairly predictable.

"Oi, you three!" The nearest of the guards said, rising to block their path. "What are you doing?" He had probably started out handsome enough, like so many of the inhabitants of the place, but there was a slightly squashed quality to the guard's features that spoke either of one too many fights or a lifetime squeezing into a guard's helmet two sizes too small for him. Probably both, Thomas guessed.

"Oh, nothing, officer," he tried in what he hoped was a calm voice. "We're just out for a stroll."

"Sure you are, and I'm just here practising my knitting. Now, you can tell me what's going on, or I can haul the three of you up to the castle and hear it there."

Thomas felt Melissa push past him, and saw her flash a brief smile at the guardsman.

"My friend is just trying to spare my reputation, sir," she said in a voice that was a distinct improvement on the one she'd tried up at the castle. To Thomas' ears it held just the right combination of faint embarrassment, openness, and a faint hint of suggestiveness for what she was saying. "When he said we were out for a stroll, we were *out for a stroll*, if you see the difference. And now I'm late home."

There was no embarrassment in the guard's face at hearing that. Quite the opposite, in fact. "Well if you're late already, darling, why not hang around here a while? Get to know some real men? I'm sure we could give you a much more interesting... walk, hmm?"

Thomas saw Melissa redden, but there wasn't time for her to answer, because Grave chose that moment to burst into the village square. The fact that he still had a boot in each hand didn't make it any less scary.

"Stop them! By order of the Queen!"

A guard dove for Thomas, who threw a punch almost on instinct. Somehow, it connected sweetly with the guard's jaw, sending him crashing to the ground. Thomas swore, trying to shake some feeling back into the hand. He turned, determined to help Melissa, but she was already standing over the guard who'd stopped them, who was on the ground, clutching himself in a way that suggested Melissa hadn't reacted well to his earlier comment.

Simon wasn't so lucky. All four of the remaining guards seemed to have decided to jump him at once, resulting in a pile of which the best that could be said was that Simon was in there somewhere. Thomas took one look at the struggling heap, and then over his shoulder to where Grave was bearing down with deliberate menace.

"Come on!" he said, grabbing Melissa's arm.

"What are you doing, Thomas? We have to help Simon!"

Thomas didn't reply. Nor did he let go of Melissa's wrist. Instead, he concentrated on moving his arms like *this* and then *this* and then like *this*, all the while concentrating on the one place, the only place, that he really wanted to be at a time like this. The air beside them ruptured in a blaze of light, and Thomas gave the scene one last, apologetic look. Having done that, he screwed his eyes shut, picked Melissa up bodily before she could protest further, and threw the pair of them forward into the hole.

Chapter Nineteen

The castle's library was a strange place, even by the standards of the rest of it. Walls stretched and shifted if you gazed at them too long, while shelves made from the bones of creatures long since extinct stretched away far further than the room seemed to allow. They held an array of books of the sort of eclecticism normally only found in a particular sort of second hand bookshop; the ones where you invariably get the feeling the owner would really rather not sell anything. The careful eye might take in leather bound covers, stacked scrolls, and even the occasional stone tablet. The even more careful eye might have noted that in amongst all this there were a few paperbacks that looked suspiciously new.

It was Erithnae's only vice. Or, at least, it was the only one of them that she thought of as a vice. She knew that risking everything just for the latest Jilly Cooper or Kathy Reichs was ludicrous, but it wasn't like anyone had ever noticed her visits to the discreet little London bookshop where she liked to browse. Even the family who owned the thing never remarked on the fact that Erithnae had been a regular customer for longer than any of them could remember. Considering how few other customers they seemed to have, maybe they just didn't want to put her off.

Even so, it was with a certain amount of guilty pleasure that Erithnae curled up on the small couch that was the place's only furniture besides the shelves, leafing through the latest book to catch her eye. Its cover featured nothing but the silhouette of some impossibly thin woman shopping and an author name picked out in what was probably supposed to look like lipstick. The contents were everything a cover like that promised.

Chicklit was a new experience for Erithnae. On the whole, she found she was enjoying it. Erithnae had tried reading fantasy, but its stories of orcs and elves and heroes just seemed too mundane. The first time she'd read through *A Midsummer Night's Dream*, Erithnae had found herself wondering how the human had found out. On the other hand this, with its hopeless heroine Judy, rapidly falling in love with suspiciously floppy-haired next-door neighbour David after walking out on a marriage where she couldn't be herself, this was *exotic*.

Erithnae was just getting to a good bit, where Judy was enjoying a night in with her lesbian flatmate Amy, whom everyone but Judy could see fancied her, when there was a sharp knock at the door.

"What is it?" Erithnae demanded. "I said I wasn't to be disturbed for at least an hour."

"Sorry, your majesty," a voice muffled by the thick oak door came back. "But it's important."

"So is this," Erithnae grumbled, but quietly. It wasn't important, of course. It was simply what she wanted to do. If you were Queen, you had to understand the difference. Duty came first. It was a bit like being in the army, only no one actually outranked you. Not that she had ever *asked* for things to be like this. When you're a princess, no one asks you what you want to do when you grow up. They all just assume.

Locating a bookmark, Erithnae stuffed the book back on the nearest shelf, and strode over to the door. On the other side stood a pair of burly guards, holding what was clearly a Figment between them, high enough that only his toes touched the floor. The manacles that they'd found from somewhere seemed a little over the top, but at least they fit in with the ripped clothing. The two guards tried to bow, which dropped the Figment onto his feet again, only for him to be hoisted into the air once more as he tried to run.

"What is it?" Erithnae demanded, in the special tone of

voice she'd perfected for situations just like this. It said that no one was in trouble yet, but that she was definitely counting down from some unstated figure in her head, and they wouldn't want her to reach zero.

"We caught this Figment down in the village, your majesty," one of them said quickly.

"And that's important enough for you to interrupt me? Just take him down to the cells and I'll deal with him in a bit."

"Begging your pardon, your majesty, but that isn't it. This one was with two others."

"Two other Figments?" Erithnae made a point of stifling a yawn.

"We don't know, majesty, but they didn't look it. There was a man and a woman, and they looked... normal. Well, right up to the point where they just disappeared."

"Disappeared?" Erithnae felt her interest rise. "Tell me about them."

"I heard the woman call the man Thomas, if it helps," the other guard said, and made a point of shaking the Figment they held between them. "I'm sure this one knows more."

Erithnae gestured for them to put him down, and they did so.

"Do you have a name?"

The Figment gave a small bow, finishing it by flashing a smile that was just a little brittle around the edges after being manhandled, or Figmenthandled, or whatever. "Simon Stranded, your majesty. And can I just say both that it's an honour to meet you, and that the stories of your beauty really don't do you justice?"

Erithnae allowed herself a tight smile in response, and raised a hand to forestall the guard who made to strike the Figment. "I'm more than capable of hurting him myself if I wish it, thank you. So, Simon Stranded, you stand here before me, knowing what's likely to happen next, and you still flirt? I'm impressed."

"I have that effect on women."

"I'm not *that* impressed. This 'Thomas' who disappeared,

would that be Thomas Greene? Think before you answer. I don't like being lied to."

Erithnae watched him consider for a moment before nodding. She waved a hand in Simon's direction.

"Very well, take him to one of the cells. I will want to speak with this Figment further. And be nice. I don't want him falling down any stairs on the way there." She thought about the physics of her castle for a moment. "Or up them, either. He's just bought himself a little while longer in this form."

"You let them take the Figment away to speak to my mother?" Siobhan asked, not bothering to disguise the incredulity in her voice. She half rose from the bench at the centre of the maze, but decided against it. If she stood up, she'd probably do something she wouldn't particularly regret later.

"There were six of them," Grave answered, "and they were in the middle of the village."

Like he couldn't deal with half a dozen of her mother's guards. On the other hand, Siobhan mused, doing so in front of a whole village's worth of witnesses might have caused awkward questions. Or at least meant getting rid of them would take all day.

"All right," Siobhan admitted. "Maybe you did the right thing. The last thing we need is a scene. Tell me again about the chase."

"Well, you see, I didn't have my boots on, and you know what it's like trying to run in socks, or maybe you…"

"Not that bit! The part where they disappeared."

"I don't know what you want, Princess. Thomas Greene just did an opening spell, grabbed the girl and jumped through before anyone could stop him. I tried to follow, but the thing closed straight after."

"And nothing about that strikes you as odd?"

"Not really, Princess. Doors never seem to stay open very long."

"How could he open one at all?" Siobhan demanded, and then wished she hadn't. The shape of a possible answer stood out in her mind like a particularly bulky piece of furniture left under a sheet. It wasn't a shape she wanted her mother's Huntsman to guess at.

"Maybe he had an amulet," Grave replied, fishing out his own and moving it between his oversized fingers like some bizarrely shaped worry bead. "Maybe someone here is helping him."

Siobhan breathed a silent sigh of relief. Trust Grave to miss the obvious.

"Yes," she agreed, "maybe they are. It would explain how they escaped you the first time." *That and incompetence*, Siobhan added in the privacy of her head. "Look into it. Find out who might have given him such a thing. Take your time. I'll handle things here."

Siobhan waited while the big lunk nodded a kind of half-hearted bow, backed away to the edge of the clearing at the centre of the maze, and hurried off to his wild goose chase. At least it would keep him out of the way for a while. Siobhan had more important things to worry about than whether Grave was suddenly going to realise that he was being manipulated.

Siobhan glanced over to the sundial, which, predictably, told her that the time was somewhere between three and nine, before deciding to start producing shadow puppets. Only the alligator was remotely convincing. Siobhan was more interested in the mirror that still sat there, alongside a surprisingly well-preserved banana. Did she want to risk it?

Certainly, she needed answers. The shape of an answer in her mind was indeed like something covered with a sheet, but it lacked any of those convenient holes that allow paint to seep in no matter how well you think you've covered things. Siobhan ran through the facts as she knew them.

The Dreaming Court was sealed off. That much Siobhan knew for certain. Oh, it wasn't a perfect seal. Siobhan had managed to get Grave through, but that was just because the barrier didn't seem to apply to the royal family. After all, her mother flitted back and forth whenever she thought no one was looking. Secretly, Siobhan even approved. Rules were things for subjects to follow, not royalty.

But that was where the problems began, because Thomas Greene had broken through that barrier not once, but twice. Had it just been the first time, Siobhan might have been prepared to believe her own lie about an amulet and a secret helper. But Grave, whatever his uselessness in other areas, simply wasn't imaginative enough to make things up. If Grave said that the half-breed had performed an opening spell, then Siobhan was certain that he had.

A barrier that could only be breached by royals. A half-breed who clearly had. Siobhan bounced back and forth between the two facts like the ball in a particularly vicious game of table tennis. She added in the apparent interference in a dream, and the definite interference with her holding cage.

Standing, Siobhan moved over to the sundial and started to reach out.

Her hand was only inches away from the hand mirror when the shadows started to shift again. Spiders and snakes and other things Siobhan hadn't been afraid of even when she was a little girl started to appear in silhouette, dancing across the sundial's face. None of them were very convincing either, but the message was clear enough.

"Sod it then. I'll do without."

Siobhan pulled her hand away. Perhaps it wasn't worth the risk after all, especially not for a mirror that was still busy working its way through every halfway good-looking woman in the known universe.

Siobhan almost wished she hadn't done that, since a good mirror would certainly have been able to confirm her suspicions about Thomas Greene. Still, this one had never been that reliable anyway. It had a tendency to talk about downloading updates whenever she tried to do anything.

Siobhan turned her mind to the problem of how else to confirm her suspicions, and smiled as she recalled that her mother kept a full-length magic mirror as a dressing mirror. Siobhan couldn't have done that. Any mirror forced to comment honestly on her choice of clothing wouldn't have lasted long before becoming the victim of an "accidentally" thrown shoe.

"I'm sure she won't mind if I borrow it," Siobhan said out loud, repeating the ancient mantra of all daughters heading for their mother's closet. And if she forgot to give the mirror back afterwards, so much the better. After all, what her mother didn't know wouldn't hurt her. What she *did* know, on the other hand, might hurt Siobhan a great deal, especially if she found out about Siobhan's efforts to eradicate someone who might just turn out to be family.

Their feet crunched along the gravel path leading to the house, the scatter of it playing in counterpoint to the rhythm of their steps. Thomas felt relieved even though he knew he shouldn't be. It was good to be home.

Not that the brick-built little house tucked into a lane that was twisting even by Devon's standards was home exactly, but it was close enough. The eyeball-meltingly bright clothes on the washing line were unmistakably his mother's, as was the VW Beetle parked in the driveway. The motorbike was Kelly's, and Thomas was surprised to see his sister home at that time of the day.

It was Kelly who opened the door when Thomas knocked, dark haired and as tall as him, dressed in leathers open just enough to reveal a glimpse of the suit underneath. It seemed she was about to head out.

"Thomas? What are you doing here? Who's this? What are you both *wearing?*"

Thomas didn't have to force a smile. "Don't ask. Is mum in?"

"She's in her 'studio,'" Kelly answered, the quotation marks as audible as the irritation. "Come in, both of you. I've got an exhibition to organise, but that can wait a few minutes."

Thomas let himself be swept up in the whirlwind of his

younger sister's welcome and pulled Melissa along in his wake.

"Who's this then?" Kelly asked. She turned to Melissa before Thomas could explain. "I'm sorry, but Thomas never seems to tell us who he's going out with until we torture the information out of him. I'm Kelly, his sister."

"Melissa."

Thomas could hear the nervousness in her voice, but Melissa took Kelly's proffered hand.

"She's not–" Thomas began, but Kelly cut him off. He was used to it.

"Lovely to meet you. So, what's with the get up? Some sort of Sealed Knot thing?"

"Sealed Knot?" Thomas asked.

"You know, dressing up and recreating battles, that sort of thing. Which side were you, cavaliers or roundheads? Actually, don't answer that. There's no way you'd ever be anything other than cavalier."

Thomas ignored the dig, grateful for the excuse. "Yes, it was something like that."

"A particularly muddy battle, was it?" Kelly asked, and Thomas had to look at Melissa before realising just how bad the pair of them had begun to look after a few fights, a brief spell of imprisonment, and a lot of running away.

"The car broke down, and we had to walk the last couple of miles." Thomas didn't worry about the lie too much. After all, if you couldn't tell lies to your own sister, who could you tell them to? "And then some caravanner forced us both to dive for cover in a hedge," he added, when that didn't seem to be quite enough to cover the state of their appearance.

Kelly nodded. "Yeah, that can happen. You should try riding a bike round here. No one ever seems to consider that someone might have a good reason to be coming the other way on the wrong side of the road."

"I can't imagine why."

"Look, I really do have to run. Melissa, was it? If you need some clothes to change into once you've cleaned up a little, mine will probably be too large, but they'll still be better than

Mum's."

"I heard that!"

"Pity you don't do anything about it then!" Kelly yelled back. "She's just along the hall. I'm sure you'll find her. When I get back, you can give me all the details of how you two got together."

You wouldn't believe them, Thomas thought to himself as Kelly breezed past him.

Melissa looked after her as she left. "Is she always like that?"

"Pretty much," Thomas admitted. "She always seems to be in the middle of something. Come on, let's get this over with."

It took a couple of attempts to find the right door, resulting in brief spells in an under-stair cupboard and a living room that seemed to have been decorated almost by argument, with bright yellow splashes along two of the walls, and combinations on the others that looked like his mother had been channelling Jackson Pollock.

The right door came around at last, revealing a room that was, thankfully, a little calmer. The place had been stripped back to floorboards and painted a fairly uniform white. Large French-windows spilled light across the space, though none of this was what caught Thomas' eye. The eight foot tall sculpture of a penguin was doing a much better job of that.

Actually, it wasn't quite a penguin yet, being mostly a steel framework covered in a patchwork of different materials. To Thomas, it looked like what might result if the *Terminator* films were re-made in the Antarctic and the props department were in a hurry. His mother emerged from behind the steel monstrosity, still holding the welding torch she'd been using.

Thomas had to fight to keep himself from seeing the younger version of her he'd seen in his dream. Unfortunately, that meant he had to see the wardrobe she was currently wearing. His mother had taken the divorce as a chance for reinvention.

"No man is going to hold me back any more," she'd declared as soon as the papers came through, and had promptly moved and set herself up as an artist, or at least as a gallery owner who did more than dabble. That also translated to a desire to dress as his mother thought an artist should, including combinations of colours more commonly associated with the brighter sort of tropical bird. In this case, it meant a rainbow coloured t-shirt, a shockingly pink shirt spattered with dried paint, blue jeans, and fluorescent green sandals.

"Thomas! I wasn't expecting you until next week. And who's this? I thought you were going out with Nicola. Not that she isn't welcome, of course."

Now that they were face to face, Thomas found some of his relief fading.

"This is Melissa, mum. And we're not... oh never mind."

"Nice to meet you, Melissa. Forgive me if I can't stop work, but this thing is supposed to be finished by the end of the week. Kelly has been very firm about that. Honestly, you should see her. I give her one little summer job at the gallery, and suddenly she's running the place." She flicked the mask down and welded another spot. "Did I hear you tell Kelly something about the Sealed Knot? I didn't know you were into that sort of thing."

This was it, Thomas realised. "I'm not."

"No? Oh, I get it. This was..." There was the inevitable pause of a parental brain trying to remember the name of a girlfriend it had been told only a moment or two earlier. "... Melissa's idea, was it? Well, there's nothing wrong with trying new things."

"Mum, Melissa isn't my girlfriend. She isn't in the Sealed Knot either. Neither of us are."

"Then why did you tell Kelly you were?"

She paused to weld another joint, and Thomas took his chance.

"It was a lie so that I wouldn't have to tell her we'd been in the Dreaming Court."

Chapter Twenty

Nicola didn't speak as the guard escorted her. She was too exhausted from the lack of sleep. Every time her head had hit the pillow, the dreams had come back. Even now she trembled at the thought of them.

The guard didn't notice. He was too busy leading her down from the tower she was in, through the castle, and up to a different one via corridors, receiving rooms, and what Nicola could have sworn was a small woodland path, if it hadn't been in the middle of the castle and lined with portraits of figures who shared an almost identical look of distaste at having to sit still long enough to be painted when they could have been doing more interesting things. It was hardly a surprise that they all bore a strong resemblance to the Queen.

Finally, Nicola's guard opened the door to a room that seemed to be packed almost to the rafters with charts, scientific instruments, and the sort of bizarrely shaped glassware that always looked as though it ought to be bubbling over with greenish liquid even when it was empty. A couple of oak chests stood in one corner, while most of the mess stood on a collection of tables that probably nested quite neatly when they weren't overflowing. The guard gave the place a nervous glance before hurrying off, leaving Nicola there.

She wasn't alone for long. After a minute or so Erithnae arrived, accompanied by an entourage that almost crashed into the back of her as she stopped at the door.

"Wait outside, all of you," Erithnae commanded in a voice that set Nicola's nerves even more on edge. Whatever was happening, she wasn't happy about something. Certainly, none of the assorted maids and guards following her dared to argue. Nicola waited until Erithnae pushed the door shut before asking the obvious question.

"Is everything all right?"

"You know," Erithnae replied, "according to all the books of etiquette, strictly speaking you should wait for me to speak first. That and curtsey, of course."

"I wouldn't know how," Nicola shot back, but cautiously. She wasn't feeling all that tough this morning.

"Oh, I'm not expecting you to. I was actually thinking that it's quite nice to have someone around who doesn't even think to do that sort of thing. Are you all right? You look tired."

"I'm fine. I just didn't sleep well."

Nicola watched as Erithnae started to move through the mess, lifting pieces of paper carefully, checking behind tables, and glancing around the worst of it.

"You could help."

"I don't know what I'm supposed to be helping *with*," Nicola pointed out. "What are you looking for?"

Erithnae stopped and pinched the bridge of her nose in a gesture that seemed less completely in control than she'd seemed before. "I'm looking for a mirror. Probably slightly larger than a hand mirror. Mine has gone missing. I suspect my daughter has decided she needs it and forgotten to give it back. It's the sort of thing she does."

"Aren't there lots of mirrors in the castle?" Nicola asked.

"This one is magical. It was my father's."

Something about that comment made Nicola take another look at the room. It was like someone had handed her the code to the place, because now Nicola could see that what she'd taken merely as the messiness of a room that didn't get used much had a still, sterile quality to it. It was a room that had been left as a mess, not because no one could be bothered to clean up, but because they'd been told in no uncertain terms what would happen if they dared touch anything there.

"This room was his, wasn't it?" Nicola guessed.

Erithnae nodded tightly in response, her face carefully blank as she continued to root through piles of papers. Nicola moved in front of her, reaching out to put a hand on top of Erithnae's as she reached for another stack.

"Will you tell me what's wrong? You obviously don't like having to search, so why bring me here?"

Erithnae went still under her touch. For a second, Nicola got the full force of a stare that made her want to back up, forget she'd spoken, and never, *ever* touch the other woman again. It subsided as quickly as it had come. A moment longer, and Erithnae started to speak.

"I've got a Figment in custody who was travelling with your boyfriend…"

"…ex-boyfriend."

"…ex-boyfriend, of course. My guards tell me that he has succeeded in leaving the Court. More than that, he did it in a way which ought to have been impossible."

Nicola was too busy to point out that almost everything in the place was impossible. Specifically, she was too busy thinking, *he's abandoned me.*

Erithnae seemed to guess her thoughts, or maybe to read them.

"He probably didn't have much choice," she said in a tone that was suddenly more soothing. "He was, after all, about to be jumped on by half a dozen guards."

Nicola didn't reply, since she suspected that it wouldn't take much to make Thomas cut and run. After all, he'd already done it to her once.

Erithnae pressed on. "I need you to tell me more about him, Nicola."

Nicola waited for the push at the edge of her mind, but there wasn't one.

"You're not going to just take what you want?" Nicola asked, with an edge of bitterness that probably had a lot to do with finding that her bo… ex-boyfriend had left her stranded.

"Or maybe you could send me some more nightmares? That was you last night, wasn't it?"

Erithnae shook her head. "Why would I do something like that, Nicola? Please, tell me about Thomas. I need to know more about him."

"Why? As annoying as he is, I'm not going to help you find him if you're just going to kill him."

Erithnae sat down on the edge of a table. "This isn't about that. I want to know more about him. I *need* to know more about him." She picked up a reasonably straight-sided beaker. "I don't even know what he looks like. Show me, Nicola. Picture his face for me. Trust me, without a magic mirror, I won't be able to use it to find him, much less hurt him. I just want to see him."

There was a note of desperation in that, a note that Nicola guessed Erithnae's subjects didn't hear too much. It was enough. She sighed and nodded, doing her best to picture Thomas' face for the other woman. It shimmered into being on the glass in Erithnae's hand, and the Dreaming Folk woman stared at it, and stared at it, and stared at it. Finally, on the edge of hearing, Nicola heard the words.

"He looks just like him."

There was the dull crack of breaking glass.

As times for imparting particularly startling pieces of information go, moments when the listener is holding a welding torch have never made it very far up the list. There's a good reason for that. Thankfully, Thomas' mother had a fire extinguisher nearby, and soon, instead of a burning penguin, there was merely a completely soaked one.

Once that was done, Thomas returned his attention to more important matters.

"Well?"

His mother stood, her mouth open. "You can't have gone there."

"How else do I know about it?" Thomas demanded. "It's

not exactly somewhere they tell you about. It's certainly not somewhere *you* told me about. Well? Say something."

His mother looked from Thomas to Melissa and back again.

"M...Melissa," she said, her voice breaking, "would you mind giving us a moment? There are obviously some things Thomas and I need to talk about."

Thomas' first instinct was to insist that whatever his mother had to say she could say in front of Melissa, but Melissa put a hand on his arm.

"I'll go and clean up a little."

"The bathroom's just at the top of the stairs, dear." Thomas' mother nodded to the doorway. "There should be some fresh towels in there, though Kelly tends to use up most of the hot water."

"I'm sure it will be fine."

Thomas felt Melissa give his arm one last squeeze, though whether she meant it as comfort or as a warning he didn't know. That's the problem with body language; if you haven't already made up your mind what you want it to mean, it can be pretty hard to decipher. Alone at last with his mother, Thomas found himself waiting for her to say something. Unfortunately, since she seemed to be waiting for much the same thing, they spent a good thirty seconds staring at one another. Finally, Thomas couldn't stand it any longer.

"Why didn't you...?"

"I should have..."

They stopped, and Thomas waved for his mother to continue.

"We should go into the kitchen. We could sit down," she said.

"Here's fine."

"Yes, I suppose it is." She leaned back against the wall. "You really went to the Dreaming Court?"

Thomas wondered how many times he'd have to repeat it before the idea sank in. "Yes! I went there, if that covers falling through a hole in space, getting chased across half the Court, dodging some frankly stupid looking Nightmares, breaking Melissa out of a prison cell, seeing you with a complete stranger in a dream quest, and then jumping back here before a bunch of guards could grab us."

"It sounds like you've had quite an adventure."

"Mother!" Thomas found his voice rising almost automatically. Given the circumstances, he thought he probably had a right to shout. "It was not 'quite an adventure'! It was bloody terrifying! And I think you owe me an explanation as to why it happened."

"There's no need to shout. Honestly, Thomas, sometimes you're just like your father."

"Which one?"

That struck a nerve. His mother looked away, as though contemplating the rebuilding of her statue. "It was all before I was married to Henry. Not long before, but I want you to know I never cheated on him."

"Just lied to him about my being his son." Thomas said the words softly, but they seemed to fill the space more efficiently than even his mother's attempt at a statue could.

"It seemed like the right thing. I was always able to say that you took after me with your looks, so it wasn't like Henry ever suspected. We'd known each other before, and after your... biological father left, he was just... there for me. After a while it even started to feel like love."

Thomas refrained from pointing out that it had hardly seemed like it towards the end of their marriage, when ducking out of the way of flying crockery had become an important life-skill.

"I saw him," Thomas said instead.

"Ceren's alive?"

Thomas didn't know which was worse, the hope in his mother's voice or having to dash it. On the other hand, it hadn't exactly been an easy couple of days for him either. "I saw him in a dream. I saw you and him, when he left. I don't know if he's still alive or not. There was a war..."

"A War," his mother corrected, a fond note touching the

words. "You could always hear the capital letter when he said it."

Thomas had been hoping not to hear that tone. "You loved him, didn't you?" He saw his mother nod. Saw too the first tears that trickled down her cheeks. Even so, Thomas couldn't bring himself to stop. Not now.

"Why didn't you tell me?"

"How could I?" his mother demanded. "What was I supposed to do? Wait until you were old enough and then say 'incidentally, your dad's not human'? You'd have thought I was mad. Besides, by that point it was obvious Ceren wasn't coming back. I thought that world would never touch you."

Thomas gestured to what he was wearing, giving his mother ample opportunity to take in the state of it.

"Mum, not only has it touched me; it's spent most of the past forty-eight hours trying to kill me. Apparently I'm not supposed to exist, and now half of the people there want me dead, while one particularly scary excuse for a princess wants to keep me locked up until she can use me for whatever psycho plan she's got in mind."

His mother's eyes widened at the last words. "But they can't. *They* of all people should be treating you better than that."

"Who?"

"His family. Or maybe that's it. Maybe it's that they can't stand the thought of you. But that can't be it. It wasn't a betrayal. She was dead long before we…"

"Mum! Could you maybe go with an intelligible version for those of us who haven't heard it before? Who are 'his family'? Who's 'She' when she's at home? Better yet, why don't you start by telling me who the man actually was?"

His mother nodded, seeming to collect herself.

"That part's easy enough. Ceren was the King."

Thomas stayed silent for more than a minute. He spent much of that time struggling to find a reply that didn't mention Elvis.

Much of the rest of it, he spent wondering how his mother could have fallen for a line like that.

"How did you fall for a line like that?" he demanded out loud when simply staring didn't seem to produce an answer.

"It wasn't a line, Thomas. Stop being so cynical. Ceren was the King of that place."

"I bet that's what he told you, mother, but even you've got to admit it sounds a bit much like a fairytale. Something from another world comes over and seduces you, only for it to turn out it's the rightful King? Come on!" Thomas held out a hand to his mother, who took it reluctantly. "You might not have seen it then, mum, but surely you see it now. He was spinning you a lie to get you into bed."

"Ceren didn't need to lie to me to get me into bed, Thomas."

His mother looked Thomas in the eye as she said it, and the incredulity started to give way, if only because there wasn't room for both it and the embarrassment.

"Besides," she continued, "he didn't tell me until he left. When we first met, I didn't even know that he wasn't human."

Thomas left it there for a second, at least until curiosity got the better of him.

"So, how exactly do you go about meeting a magical 'King'?"

He couldn't help the note of doubt that came with that last word. As far as Thomas was concerned, the royalty of his parentage was still very much up for debate.

"We met at a party."

Thomas shot her the most sceptical look he could manage.

"It's true! Well, I suppose technically we met just outside a party, in the garden. You see I had this friend, Wendy, whose family had quite a bit of money. She organised a party up at her parents' big house in the country one weekend while they were away. It all seemed very daring, but really, after the first few hours it was all a bit much. You know what I'm like at parties."

Thomas knew. His mother was, to say the least, one of life's natural kitchen dwellers when it came to parties. She just never seemed to get the hang of them.

"Anyway, I ended up wandering out into the grounds. Truth to tell, I was probably a bit tipsy by that point. I found Ceren sitting on the edge of an ornamental bridge, looking so utterly... sad. Maybe if I'd been a bit more sober I'd have kept away from him. He certainly looked tattered enough. Later I found out that he'd just been wandering around, living rough. When I asked him how long once, all he would say was 'years.'"

"You stopped to talk to him?" Thomas asked, wanting to redirect his mother's attention to something more important than her former lover's clothes.

"I asked him what was wrong," she confirmed. "And he just looked at me. He said it was a long story, and that I should just leave him alone, but I said I wasn't going anywhere. I had all the time in the world, I said, which was the first time I saw him smile. Of course, I didn't know why at the time, not even when he said 'no, *I* have all the time in the world, and that's half the problem.'"

Thomas continued to listen. He listened while his mother spoke about the instant connection they seemed to have, and about how she'd gently poked and prodded until that strange man had opened up. He listened while she spoke about the pair of them talking until well past the sun coming up. He even listened to the part where Ceren had mentioned how he'd been living, and where his mother had insisted on taking him home with her, though Thomas couldn't avoid a disapproving look at that part.

His mother snorted. "Oh I know it seems silly to you, but what about that girl upstairs?"

"Melissa."

"Haven't you done almost the same thing with her?"

"Yes, but we're not...that is, she just needed helping."

"If you say so, dear." With that, his mother went on with her story. It was a simple enough one. She'd taken Ceren home to her flat, where he stayed the night, and the next, and the next. There wasn't anything sexual in it at first; he slept on the sofa, she on her bed, "which was frankly less comfortable than the sofa, let me tell you…"

Except when in the depths of his darker moods, Ceren turned out to be helpful, and gentle, and considerate, not to mention stunningly good looking. Eventually, the inevitable happened, and the flat got its sofa back, but even that didn't take away the moments when he would just stare into space, or turn away so that she wouldn't see tears.

"And then one day, about a month after he moved in," his mother continued, "Ceren told me everything. About the Courts, the War, his dead wife… everything. I didn't believe him at first, but there was something about him… not to mention the fact that he suddenly started doing magic in my front room. I'll tell you, Thomas, that came as a shock."

"I can guess."

"I know you can. And then, almost as suddenly as he'd shown up, Ceren said that he had to leave. He said I'd showed him that he couldn't hide from his responsibilities, or from life. I… I waited as long as I could, before I gave in and said yes to Henry."

If Thomas remembered his dream correctly, that wasn't exactly what Ceren had said, but it was close enough. He tried to wrap his head round it.

"So you're telling me that my biological father is the King of the Dreaming Court, who loved you without revealing who he was, and who left you because he couldn't abandon his duty to his people. I still think it sounds a lot like a fairy story."

"From what Ceren told me," his mother countered, "that whole place runs like a fairy story."

That, at least, Thomas had to concede. What was worse, he couldn't see a good reason for the man to have lied about who he was, not after so long. Which meant…

"Does this mean that technically I'm a handsome prince?"

Chapter Twenty One

Were Grave ever to get round to writing his book on hunting, as-suming he could overcome associated problems such as remem-bering which pocket he'd put the manuscript into, not to mention managing not to get blood on it, he would have to include a chapter on string. *Yes*, Grave thought as he fished yet another ball of the stuff from one of his pockets, placing it delicately on the floor of his abandoned barn, *definitely string*.

String, thread, rope, it was all such useful stuff. From tying flies to setting snares, there was hardly a problem that couldn't be solved with enough string. Grave remembered having to chase down a were-tiger once. Was it a hundred and fifty years ago? Now, any other hunter would have blundered around with elephants and guns and silver bullets, and would probably have been eaten ten yards into the jungle as a result. Grave had just trailed a sufficiently long length of string in front of the best hid-ing places until the thing had done what all cats do when con-fronted with the stuff. Twenty seconds later, the were-tiger had managed to tangle itself up so badly that Grave had hardly needed to tie any extra knots.

"Are you going to do something, or do I have to stand here until both your brain cells decide they like each other again?"

Grave shook himself out of his remembrances, grumbling an apology to the Princess, who stood in the middle of his barn holding a mirror Grave could have sworn he'd seen in the Queen's chambers. At least, by the time it reached Siobhan it probably sounded like an apology. It didn't start out that way. He swore a little more as his massive fingers pried at a particularly stubborn tangle. Siobhan didn't seem to notice.

"Are you sure this place is secure?" she demanded.

"Yes, Princess. No one comes here except me."

"I can see why. It's a dump. Not to mention that all this 'out of phase' stuff is just... weird."

Grave spared the bales of hay and only semi-opaque walls a brief glance.

"I've never given it much thought, Princess."

"*And* I almost stepped into one of those damn traps."

A pity she hadn't, really, Grave thought. Still, it had been careless to leave any of the things down. One little thing like being caught in a bear-trap, and Siobhan would probably go running to her mother. Well, not running, obviously, but certainly limping. And then...

Grave managed to get the last of the tangles undone. "I still don't see why I can't go after them," he muttered, and it seemed that Siobhan heard him that time, because she glared back.

"Because I say so, all right? Your antics over the last few days have drawn quite enough attention. The last thing I need is you blundering around in their world any more. We'll just have to wait for them to come back."

Grave shrugged and set to his work, but he didn't miss the look of relief that touched Siobhan's features so briefly that it might have been trying for some sort of speed record. If he didn't know better, he'd think he'd just been lied to. But then, it wasn't like it mattered.

"And you're sure they'll even come back? I wouldn't't."

"They'll come back. My mother has the human girl, remember?"

Grave wasn't so sure. Thomas Greene didn't seem much like the sort of person who would play the hero. He didn't say it though. His job was just to do what he was told, even if the little brat was trying to tell him how to do something Grave had been doing a millennium before she was born. Grave contemplated the usefulness of string as a garrotte, and thought better of it.

"How much longer?" Siobhan demanded, practically on cue.

"Not long, Princess."

Grave started picking out lengths of string, more by feel than through any sense of measurement. He couldn't quite remember where he'd learned to do this. Had it been that old witch out on the Greek islands, the one who'd made Grave think he was a pig for almost a week? Or perhaps one of the mad old hermits who seemed to occupy almost every wood once upon a time, waiting for some young hero to pass so they could leap out and babble something that might have passed for wise advice if they'd been on slightly fewer mushrooms? You just didn't get proper mad hermits any more, for some reason. Maybe the mushrooms had changed.

Grave worked carefully, methodically, weaving together the string, tying knots, occasionally unravelling sections that didn't look right and starting again. At last, it was done. Grave stepped back, or would have done, if such a careless movement wouldn't have left him trapped like an especially hairy fly in the web of some giant spider. As it was, Grave stepped more sort of sideways, ducking a little so that he could ease his way out of the network of lines strung from every point on the walls that would stay solid long enough to hold them.

The whole looked like the universe's largest game of cat's cradle, woven around the mirror that Siobhan had brought, a mirror that was currently showing Thomas Greene's face. Some of the strings ran from it to the walls. Some tangled with each other on the way. A few seemed to disappear in mid-air, still perfectly tightly strung. Tied in the middle of the whole mess there sat a tiny golden bell.

"It's done," Grave announced. "If he arrives, the bell will ring, and then…"

"And then we catch him," Siobhan instructed. "Just one thought though. How are we supposed to hear such a tiny bell from the castle?"

Grave swore. He *knew* he'd forgotten something.

Siobhan just grinned. "It looks like you'll be staying here until he shows up then."

Grave didn't bother pointing out that such an event could take days, if Thomas Greene bothered showing up at all. He was fairly sure the Princess already knew that. Grave watched her walk to the barn's open doorway, where she paused.

"Don't forget to come and get me when he arrives, Grave. I'm sure it won't take *too* long."

"Thomas, why is your girlfriend passed out asleep on my bed?" Kelly demanded, about five minutes after arriving home. Her arrival had managed to break through the silence between Thomas and their mother; a silence punctuated only by the occasional flare of the welding torch as she attempted to repair her sculpture.

"I didn't realise she was. And she's not my girlfriend."

"You brought her home and she's not your girlfriend. Yeah. Right."

"Did you wake her up?" he asked.

"No, I thought I'd leave that one to you. Mum's still creating? Then I'll see if there's anything worth having for lunch."

Kelly sloped off into the kitchen and Thomas headed upstairs. Sure enough, Melissa was laid out on the bed, dressed now in jeans and a lilac t-shirt that fell baggily around her. She snored gently.

Thomas reached out and shook her, waiting until her eyes opened before he stopped. He had a feeling that otherwise, Melissa would just roll over and go back to sleep.

"Wssgl... oh, hello Thomas. I must have fallen asleep."

"Just for an hour or two."

"Well the bed was so comfy, I must have drifted off."

"As Goldilocks said to the bears."

"Ah, but there's only penguins here. Besides," Melissa ran her fingers through her hair, "I'm about a dozen shades too dark for that story."

Thomas offered her his hand and Melissa took it, rising smoothly to her feet.

"We should head downstairs. Kelly's making lunch. I'll warn you now, she thinks you're my girlfriend."

Melissa gave him a smile that was still sleepy. "Would that be so bad?"

Thomas was almost too surprised to say anything. "Well, that was unexpected," he admitted. "I mean, I've only just broken up with Nicola, and we've only just met, and…"

Melissa nodded. "Yes, there are a lot of 'ands,' aren't there? And I'm not saying that we should. But maybe, afterwards… who knows?"

"Who knows," Thomas agreed. "We should head downstairs before Kelly gets too many ideas about what we're doing in her room."

"Probably. How did your chat with your mother go?"

Thomas was silent for a moment, and Melissa squeezed his hand. "That well?"

"According to her, I'm the love child of the Dreaming Court's old King, but it's all right because she really loved him and only hooked up with my fa… my… her husband on the rebound."

"Probably she just meant that you came out of something special, not just some one night stand."

Thomas tried that for size, and somehow the thought was a little more comforting. So he told her the rest of it. "Of course, this means that I'm technically a prince of the place, which sounds like a tremendous coincidence. They start hunting for us and the first one they go after is royalty? At this rate there will probably be some sort of ancient prophecy that says I'm supposed to save the world."

Melissa gave his hand another quick squeeze. "Are you always this cynical?"

"Only when I've spent the last few days running for my life."

"Well, that's over, so you can stop now. Anyway, they

didn't come after you first, did they? Siobhan grabbed me well before you, and then there were all the ones they..." it seemed that the word "killed" wasn't one she wanted to say out loud. "You're just the first one who was able to jump into their world to escape. And if I understand it, that's *because* of who your father was. You should count yourself lucky. I know I do. If you hadn't come along, who knows when Siobhan would have got bored with me?"

There was that, Thomas had to admit, though it threw up disturbing thoughts too. How many like him had been killed before they got round to him, just to keep some secret? How many more would they kill afterwards? More importantly, did it mean he should he be grateful that his mother's taste in men appeared to run to royalty?

"It's still weird to try and wrap my head around," Thomas said. "You think you know everything there is to know about your parents, and then it turns out that one of them spent her youth sleeping with extradimensional men. *Parents.*"

That last word was the sigh that presumably every creature with discernable parents has uttered at one point or another. It doesn't matter if they're born, hatched from eggs, or produced by splitting carefully into identical halves, at some point, they still feel the need to express in whatever the local equivalent is of that word the sheer bewildering hopelessness of having antecedents.

Melissa started, and Thomas raised a questioning eyebrow.

"Is there a phone around here I can use?" Melissa asked.

"There will be somewhere. Is everything ok?"

"It's just, I've been away so long... I should probably ring my own family."

Thomas stopped. He hadn't thought about that. He'd only been gone for a couple of days. Melissa had been missing much longer. Had her family and friends been going frantic, looking for her? Had they contacted the police? Had they started to assume, after a month with no contact, that the worst had happened?"

They went downstairs and repeated the request to his

mother, who led them to the phone in the living room. Melissa dialled a number from memory, and Thomas stayed only a little way back, trying for that combination of listening in while appearing not to that is the mainstay of any polite but fundamentally nosey person.

To Thomas, the phone call sounded worryingly normal. After a minute or so, Melissa said a perfectly ordinary goodbye and set the phone down carefully. Thomas could see the tightness around her eyes.

"What's wrong?"

Melissa shook her head. "I should have seen that coming. I know we've never been close, and it's not like I was living at home, but..."

"They didn't notice you were gone?" Thomas asked. Melissa nodded silently, before letting him wrap an arm around her. After a minute or so, a thought came to Thomas. "What about friends?"

He found himself interrupted by a yell from Kelly, saying that if they wanted lunch, they should hurry up and get in the kitchen, and that if they'd been at it in her room she was going to have to burn the sheets, not to mention never speaking to Thomas again. That managed to bring the faintest smile to Melissa's lips.

"After lunch. We wouldn't want your sister getting the wrong idea."

~~~~

"Enjoying yourself down here?" Siobhan asked as the door to the cell swung open. Simon Stranded saw her gesture to one of the guards. "Leave us alone for a while."

"We're not supposed to..."

"I don't care what you're not supposed to do. Look at him. It's not like he's ever going to be a threat."

Simon did his best to ignore the jibe. Of course he wasn't enjoying himself. He was locked up, banged up, in the clink, imprisoned, and clapped in irons. He'd had enough time to think of more than a few synonyms for his current state. Even the island had been better than this.

It didn't help that his imprisonment was likely to end in a brief spell of extreme pain, followed by a rather longer one of drifting around as a grey mist. Almost anything was better than that, though as the guard sloped off, leaving him worryingly alone with the Princess, Simon began to wonder if maybe there were a few things not entirely covered by "almost anything."

"So you're what has been helping Thomas," Siobhan said, stepping into the tiny stone box. "How has that worked out for you, do you think?"

"Well, I find myself being visited by beautiful women, so it isn't all bad."

Simon couldn't help himself. It was probably something genetic, if Figments had genetics. In answer, the Princess gave the sort of laugh that would probably have turned heads in a bar.

"Unfortunately, in a little while the woman will be my dear mother. And then… death? The extinction of who you are now, at least. But before that, she will no doubt have questions."

Simon noticed that Siobhan didn't mention the words "horrible torture." But then again, the way Siobhan *didn't* mention them that was almost as good as putting them on a sign. In any case, they were the sort of words that didn't really need mentioning. Under circumstances like these they had a knack of showing up in a mind of their own accord. They were very reliable that way. And there was no way that a castle that looked like this wouldn't have the complete catalogue's worth of racks, hot irons and thumbscrews. They probably came with the place, like the curtains in a new house that don't really go with any of the furniture.

"You've made your point."

Siobhan moved closer, tracing a finger down the line of his jaw. "Have I?" The tracing finger was suddenly a grip that drew him forward to meet her lips.

"Is this really all you've come here for?" Simon asked when she released him, knowing that it wasn't, even as he admitted to himself that he wouldn't really mind if it were. Siobhan was probably attractive enough to normal men, but to him... it was like taking a man crossing a desert and offering him one of those fancy bottled waters that cost more than any other drink in a bar. Siobhan just laughed again.

"You think highly of yourself."

"No, I just don't think that much of you."

"Oh, I'm sure that's not true." She moved back a little, and Simon Stranded found he could think again. "But as it happens, I'm wondering if you can help me."

"Of course you are." He decided to play his own card. There was no point in holding it back. "And this has nothing to do with the part where I saw you hunting for Thomas with the Nightmare Hunt when you were supposed to be looking for someone else? Nothing to do with the fact that you knew about him being here when no one else did?"

As Simon hoped, that made her pause.

After a second or so Siobhan sighed. "You know, all that means is that I can't let you talk to my mother. I could accomplish that just by rendering you down now. I could say I was trying to be helpful."

Simon hadn't thought of that. On the whole, he really wished he had.

"What was it you wanted again?" he asked.

"Very good." Siobhan smiled in a way that reminded him uncomfortably of a cat. Simon had never trusted cats. "All I want is for you to tell me about Thomas Greene. Well, that and to help me capture him when he eventually shows up here. See? It's hardly anything really."

Simon leaned back against the nearest wall, ticking off points on his fingers. Given the length of the digits in question, they were good fingers for ticking things off on.

"First, he's a friend, so why would I betray him like that? Second, what would stop you from killing me the moment I've helped you? Thirdly, and I think most importantly, Thomas won't be coming back. He just isn't that stupid."

Siobhan quirked a lip in response. She moved close again, folding Simon's fingers back towards the palm in reverse order.

She managed to make it more suggestive than it should have been, but then, Siobhan seemed like the sort of person who could make "how are you?" sound like an invitation to bed. Her voice, when it came, was, predictably enough, a sultry purr.

"One, he'll be back. I'm sure of it, even if no one else seems to be. Two, how about I send you back to your island? It's nice and far away, so there's no chance of you talking to my mother, which means I don't need to hurt you. Which brings us nicely to three. If you don't help me, I'll kill you."

Simon wished she hadn't put it like that, but it seemed the Princess wasn't done.

"What do you even owe him?" she demanded. "You help him, protect him, and then he abandons you to be grabbed by my mother. What has Thomas Greene done for you? Nothing. While I'm offering you everything. You've got your whole life in front of you. Or you will have if you accept, anyway. Think about it."

Simon thought about it. Then he thought about it some more. Then some more. Mostly, he was trying to find a way of thinking about it that didn't make him feel uncomfortably like a traitor. On the other hand, if he accepted, at least there would be a *him* to feel that way. Put like that, it didn't sound quite so bad.

"If it helps," Siobhan finished, "I don't plan to hurt him. I need him."

Finally Simon nodded.

"Oh good!" Siobhan managed to invest those two syllables with all the enthusiasm of a girl being told she's being given a pony, and that someone else will be doing the cleaning out. The way her fingers traced down his chest was rather less innocent. "Now, where were we?"

Chapter Twenty Two

Lunch was… awkward. Thomas knew that Kelly didn't mean it to be that way, but she was curious about Melissa, and Kelly didn't believe that phrases like "none of your business" ever really applied to her. She also wouldn't accept the fact that they weren't going out. Since Thomas was pretty sure that the truth would have her accusing them both of being completely insane, that only left lying. That was fun for a while, inventing details for how they'd met, and how the car had broken down, but eventually it occurred to Thomas that it was only a step away from the sort of lie their mother had been telling him all his life. That took some of the joy out of it.

Thankfully, by that point Kelly had obviously decided that she'd shown enough of an interest in her big brother's life and the coast was clear to talk about her efforts at the gallery. After five minutes of stories about how Kelly was the only one who seemed to run the thing as a business, Melissa excused herself to try the phone again. Thomas, however, was stuck with the full twenty-minute version. He was almost glad to have one thing in his life stable, even if it was his sister's inability to shut up for more than a second or two at a time.

"There was this one customer, he'd come in and stare at the paintings for an hour at a time, and mother would always chat to him, give him a cup of coffee, that sort of thing. It turns out, he never had any intention of buying anything, he just liked the free coffee. Naturally, I put a stop to that straightaway."

"That's great, Kelly," Thomas lied, "I should go and make sure Melissa's all right, it's been a little while now."

"Ok, but no going at it anywhere I might see," Kelly said. "There are some images I just don't need."

"Kelly, we're really not..." Thomas began, but gave up. There didn't seem to be much point.

Melissa wasn't in the living room. Instead, Thomas found her out in the garden. Garden was probably the wrong term for it, since it implied more in the way of living plants than was currently the case, though Thomas noticed that the plants behind where Melissa had been walking were doing a lot better than the ones in front of her. She looked up as he approached, and it seemed to Thomas that she looked happier than she had before.

"You managed to get in touch with your friends?" Thomas asked, guessing. Melissa nodded.

"A couple. They'd thought maybe I'd gone to see my family, but they didn't know how to get in touch. When I didn't come back, they got worried and phoned the police."

"What did they say?"

"That if my friends didn't even know if I was missing for sure, then they couldn't really do much. It's just good to know that *somebody* missed me. I was beginning to think that nobody had noticed I'd gone."

Melissa reached down and put her fingers to a fuchsia, which bloomed under her touch. She looked up and pinned Thomas with a sharp look. "I think it's probably about time for us to go back and help your ex-girlfriend."

Thomas paused, unsure of what to say. After all, what did you say to the suggestion that you should go on a possibly suicidal trip to rescue your ex? Especially one that you'd already hinted you'd go on.

"How did we even get from me asking about your friends to you suggesting we should take on the entire Dreaming Court?"

Melissa stood, brushing some of the dirt from her hands. "My family didn't notice I was gone, and that was bad enough. It got me thinking that everyone should have someone who cares.

Phoning my friends was worse. They did care. Who cares about..."

"Nicola," Thomas supplied.

"...Nicola being gone? Who is that going to hurt? Those people deserve better than for us to leave her there, and Nicola deserves better than for you not to care about it."

"I care." The words came out rather more petulantly than he intended.

"Do you?"

"Yes."

"Then don't you think it's time to do something about it?"

Thomas didn't answer that at once, giving himself time for some of the more obvious possibilities to resolve themselves into words. "You do realise that we could be killed?"

Melissa reached out and took his hand. "I don't want you to be killed, Thomas. I'd quite like to see more of you, and I'm pretty sure that needs you to be alive. At least if it isn't going to be worryingly weird. But what do you think will happen if you stay here? They've already attacked you in this world. It wouldn't be hard to do it again. You need to go back and deal with this, get Nicola back, and make sure no one's coming after you, or you'll spend the rest of your life looking over your shoulder for large men in bad coats." She took a breath. "We both will."

Thomas sighed. "You know, life would have been easier if my mother's big fling had been with someone vaguely normal."

"I suspect that eventually everyone suspects that life would be simpler without parents. Now, are you going to go back and help Nicola, or am I supposed to conclude that you like the idea of leaving your exes in alternate worlds?"

"You've got to admit," Thomas said with a smile, "it does cut down on the chances of running into them again."

"*Thomas.*"

"I'm kidding. I'll go. Though what I'm going to do when I get there, I don't know."

"*We'll* go. Someone has to keep an eye on you."

"You're going somewhere?"

Thomas turned to find Kelly only a few feet away. Since she didn't have the mildly stunned expression of someone who'd just found out about the existence of other worlds, Thomas guessed she'd only just shown up.

"We're just going out for a little while."

"Really, where are you going?" Thomas heard the unspoken *is it interesting enough for me to want to tag along* as clearly as if Kelly had said it. Still, lying to his sister was easy enough... except that he suddenly found he couldn't do it.

"We're going to another world to try and save my ex-girlfriend, you remember Nicola, from the Queen of the dreaming folk and her psycho daughter." The sentence came out in a rush. Even so, there was plenty of time for Kelly's eyebrows to narrow.

"Look, if you don't want to tell me, fair enough, but there's no need to be sarcastic about it."

Thomas didn't really know what to say to that. Of course, the right thing to do was apologise, say they were both heading down to the shops, and zap out of there as soon as he and Melissa were out of sight. He couldn't do that, either. Instead, Thomas just moved his arms like *this* and *this* and then like *this*, letting the light of the portal swallow them up. The last sight he had before the thing closed behind them was of Kelly standing open-mouthed on the lawn. Oh well, his mother could probably explain.

"Let me see your hand." Nicola didn't particularly expect Erithnae to let her check it, but she didn't expect to be shoved back hard enough to set her stumbling either. People don't, as a rule, any more than they expect delicate, refined fairie queens to suddenly start tearing apart a room like a gorilla searching for its car keys.

That, though, was exactly what Erithnae was doing, tossing aside papers, tearing open drawers in the desks, and even brushing aside glassware so that it formed a brief symphony of crashes. This wasn't the time to start interrupting. If anything, it was the time to find something nice and solid to hide behind. Possibly a small country. Unfortunately, since Nicola was stuck in the same room with her, all she could do was follow in Erithnae's wake, trying to keep out of the way and attempting to keep her footing on a floor increasingly covered with glass shards.

More papers found themselves sorted through, then tossed aside. They were followed by a couple of ancient looking books, a folder full of sketches for creatures that seemed to defy common sense as often as genetics, and a particularly ugly lump of glass that could only have been a paperweight. That rush seemed to take a little of the energy out of Erithnae, and Nicola finally dared to step forward. Not quite in her path, but near it.

"If you're still looking for a mirror, this will only break it."

That earned the sort of look that always results when people start being unreasonably reasonable to someone who's upset. Since Nicola couldn't think of many other ways of being, she pressed on anyway.

"Why don't you let me help?"

There was an awkward moment, when Nicola suspected that she'd just done the equivalent of deciding that Ground Zero would be a lovely place for a picnic, but then Erithnae nodded silently.

"It would help if I knew what we were looking for," Nicola said gently, but Erithnae ignored her. Nicola pressed on anyway, trying to balance not getting in the way with making sure she was the one who searched through anything particularly fragile looking. Nicola had the feeling that afterwards, Erithnae would look round at the mess she'd created and it would only make her feel worse, even if, as Queen, she probably wasn't the one who was going to have to tidy it up.

It was another minute or two before Nicola saw the other woman's eyes fix on the chests pushed against the far wall. Nicola walked over with her and tried the lid of one. It was locked.

"I didn't see a key anywhere," she said.

Erithnae gave her a look that was far emptier than it should have been. "There isn't. I threw them away. I thought some things were better left alone. I don't suppose you can pick a lock?"

Erithnae knelt by the chest and Nicola took a second look at it as she did so. The lock on the thing was big and solid looking. It didn't seem like the sort of thing that was about to open to a bent hairpin and a lot of hoping.

"That's a bit more demanding than a stuck bike lock."

"Never mind then."

Nicola watched as Erithnae placed her hand flat on the plate of the lock. A second later, and it simply wasn't there. Neither was the remainder of the chest. The whole thing had just... gone, leaving what were presumably the contents to fall across the floor in a tidal wave of old clothes, pictures, and letters.

It was a bundle of those last that Erithnae snatched up, bound together with green lace tied in a bow. When she spread them out on the nearest of the tables and started to look through them, Nicola had the sense to stay back. Whatever lay in those chests was more private even than the rest of the room, and upsetting someone who could make solid wood and metal vanish didn't sound like a very good idea at all.

Instead, Nicola stood there as silently as she could manage while Erithnae read, tracing the lines of the letters with a fingernail. She read through one before tossing it aside and turning to the next, and the next. She kept going in utter silence until Nicola ached to say something, if only to fill the space with sound. She didn't though, because a small voice kept telling her this was something Nicola shouldn't interrupt.

The tears began on about the third letter, falling silently as Erithnae read. By the last, Nicola couldn't contain herself any longer. She stepped forward, reaching out for the other woman. As mistakes went, it was roughly equivalent to being the first person to open the door on a tiger that had been locked in a very small broom cupboard. However kind the intentions of the person letting it out, they still needed to be wearing a great deal of armour.

Nicola found herself glancing down as Erithnae wheeled

on her, probably in some unconscious attempt to avoid the fury of her gaze. Either that, or curiosity finally got the better of her. Either way, she had the chance to make out the words *My Darling Gwen* at the top of one of the letters in the moments before the nightmares hit. Her one thought as she collapsed was that having something like this happen twice in one day was just wrong.

Or at least, it would have been her thought if she hadn't been too busy screaming.

Grave didn't know how long he'd been watching the contraption when the strings began to twitch, sending the bell at the centre into clanging, clattering motion. It might have been five minutes, or an hour, or three days, he didn't really know. After the first few minutes, waiting was all the same to him. As skills went, it was a useful one for a hunter, though he could probably also have made good money teaching it to rail passengers.

Grave checked his watch, a great silver-fobbed thing, thought about it, then took off the five minutes it had taken to find his watch in the deeper recesses of his coat. After a moment's consideration, Grave decided to add it on again on the basis that he wanted to know what time it was now, not five minutes ago. Shortly after that, he gave up and started out purposefully for the castle. Since there was still quite a lot of string in the way, that resulted in Grave trailing most of it behind him like the trail of some great brown-coated comet.

Grave went straight to the rose gardens, picking the last of the string from himself and depositing it on a stray rose stem. The doorway was shut, so he had to knock. In the time it took for the brickwork to peel back, revealing the Princess, the rose had managed to tie together a passable net.

"What do you want, Grave?" Siobhan demanded. "Can't you see I'm in the middle of something?"

Grave found his gaze drawn to the silky robe she wore, not to mention to the flashes of smooth flesh where the breeze caught it, and found that it was fairly easy to guess exactly what sort of something the Princess was in the middle of. Nice to see that while Grave was staring at pieces of string, Siobhan was enjoying herself.

"The bell has sounded, Princess."

"Bell, what bell? You mean the one in your little web?"

"Yes, Princess."

"So soon? You're sure it's not just the wind?"

Grave frowned at this latest slight on his professionalism. "It was in the barn. There is no wind."

"Then they're back," Siobhan said.

"Yes, Princess. I will bring them to you at once."

"You'll do no such thing."

"Yes, Prin… *what?*" That came out about an octave higher than his normal baritone, and Grave repeated it, making sure it was back to his standard ominous growl. "What? I am the greatest Huntsman of this Court."

"One who's already lost Thomas Greene twice. At least."

"Those were both…" Grave began, but Siobhan raised one delicate hand.

"No. I don't want to hear it. I've made my decision. I'm going to deal with this myself. At least that way, I can be sure it's going to be done properly."

"But Princess…" Grave didn't finish. He was talking to a wall by that point. Grave took a long, calming breath. Then another. Then he punched the wall hard enough to crumble brick. At about the same time, the rose bush threw its little net. It landed on Grave's head, and settled there forlornly.

Chapter Twenty Three

Siobhan heard the thump against the brick, but it wasn't like it mattered. The big fool would go off and sulk for a bit, but this was too important to let Grave mess it up. There were far better ways of working.

Siobhan made her way back down the corridor to the cavern at the end. The syrup was gone, but the throne and bed were still there. The shape of Simon Stranded stirred in the latter, rising to a sitting position. The expression he wore was that particular mix of exhaustion and worried fascination that her lovers always seemed to end up with, for some reason. Still, Siobhan was more than glad she'd brought him from the dungeons.

That, at least, had been easy. All she'd had to do was walk out of there with him. The guards hadn't even asked for a reason. It was her mother's dungeon, after all, and asking questions of royalty was traditionally a pretty poor way of ensuring job security. No doubt they'd assumed Siobhan had taken the Figment for… well, everything that she'd spent the last few hours doing. The point was that they wouldn't think to look *beyond* that. Her mother certainly wouldn't. It was one of those times when a bad reputation was a good thing to have.

Over in the bed, the Figment groaned.

"Not worn out, surely?" Siobhan purred, enjoying his reaction, which was to squirm away uncomfortably. "Relax, Simon. It's time for you to do your real job."

Siobhan heard the sigh of relief even as the Figment started looking round for his clothes. It took a while to find them. Eventually though, he stood in front of her.

"Now, you remember what you have to do?"

She saw him nod reluctantly.

"You're not having second thoughts, are you?"

He shook his head, and Siobhan smiled, pressing close to him and tracing fingers down his jaw.

"That's good."

"Ow!"

Siobhan withdrew her fingernails after a moment.

"Just so you remember. I don't much want to kill you, Simon, but if you don't play your part... well, I would be terribly unhappy. And that would be a pity. For you, at least."

Siobhan let him go. He hurried for the door. It was so easy to control people. A little fear, a little lust, the promise of what they wanted, and they'd do almost anything. It was hardly a great feat for her mother to do it, when Siobhan could do it every bit as well, if not better. She would prove that. Siobhan could just imagine the look in her mother's eye when she told her about this. If she told her. The promise of real power dangled in front of her just as surely as she'd dangled freedom in front of the Figment.

Of course, Siobhan thought, wiping the flecks of blood from her fingernails with distaste, just because you gave people the promise of what they wanted didn't mean you had to *keep* that promise.

To say that Erithnae was angry would be rather like suggesting that Viking berserkers were a little touchy. Rage and betrayal and a dozen other emotions seemed to be swimming round her head, doing the backstroke as it happened. When the human girl made the mistake of touching her, all Erithnae could think of was the human bitch who had seduced her father, who'd made him betray her mother, betray *her* like that. It was hardly surprising, really, that Erithnae lashed out.

Nightmares poured down her arms and into the human be-fore Erithnae even stopped to think. Things that made her Night-mare Hunt look like amateurs. Things that made the girl scream, and collapse, and then scream again. Things that could drive strong men mad and make heroes run home to their mothers.

None of them, Erithnae felt, were a patch on what was go-ing on in her own head. How could he have done something like this? There was a war... sorry, a War, on and her father had run off to start an affair with some human? How could he do that so soon after her mother's death? Didn't he love her at all? Where was that screaming coming from?

Oh yes, the human girl. She lay on the floor; her eyes fo-cussed on some terror only she could see, her mouth open in a plea to something that wouldn't listen.

Erithnae blinked. What was she doing? She waved a hand once, and the sound stopped, to be replaced by the softer sound of sobs. Nicola looked up at her with the sort of fear that was only a step away from panic.

"*Why?*"

Erithnae looked away. Did you get to apologise, as a Queen? To explain? *Could* she even explain?

"Why?" Nicola repeated, and Erithnae was shocked to feel the human's hands on her, spinning Erithnae round to face her. She should have been a quivering wreck. She certainly shouldn't have wanted to manhandle the Dreaming Queen. Obviously no one had told Nicola that.

"Because he cheated on her!"

Erithnae reached out for one of the letters, waving it the way a lawyer in a certain sort of courtroom drama might wave the crucial bit of evidence.

"You know what these are? Love letters!" Erithnae spat the words with the sort of contempt normally reserved for "tax returns" or "letters to the editor." "Unsent love letters to his hu-man and her brat. He went out after the death of my mother, and he had a child with some human..." Erithnae struggled to think of a term bad enough, and that was enough to let her realise that she was on the verge of ranting. Actually, well past the verge and about halfway up the embankment of ranting, if you could have such a thing. She stopped herself, then gently pried Nicola's hands from her.

"I... I looked at you and I saw her. I'm sorry. I shouldn't have done it."

"No, you shouldn't."

There was a fragile note in those words as Nicola let her go. But it was far too late to do anything about that.

"That's the worst part about being Queen," Erithnae said, as much to herself as to Nicola. "I have to be so careful. Everything here depends on me, and if I make the wrong choice, or I lose my temper... how many people get hurt? I thought my father left because he couldn't handle the War, or Mother's death, or both, and I was angry enough at being left with all of that. But to leave just so he could hook up with some *strumpet*, that's worse."

She saw the human girl raise an eyebrow.

"What?"

"Does anybody actually *say* strumpet?" Nicola gave a giggle that seemed completely at odds with the situation. "When I was little, I heard that word, and I thought it was a musical instrument, like a trumpet. I thought people marched around in marching bands playing strumpets."

"You're not making sense, Nicola."

"Is it any wonder? I've got a head full of nightmares that should be leaving me a gibbering wreck, not to mention a back full of glass. I'm entitled to be a little... oh..."

Erithnae caught Nicola as her knees gave way. Sure enough, her back looked like it had been mauled. Fragments of glass dusted her clothing, while here and there shards stuck through it.

"Try to hold still while I fetch help," Erithnae said, and sighed. "That's what comes of smashing things, I suppose. I'll get Poppy. She was able to help before."

Nicola's touch on her arm stopped her. "Wait."

"If you're feeling faint, there isn't time to wait."

"*Wait.* I want to say something. Also I want to stare at this ceiling a bit more. It's really pretty..."

"You're getting light-headed," Erithnae said.

"Yes, so shut up and listen. You're angry that your dad ran off. You're angry that he found someone that made him happy so soon after your mother's death..."

"You don't know what you're..."

Nicola put a finger to her lips, and giggled again. "Shush. I'm the one who's deli...deli... out of it here, so I get to talk. That doesn't make sense, does it? Anyway, you've got to listen, because you pushed me over. All I'm hearing is *your* dad, *your* mum, *your* pain. Well, he was probably in pain too. He'd just lost his wife. And yes, running off was a pretty... pretty... something thing to do, but you shouldn't be angry with him for finding someone who made him happy. How long was the War?"

"Centuries," Erithnae supplied.

"Well, exactly then."

"Exactly what?"

"What? Oh, right. It was hundreds of years after your mother died. I think he was probably due some happiness. Did I say that already?"

Erithnae nodded. "Yes. Go to sleep now, Nicola."

"Don't wan' to sleep..." she murmured. "'ghtmares."

"I promise you there won't be."

Erithnae passed a hand over Nicola's eyes, sending the girl to sleep. She carried her to the door, handing Nicola over to a guard. "Take her to Poppy, would you?"

"And then back to her room, Your Majesty?"

Erithnae shook her head. She probably owed Nicola something to make up for this. Actually, she probably owed her a great deal to make up for this, but sometimes you had to settle for what you could give.

"Let her have free rein of the castle and the gardens. After all, it's not like she can go anywhere."

Grave contemplated the mess that was the floor of his barn

through a haze of anger. No, that wasn't right. Grave was more than angry now. He was... *angrier*. Angry was a place where people stomped about and shouted. He was all the way through that, and at a point that could probably pass for thoughtful right up to the point where anyone went near him. He picked up a handful of string.

"All this mess," Grave observed to no one in particular. "And who has to clean it up? Me, the same as always. I've been cleaning up their messes since..." Actually, Grave couldn't re-member quite when he'd started, only that it had been a long, long time ago. Long enough that it made centuries seem short by comparison. Grave made his way through the mess of string, tossing it aside.

"If you don't mind my saying so, you look very upset."

Grave whirled at the sound, his eyes fixing after a moment on the mirror that still sat propped against a vaguely translucent bale of hay. He felt his eyes narrow. Grave thought he heard the thing gulp.

"I was just saying..."

"Don't."

Grave left the thing to silence for a moment, but the prob-lem with that was that he *wanted* to talk, and even talking to the mirror was better than talking to himself.

"I did all the hard work," Grave said, not looking at it, con-tinuing to clean the place. "I tracked him. I found him, and now she won't even let me finish the job."

"That's..."

"*Let* me," Grave repeated, rolling the words round in his mouth like someone who was pretty certain he'd just bitten into something he didn't want to eat. "Since when do they get to de-cide that?"

"Well..." It was obvious the mirror hadn't been pro-grammed with any sense of self preservation. "...I suppose that technically they've always... er, could you put me down please?"

Grave hoisted the mirror, checking the shape of the thing, weighing it like a man considering whether the axe he held would actually make a dent on the tree he was eyeing.

"It *wasn't* always the case." As Grave muttered it, he knew that it was true. It used to be that when he hunted someone, that was it. You called in the Huntsman only when you wanted someone dead. And then they died. There was none of this calling him back business. None of this calling him an idiot. They used to respect him.

Anyone else, of course, would simply have walked away long before now. That was what they did, these days. Grave had seen it on his visits to the human world. They'd just walk out and get another job, just like that. Well, sometimes not just like that, but to Grave the timescales involved were as near as made no difference.

The trouble was, Grave just couldn't see himself doing that sort of thing, and not just because his life expectancy after marching up to the Queen and telling her where to stuff her job would be about the same as that of a snowman faced with a flamethrower. His job was his life. It was all he'd ever done, and for Grave, "ever" was a word that took on a whole new meaning. Grave had been raised to believe in honour, duty, respect and never pulling faces in case the wind changed. At least three of those four applied here.

Respect, that was the thing. It used to be that the old King had valued him. Even his daughter had seemed to, though she didn't seem to want nearly as many people hunted down and put to death, for some reason. Siobhan though... no. There was a time when Grave had been a terror of the night, the thing mothers had scared their children with, when they weren't persuading them that if they kept biting their nails they'd end up with no arms. Humans were good at making up their own scary things, but Grave had been worse than all of them.

Maybe it was time to get that back.

Tucking the mirror under his arm, Grave stomped the few hundred yards to a patch of grass that looked the same as all the other patches of grass around it. The expression he wore while he did it was the sort of thing that might convince anybody watching not to start reading any long books.

He looked around, making certain. This he remembered.

Grave took one last look at the mirror, before using it to scoop aside grass and sods of earth like some particularly shiny spade. The mirror gave a cry of indignation.

"Hey! I'm supposed to be a valuable magic mirror! If I wanted to do manual work, I'd have become a ploughshare."

"*Shut up.*"

"Um... right. Shutting up."

Grave kept digging. It wasn't easy; partly because the ground had lain undisturbed for years, and partly because mirrors don't make for particularly good digging tools. When he heard the thump of mirror frame against wood, Grave cast it aside completely, brushing away earth with his hands like some huge, hairy mole. With a grunt of effort, Grave dragged an iron bound chest into the light.

It took longer to find the key. Eventually he found it wrapped up in two shopping lists and an expired railcard. When had he...

No. Enough.

He extracted the iron key from its wrapping, shoved it into the lock, and turned it with the sort of precision normally associated with defusing bombs. Though this, of course, was almost exactly the opposite. As Grave lifted the lid, black steel refused to glitter in the sunlight.

Grave took out the armour piece by piece. Each held the sort of runes that invariably looked like you didn't want to know what they meant, picked out in a rusty red. He pulled out the pauldrons, and the greaves, the gauntlets, and the massive breastplate, big enough to use as a coffee table. More pieces followed. Finally, lovingly, Grave pulled out the great black helm, letting it spin between his hands for a moment the way a golfer might spin a favourite club. It left the face open, but not much more.

Grave stripped off his outer clothing and slid the stuff on, locking its plates and its chain and its straps together like the carapace of some huge insect. Finally, he slid the great helm onto his head. It was strange and claustrophobic after so long, but it didn't take long for it to feel... right again. Except for one thing.

With a certain amount of effort Grave just about managed to slip the coat back on over the armour. The rat in his pocket poked its head out, took one look at him, and went back to sleep. Grave stalked over to the mirror. With the addition of the helm, his voice boomed even more than usual.

"Mirror, mirror, on the... floor, tell me, who's the scariest of them all?"

The mirror only went blank for a moment. "You, boss. Definitely you."

"Good."

Chapter Twenty Four

"Hey, Thomas!"

Thomas froze as he tried to get his bearings, startled by the sudden addition to a small field outside the castle village of Simon Stranded's voice. He'd been aiming for somewhere inside the castle, but instead he and Melissa found themselves knee deep in mud. At least, Thomas hoped it was mud. Given that there were cows at the other end of the field, at least one worse option was available.

"What are you doing here?" Thomas demanded as the Figment hopped over a hedge, making his way through the mire towards them. Well, not through exactly. Simon Stranded seemed almost to float over the mud, his sandals barely touching it. "And how are you doing that?"

"It's just like walking on sand, isn't it? You've just got to kind of take things lightly. I've had lots of practise at that."

Melissa hugged Stranded as soon as he was near enough, which made Thomas... uncomfortable. *On a mission to rescue your ex,* he reminded himself. Still, he wasn't nearly as uncomfortable as it seemed to make Simon. After only a second he pulled back, without so much as a flirtatious smile.

"You're angry at being left behind, aren't you?" Melissa guessed. Thomas could almost see the effort that Stranded put into forcing a smile.

"No, no, it's all right. I don't blame you. There are times when you just don't have any choice. Believe me, I know."

That was remarkably forgiving of him, Thomas thought. Still, it didn't explain the most important thing. "How did you get away?" he asked. "The last we saw of you, you were buried under a pile of guardsmen."

"The thing with piles of guardsmen is that they're never quite sure who's got hold of what. I just waited until they'd all got each other in an inescapable grip and then slipped out between them."

Melissa laughed at that. "You're not serious."

"I'm never serious. Actually, I just waited until they took me up to the castle, seduced the daughter of the Queen, and got her to let me go in exchange for a promise that I'd hand you over as soon as you showed up."

"You what?" Thomas started to gather himself to jump out of there with Melissa, but Simon held up a long-fingered hand.

"Relax. I only said that so they'd let me go. It's not like I have any intention of doing it."

"How do we know that?"

"I led you across half this Court, didn't I?" There was suddenly a hurt note in Simon's voice. "I let you get me into this mess. I'm not about to abandon you now. But if you don't trust me…"

"Of course we trust you," Melissa said, taking Simon's hand and shooting Thomas a remarkably eloquent look. "Don't we, Thomas?"

"Yes, of course we do," Thomas repeated dutifully, even though he did no such thing. "Won't Siobhan be upset to find out you've betrayed her?"

Stranded grinned. "I prefer to think of it as moving on after a brief but enjoyable relationship. You get used to it. Besides, she'll be too busy being upset that she's also lost your ex-girlfriend. While Siobhan was trying to get me to agree, I was finding out about the castle, including the way in that no one knows about."

"You found a way in?" Thomas couldn't help but hear the optimistic note in Melissa's voice. He had to admit, it sounded good. No sneaking in backed by nothing more than a pie, no trying to take on all the guards in the place, just a nice, convenient secret entrance. Actually, when you thought about it, it sounded a bit too good to be true.

"Are you sure this isn't a trap?"

"*Thomas!*"

"It just all seems very convenient. I mean, how did Simon even find us?"

The Figment grinned.

"I guess we're just fated to be together. The hero and his loveable but ultimately rather stupid human sidekick... ouch! There's no need to hit me!"

"I don't know," Thomas said, rubbing his knuckles where they'd connected with the Figment's shoulder. "It felt fairly necessary at the time. So, where is this secret entrance?"

Stranded stood there sulkily until Melissa sighed.

"Simon, please tell us. I'm sure Thomas didn't mean to hurt you."

"I'm sure he did," Thomas muttered, but not loud enough to be heard. In answer, the Figment swept a hand in the direction of the trees that were just visible over the fields.

"It's in the Orchard. As far as I can tell, the royalty want a safe way of going out to interfere with dreams. One that doesn't run the risk of coming into contact with anybody less important."

That made a sort of sense, Thomas had to admit.

"I suppose if it's a trap, at least there will be lots of places to hide."

Melissa just shook her head. Simon sighed.

"It's all right. I wouldn't trust me either. After all, I've only saved your life a couple of times, led you to a wise woman you wouldn't have met otherwise, and generally kept you in one piece. How is that going to offset the fact that I'm just a Figment?"

"What?" Thomas demanded. "This has nothing to do with you being a Figment."

"No? The first time you saw us, you practically jumped out of your skin."

"Keith had a beak!"

"So? Still, I suppose it's all we can expect from a blue-blood like yourself."

"What? I only found out about that yesterday!"

"And already you're too good for the likes of me." Simon managed an aggrieved look that said clearly that, if ever there was a downtrodden mass, it was him.

"No I'm not! I mean... I..."

Melissa took hold of Thomas' arm.

"We've got to get in there somehow, Thomas. Trusting Simon seems like a better bet than trying to get in on our own. What else are we going to do? Stand in this muddy field until a music festival shows up?"

There came a time, Thomas thought, when you just had to give in and accept the inevitable. He threw up his hands. Well, hand. Melissa still had hold of his other arm.

"All right! Simon, I believe you. If you'll look me in the eye and tell me that this isn't a trap, then it isn't a trap."

Simon Stranded looked Thomas squarely in the eyes.

"It isn't a trap."

Nicola did her best to hold still as Poppy got the worst of the glass out of her. She lay on a bench that had held an assortment of flowerpots only a few minutes before, which mostly meant that Nicola was having to try very hard not to think about how easily this many cuts could become infected. She bit her lip as Poppy tugged another shard out with tweezers.

"There," the other woman said, "that's the last of it, I think. Now, you should drink your tea."

She'd put together the same noxious concoction as last time. Nicola forced herself to drink it. It helped, at least with the physical side of things. The rest of it... well, that wasn't so good. She hardly dared to blink at the moment, so what would it be like when the time came to sleep again?

"Poppy," she asked. "Do you think I'll ever be able to get out of here?"

"Oh yes, of course. Her majesty has said that you can go down into the gardens any time you like. I think she feels a bit upset about what happened."

"She should." Nicola said automatically, sitting up as she did so. Her back ached, but it didn't feel like molten lava was pouring down it, so that was a good sign. "And that wasn't what I meant, Poppy. I meant, do you think I'll ever be able to go home?"

Poppy bit her lip.

"I don't know," she said, but from her tone Nicola could guess.

"I'm stuck here, aren't I?"

That just made Poppy look more uncomfortable. It probably wasn't very fair of Nicola to press her like this. After all, it was hardly the gardener's fault. Nicola reached out and put a hand on her shoulder.

"It's all right, Poppy."

"Maybe her Majesty will change her mind," Poppy said hopefully. "And if not, well, it's not such a bad place to live. We've got the gardens, and the Maze, and the gardens, and all *kinds* of plants. You've already met the roses, and…" Nicola got the feeling that Poppy was struggling to think of something non-plant related, having been told at some point that other people occasionally found those things interesting. Nicola decided to save her the trouble.

"How about we go down to the garden? If I'm trapped here, I might as well be out in the fresh air."

Poppy nodded and helped her to her feet. "And who knows, your boyfriend might still come to rescue you. Though I don't think the Queen will like that really. Still, you can hope, I suppose. But obviously I mustn't."

"It's a trap!"

It takes a special sort of effort to cram both "oh my God, we're going to die!" and "I told you so" into three short words, but, as hideous creatures poured from behind every tree he could make out, Thomas gave it a good go. Melissa was more straightforward.

"You betrayed us, Simon!"

"I didn't have a choice."

"Of course you had a choice," Thomas snapped back. "You could betray us, or you could *not* betray us. See, it's a choice."

"Siobhan would have killed me!"

"It's a pity she didn't."

Melissa made a small sound of fear. "What are those things?"

They certainly weren't clowns and old ladies. Instead, there were creatures with claws like those knives that were supposed to be able to cut through tin cans, others that had more teeth than a dentures factory, and a few that were little more than big clusters of spikes. They poured from the trees in smoky masses, taking shape as they hit the ground. It took Thomas a moment to realise that they were actually coming from the fruit that those trees bore. Someone was dragging them straight out of dreams.

It was fairly easy to guess who. Particularly when she stepped out to just beyond the ring of creatures, leaning casually against one of the tree trunks.

"So," Siobhan asked in an amused tone, "who wants to know what I'm going to do to them for getting syrup all over my floor?"

Thomas looked around hurriedly, trying to find some gap in the wall of hideous creatures that surrounded them. All he found instead were more teeth and claws. Melissa's hand tightened on his arm. When he looked, her face was absolutely white.

"I can't go back to that, Thomas. I can't."

He saw Siobhan step forward closer to the line of monsters. It parted for her, but not by much. Certainly not by enough that making a run for it would amount to anything other than charging head first into a blender.

"Give up and I won't hurt you," Siobhan promised. "Just come along nice and quietly, and everything will be all right."

To Thomas, it sounded far too close to "this won't hurt a bit."

"What did she promise you?" he demanded of Simon Stranded.

"A way out. I go back to my island, and I don't have everything in the Court trying to turn me into a fine grey mist. And she promised she wouldn't hurt you."

"And you *believed* her?"

Siobhan drummed her fingers impatiently on the back of the nearest creature before seeming to remember exactly what it was. She wiped her hand discretely on the filmy dress she wore.

"I'm not going to kill you, Thomas. After all, you're family. Yes, I know. Now, as fun as this all is, I don't have time for it. Either surrender, or you'll find out what it's like to be torn apart by a real Nightmare Hunt, not that pack of idiots my mother keeps."

Thomas grinned, suddenly unable to stop himself as he stared over Siobhan's shoulder.

"What, *that* pack of idiots?"

Siobhan's head snapped round, and she ducked with inhuman quickness, allowing a custard pie to sail past her. It struck a thing with half a dozen mouths, which started to dissolve.

"Allergic to custard," Thomas said. "Who'd have thought it?"

The Nightmare Hunt barrelled into Siobhan's creatures with all the gusto of... well, insane nightmare things spoiling for a fight. The gremlin tripped up a tentacled thing. The clowns kept up a constant volley of custard. Even the little girl stared at something with six-inch claws until it got embarrassed and backed away. And at the centre of the charge was a huge figure in outsize black armour covered by an even bigger overcoat.

"Take my kill away from me, will you?" Grave roared, hitting one creature hard enough to send it sprawling. "Call me useless, would you?"

He picked up a strange, chitinous thing and flung it at two

others.

"I hunted them down! I get the kill!"

"What's he doing?" Melissa demanded, and Thomas shrugged.

"I haven't got a clue. But with all this talk of killing, I don't think we're going to want to be here when the dust settles."

He looked around, trying to find an opening. Thomas knew they'd have to act fast. There was only so long that a force whose primary weapons seemed to be custard, a pair of viciously applied knitting needles and the knack of staring unnervingly was going to last once the other side remembered that they had claws. The only reason it was going so well was that a couple of the original Nightmare Hunt were genuinely dangerous. The floating thing with all the tentacles picked up creatures at random and slammed them into trees, the gremlin happily ran round tying legs together, while in the middle of it all a giant boot stomped merrily on some sort of blade-footed beetle.

Thomas ducked to avoid a flying body, realised that he'd lost track of Melissa, and looked around for her in near panic. He found her locked in the grip of some claw-handed thing with no apparent face, just a blank, flat oval of skin. With a roar that surprised even him, Thomas lashed out, catching the thing on the side of the head. It let go of Melissa and turned to face… turned so that Thomas was in front of it. It occurred to Thomas that this wasn't the best place to be, given the claws. The thing raised one hand to swipe at him… and neatly toppled over.

Melissa put down the branch she'd hit it with.

"We need to get out of here."

Thomas scanned the melee as best he could, trying to find an opening. Finally, he spotted something that might work.

"This way!"

Thomas darted forward between two clowns, tapped them on the shoulders, and ducked. They spun in perfect unison, felling one another with expertly timed pies, and leaving a gap just big enough to slip through. Which is exactly what Thomas and Melissa did.

"Now run!"

~~~~~~

They ran. They sprinted, scarpered, legged it, made a dash for freedom, and ran as fast as their respective legs would carry them. Thomas, being a fan of what might be called the classical school of running away, ran with eyes fixed firmly forward, quite emphatically not looking back. Perhaps if he'd done so he'd have come to a rather important conclusion, which is that, in a joint escape attempt, it's usually a good idea if everybody runs away in broadly the same direction.

As it was, Thomas was only able to come to this conclusion at a point when it was rather too late to make use of it, namely when he stopped with burning lungs and a heart that seemed to want to be on the other side of his ribcage only to find that Melissa wasn't anywhere to be seen. Neither was anybody chasing him, though some muffled shouting in the trees suggested that was a state of affairs that might correct itself in the near future.

What there was, was a clearing.

A clearing with a cave in it, to be precise. Thomas had never seen a cave like it, since those he had seen had mostly been dingy little things in the side of cliffs rather than neat holes in the side of roughly circular mounds of earth. Besides, none of the caves he'd seen before featured giant lizards basking in front of them. Thomas took a step towards the thing from sheer fascination before it occurred to him quite how stupid walking towards something with quite so many teeth might be.

A yellow eye snapped open with the sort of laziness that cats, lizards and university students seemed to have divided up between them in the dawn of time. Thomas wasn't fooled. He'd seen that look on a former neighbour's tabby, usually when faced with something small that went "squeak!" It was a look that expressed a fundamental disinterest in the universe, right up until the thing it emphatically wasn't watching made the mistake of moving.

Unfortunately, Thomas had a pretty good idea that somehow, he'd managed to cast himself as the small squeaking thing. He thought that was probably a bit of a stretch of his acting abilities, but clearly the lizard-thing didn't, and in these situations it's the opinion of the thing with all the teeth that counts.

Another shout from somewhere behind him reminded Thomas that he couldn't just stand there all day. Neither could he simply keep running. At least, that's what his heart and lungs were saying, and Thomas was inclined to take their word for it. He supposed he could just jump back into his world, but that would mean abandoning Melissa and Nicola, probably for good. He needed somewhere to hide.

Thomas' eyes fixed on the cave with a certain amount of inevitability.

Slowly, at the sort of speed normally associated with tectonic plates, Thomas searched the grass around him for something he could use to get past the lizard. Despite his best efforts, Thomas couldn't force his eyes to present the image of a small tank. Instead, the persisted in showing him nothing more than a collection of assorted fallen branches. Thomas picked up a reasonably hefty one, weighing it in his hands.

Through it all, the lizard continued to watch him, as if waiting for the moment when Thomas would finally do something interesting enough to make him worth eating. Thomas' eyes went from his makeshift club to the creature and back again. As if on cue, the lizard-thing yawned. At least, it opened its mouth wide, displaying a collection truly ferocious dentistry that made Thomas consider his chances again.

"Who am I kidding? I'll never get past that with this."

Thomas hurled the branch away. He was quite surprised when the lizard thing set off after it, snatching it from the air with the longest tongue Thomas had ever seen. It hurried back to deposit it at his feet, looking up at him expectantly.

Why not? Thomas thought, and picked the thing up, before hurling it out into the trees.

"Fetch!"

The lizard-thing bounded away with an expression of delight matched only by Thomas' as he darted to the cave, all but throwing himself inside. That quickly became throwing himself headlong into the dark interior, as Thomas' feet caught on something he couldn't see. Thomas tumbled down a short slope, rolling and jolting, finally coming to rest on what felt like a rough earth floor. He had to work by feel, because the cave was in complete darkness.

"You'd think a little light wouldn't be much to ask for," Thomas muttered, and was rewarded with a soft glow that seemed to come from all the walls at once. The glow revealed a huge stone walled room. Cathedrals would have seemed pokey by comparison. Even some smaller aircraft hangers would have been marked down by estate agents as compact after viewing the place. Like so much of the rest of the Court, it seemed to have done away with the idea of the space available on the insides of things having something to do with the space on their outsides. And almost every inch of this space was filled with nothing except row upon row of fruit trees.

The same as outside, Thomas thought. Only, why are these locked away behind some sort of guard… thing?

Thomas examined the trees more closely. As with the others, they bore fruit, but no two fruits were the same. Some were misshapen and odd, while others seemed to glow from within with whole rainbows of colour. Each tree stood in a plant pot that might have doubled as a bathtub if it ever gave up arboriculture, and each pot had words printed neatly on the side. The first he read said *Flower Court 304*, the next *Flower Court 303*.

On instinct, Thomas hunted around until he found those marked as the Dreaming Court's. They were, he found, arranged in a single long line along the back wall of the place. He followed them along. *Dreaming Court 105… Dreaming Court 47… Dreaming Court 18…* Thomas kept walking. Finally, he came to the pot marked *Dreaming Court 1*.

Ten minutes of random fruit sampling later, Thomas picked up a piece that seemed almost too bright to look at, put it in his pocket, and headed back towards the mouth of the cave.

Chapter Twenty Five

Grave was enjoying himself more than he had for centuries, bellowing and bludgeoning and hitting Figments with whatever came to hand. Quite often, this turned out to be another Figment. It didn't slow Grave down. Even in the War, he hadn't had a chance to get properly angry like this, and Grave intended to make the most of every minute of it.

He was enjoying himself so thoroughly, in fact, that it took Grave a little while to realise that there didn't seem to be any sign of Thomas Greene or the girl in the general melee. For a brief moment, he was simply too busy savouring the thrill of a really good fight to care. Gradually though, a nagging feeling that he ought to be going after them chipped away at Grave, rather like the gremlin who was hanging onto his helmet, tapping away with a tiny hammer.

Grave plucked it off and held it between thumb and forefinger as he lifted it to eye level.

"You're supposed to be attacking the *other* side."

Grave hauled the thing back, winding up his throwing arm.

"Oh, sorry. I got a bit carried awaaaayyyy…"

The nagging feeling wasn't so easy to get rid of. Grave was a hunter, not just a random brawler. He saw the hunt through, no matter how arduous it was. He couldn't let a little thing like a really good scrap get in the way of that, no matter how much he might want to. Besides, Grave thought as he sidestepped and stuck his arm out, letting a bulbous, horned thing knock itself flat, he had a reputation to maintain.

Decision made, Grave set about extricating himself from the fight. The Nightmare Hunt could handle things without him. Or, if they couldn't, he didn't much care. Pulling out of the mass brawl was rather more difficult than getting into it. Almost by definition, fights are the sort of things where no one is inclined to get out of the way if you simply say "excuse me," not that Grave had any intention of doing so. Instead, he picked the nearest clear space, and forged a path towards it with shoves, punches, and the occasional vicious elbow jab. At least one of the Figments in his way took a good look at Grave, decided that the fight would be an altogether more pleasant place without him, and stepped neatly out of the way.

Pretty soon, he was in clear space. Grave sniffed the air. This close to the fight, of course, he could mostly just scent that mix of anger, blood and "I really want to get out of here" fear that was the mark of any good set-to, but if he made an effort… yes, there was the human scent. Or rather, scents. After only a little way, a pair of distinct scents split onto different paths through the trees. Grave sniffed the air again, and loped off after the one with the male taste to it. The young lady could wait.

Grave set off after the scent with a speed that belied his size. In the armour, it made him look like the one American football player no one would ever want to try and tackle. That, or a rhino in an overcoat. The effort involved only made him angrier. Grave didn't like to run, and Thomas Greene had already made him do it once before. He'd pay for that too.

The scent stopped at the clearing that held the cave. Sadly, Grave didn't. Once actually running, someone his size didn't stop easily, and this time it required the aid of a tree on the far side of the clearing. The tree in question considered the possibility of staying upright for only the briefest of moments before toppling with a crash. The Queen's pet guard monster trotted up to him with a branch in its mouth, which it dutifully laid at Grave's feet.

"What do you call this?" Grave demanded. "You're supposed to be guarding, not…"

Grave let the thought trail off. Partly that was because the lizard hissed at him, and even Grave knew enough to be careful around the beast. Mostly though, it was because it had occurred to him that if Thomas Greene had got past the thing, then he was probably somewhere in the cave.

He looked back to it just in time to see the half-breed step outside.

Grave let out a roar and barrelled forward, or he would have if something hadn't grabbed hold of his coat. As Thomas Greene took one look over at Grave and sprinted off in the opposite direction, Grave looked down to see the lizard holding the hem of the thing in its teeth. It looked up at him with a plaintive expression before glancing pointedly at the branch.

"I don't have time!" Grave roared. The lizard just kept staring. It was clear that it could continue to do so all day if it had to, just as it could continue to hold onto his coat.

"Oh, very well!" Grave snarled, and heaved the branch away. As the lizard bounded after it, Grave did much the same in the direction that his prey had just taken.

He could feel the pulse of the hunt now, beating through him with every heavy footfall. He could almost taste the closeness of his victim, follow the tang of the fear as surely as he'd tracked the scent of human before. Soon Grave would catch sight of him again, and then… the final sprint, the spring, and the satisfaction of finally finishing this bloody awful job.

Grave loped out of the trees, and, in the sudden glare of the sunlight, he saw him. Thomas Greene had almost made it as far as the entrance to the Maze, which was further than Grave had thought he'd get. But still, even he wouldn't be foolish enough to try and lose Grave in *there*. *Then again*, Grave thought as his prey slipped through the entrance, *maybe he would*.

Siobhan stood back from the fight, watching the mess but being very careful to keep out of it. Not that she couldn't more than hold her own against Figments, of course, but that wasn't the point. What was the use of having horrible nightmare things if you had to do your own fighting?

She was, however, having a certain amount of trouble keeping track of who was winning. It wasn't exactly as though the assorted Things were wearing uniforms, and for the most part, it was just a mess. Even as Siobhan watched, a tentacled creature from her side leapt at the floating tentacled mass that Grave had brought with him. The result was the sort of knot that would probably require some sort of Greek general to undo.

Siobhan ducked a custard pie and checked the heaving mob of fighters again. Grave had, of course, run off. She'd seen that. It was almost impossible to miss an eight-foot tall man in black armour charging out of the fight, even in all the chaos. What was proving more difficult was locating either Thomas or Melissa. Siobhan bit her lip, wondering why Grave should have run off like that, if not to…

Siobhan used several words that princesses probably weren't supposed to use, and waved a hand at the melee. The nearest of the Figments screamed before vanishing into the familiar grey mist. More followed, and still more. The giant boot vanished in mid-leap. The little girl gave Siobhan one last, accusatory stare before turning into mist. Even those on her own side weren't immune. With Grave gone, Siobhan was sure she could handle whatever would be left afterwards, so she just had done with the lot, leaving nothing but a clearing filled with hanging grey forms.

"They've gone." Siobhan said it coldly, letting the anger bubble under the surface. She almost wished she hadn't transformed all of the Figments now, because she needed something to take her mood out on. The snap of a twig answered her prayers. Siobhan darted around a tree, grabbed a double handful of cloth, and slammed Simon Stranded back against the trunk before he could do more than yelp.

"I was wondering where you'd got to."

"I was just… trying to keep out of the way."

"Of course you were. Did you see which way they ran?"

"Which way who ran?"

Siobhan slapped him. She wasn't in the mood for being messed around. "Who do you think I mean? Which way did they go?"

"You said you wouldn't hurt me," the Figment reminded her.

"I'll do worse than a tiny slap if you don't tell me which way they went."

Siobhan watched as, trembling, Simon Stranded raised an arm to point back towards the castle.

"You're certain?"

He nodded.

"Good."

Siobhan pushed him back, and made a dismissive wave of her hand. Simon looked at her in utter puzzlement for a moment, before opening his mouth in a howl that would have done any wounded animal proud. It rose, and then fell, and then ended with the sudden *pfft* of Figment exploding into the familiar fine mist.

"Now, let's see if we can't make you into something more useful."

Melissa wasn't sure when she and Thomas had managed to get split up, but she didn't dare stop and turn back. All Melissa could do was hope: that he was all right, that he'd manage to find her given time, and that the path she ran along would lead somewhere. Somewhere that wasn't crawling with spike-covered Figments, for preference.

After another couple of minutes, she found that it actually led to a garden. And not just to any garden. Just from the scent and the patterns of the flowers Melissa would have known it as one of the royal gardens anywhere. Being dragged through it to your prison tends to fix a place in your mind. Besides, the looming presence of the castle above it was a bit of a clue. It wasn't a good place to stay. Or was it? Sooner or later Thomas was bound to look here, wasn't he? Even so, it seemed like an awfully large risk to be wandering around the castle gardens, where there might be guards, or dreaming folk or...

"Oh, hi."

The woman who said it looked to be about Melissa's age, in as much as that was ever a guide here, slender, blonde, and wearing jeans and a grubby international food aid t-shirt. She was accompanied by a taller woman with green and blonde hair, who clung to her elbow like a mother hen.

"Nicola, I'm not sure we should be talking to people. The Queen will be..."

"Funnily enough, Poppy, I don't care what she thinks at the moment."

The taller woman fell silent. In that silence, Melissa calculated the odds of one of the dreaming folk being called Nicola and wearing a t-shirt that wouldn't have been printed when the War started. Her eyes widened.

"Nicola? Nicola as in Thomas' ex? We've been looking all... oh." Melissa clamped her mouth firmly shut as she realised that the other woman was almost certainly one of the dreaming folk. Judging by the look she got, it was probably too late.

"Who are you?" the taller woman demanded. "Are you another one?"

Her hand clamped onto Melissa's arm, preventing any escape.

"Another one what?"

The taller woman looked puzzled for a moment.

"I don't think I can say. It's supposed to be a secret."

Beside her, the woman who was probably Nicola sighed.

"Another human. There, I've said it. Happy? If you are, I'd recommend running for it."

Melissa lifted her captured arm by way of answer. Something about the movement must have turned her to just the right angle, because a rapidly approaching shape caught her eye.

"What's that?"

The woman who had hold of her shook her head.

"Oh no. I'm not falling for that. Her Majesty said I had to be careful."

"Poppy," Nicola said, "I think there really is something."

There was, but Melissa couldn't quite make out what. She tried shielding her eyes with her free hand. That just made the thing a slightly shadier blur. Another second of staring though, and it swam into focus like that picture where you suddenly see what all the fuss with the candlestick and the two faces is about.

"Is that Siobhan? What's that she's riding? Is that a unicorn?"

Chapter Twenty Six

Thomas' parents, or, he corrected himself, his mum and the man she'd married, had once taken him to a maze when he was a child. It was one of those family days out that a great many children find themselves subjected to, usually without the parents considering such basic questions as "does anyone actually want to do this?" "wouldn't we all be better off at the zoo?" and crucially, "what if my child runs off and gets stranded in the maze for an hour while we try to find him?"

If they'd brought him to *this* maze, it would have been a lot longer than an hour. The walls on either side changed between hedges, stone and rustling wheat seemingly at random, while the turnings were complicated, twisting things that seemed to make no sense. Thomas quickly found himself lost. The only advantage to that was that if he didn't know where he was, it was a pretty good bet that no one else did either. But he couldn't stay there forever. He'd only ducked inside in the hopes of losing Grave. Eventually, that goal achieved, Thomas would probably want to get out again, find Melissa and probably Nicola, and get them all out of the Court. It wasn't too much to ask, was it?

For the moment, at least, it apparently was. The maze took turnings that it couldn't possibly have managed without running into itself. Either that, or Thomas just wasn't keeping track very well. It might have helped if he could remember what it was you were supposed to do in mazes. Was it right turns on the way in followed by lefts on the way out, or vice versa? Did that even apply when the maze in question didn't seem to let silly things like the locations of its own walls stand in the way of getting someone hopelessly confused?

Somewhere behind him, Thomas could hear the particular mixture of heavy footfalls, sniffing and occasional swearing that could only mean Grave was on his trail. Eventually, if he stayed here, Grave would catch up. Probably, anyway, though given the apparent impossibility of the maze, there was always a chance that they might both wander round forever, never quite finding a way through the maze, never quite running into one another.

Almost as soon as he thought it, Thomas wasn't lost any longer. Or, at least, he stepped through a gap between two hedges and into a clear space that was almost certainly the maze's centre. A bench sat there, alongside a sundial that, for no apparent reason, had a small hand mirror and a banana sitting on its surface. The mirror was clouded over, literally. It looked like someone had decided to employ it as a way of letting storm clouds check their appearance, though not for long. A face, though one that looked like it had been put together by the simple expedient of stealing one from a statue, filled the frame.

"Judge Tina Van Veebling!"

"What?" Thomas asked, carefully since he didn't really know what you were supposed to do when mirrors started talking, or at least when they started calling out the names of members of the judiciary. He reached out for it.

"I wouldn't do that, if I were you," the mirror said in a bright voice. "That banana used to be a butterfly, before it touched this thing. Use a stick instead. There's one by your feet."

There was. Somewhat gingerly, Thomas pushed the mirror from the sundial, catching it before it could hit the ground.

"You'll need the banana too. That's good. Place it about two metres in front of you. Left a bit. Yes, right there."

Thomas did it, and only then wondered why he was taking instructions from a common household object.

"What are you?" he asked.

"Oh, just your basic magic mirror. Well, not exactly basic. Not after what I just managed."

There are moments when you just know that your half of the conversation has been scripted in advance, and that no amount of wishing you were somewhere else, looking pointedly at your watch, or even running in the other direction will change it. Thomas decided to yield to the inevitable.

"What was it that you managed?"

"I managed to answer *the question!*"

"What question?" Thomas asked, nonplussed.

"What question? What question? The question! You know, the one that they all want answered. The one that's supposed to be impossible unless you're some big shot MM780 model."

"What's an MM780?"

"A bunch of flash bastards who hang around in their big gilt frames, that's what, lording it over the rest of us because *they* can answer the question."

"*What* question?" Thomas repeated, trying his best to be patient and largely failing.

"Oh, surely you must know it? Look, I'll start. Mirror, mirror, on the wall, who's the…"

"…fairest of them all?" Thomas finished.

"Judge Tina Van Veebling!"

The image of a woman filled the mirror's frame. Thomas had to admit that she was beautiful. She seemed to be wearing an especially low cut version of a judge's gown. Of course, she was also biting down on the neck of some helpless man, which rather spoiled the effect.

"She's a vampire." Thomas thought about it for a moment. "And I can't believe I've got to the stage where I can say something like that as though it's normal. Anyway, are you sure? I mean, it seems a bit… subjective for something like beauty."

"Of course I'm sure. She's beautiful, she's a judge in the Court of Blood, *and* she burns easily."

"Because she's a vampire," Thomas pointed out.

"Fair in every sense. I like her, anyway."

"So you've cheated."

The face in the mirror looked vaguely affronted by that. "I haven't. I've just shown what I think are admirable decision-making skills in coping with an otherwise tricky selection process. And if you don't agree, you can go and compare all the other women in the universe for yourself. Not that you can. There's that huge bugger, Grave, in the way. Look, he's just about to come in here."

"What?" Thomas looked around the centre of the maze. There was only the one entrance, so that was out. The trouble was, there wasn't much in the way of cover either. The bench would hide him for approximately the same amount of time he would survive after being found, while as for the sundial, Thomas really didn't want to risk touching it by accident.

"What am I going to do?" Thomas demanded.

The face in the mirror grinned. "Just relax. I've got it all well in hand. Or I would have, if I had hands. What did you think the banana was for? All you need to do for now is stand in front of the sundial. He'll charge in, slip on the banana, and go flying straight into it. All you've got to do is dodge."

The mirror sounded very certain, and Thomas had to admit that, put like that, it did sound very easy.

"Well," Nicola heard Melissa mutter, "since it's Siobhan on top, I think we can be pretty sure that's not a real unicorn."

"What?" It took Nicola a moment before she got it. It had been a rough day. "Oh, I see. You know her then?"

"The Queen's daughter," Poppy supplied from beside her. Nicola noticed that her usual smile was missing. "She is… not a very nice person."

From Poppy, Nicola thought, that was approximately the same as someone else calling the approaching Princess a murderous psychopath.

"She seems in a hurry."

"She's chasing me," Melissa admitted. "She wants to control Thomas and me. Please, we need to run."

"She's the Queen's daughter," Poppy repeated, as though that was an answer.

"And does that mean that she won't do anything to us?" Nicola asked.

"Um… probably not."

"Then I think I've had enough of a walk. We should probably head in. Quickly."

"You know," Poppy said in a vague sort of way, "I'm sure it's all a misunderstanding. Though I'd never noticed how *pointy* unicorns are until now."

Nicola sighed, and looked over to Melissa, who nodded. They grabbed an arm each, and hauled Poppy backwards as quickly as they could. It wasn't quick enough, which is hardly surprising really. Horses, even pointy ones, move faster than people dragging someone between them. The unicorn slammed into them with the force of a minor car accident, knocking Nicola away from Poppy and to her knees on the garden's grass. Nicola looked up in time to see the beast pulling its horn out of the hole it had punched in Poppy, dripping with blood. The injured gardener fell to the ground, and the unicorn reared up, looking for all the world as though it would trample her.

It didn't get the chance. The grass around the dreaming Fey woman rose up in a kind of tide that washed over her and then wove itself together into a sort of rough cocoon. It was hard, too, because the unicorn's hooves crashed down on it with a clang. Nicola was still staring at it when Melissa dragged her to her feet.

"I've done what I can to keep her safe, but we need to *run*."

As if to reinforce that message, Nicola saw Siobhan dismount from the unicorn. Her expression promised pain. Nicola nodded and started to run back towards the castle.

"There's a gardener's door just back here. Hurry."

They hurried, squeezing through the door and slamming the thing behind them. Nicola bolted it, and then nodded to the thick length of wood propped against the wall as casually as a walking stick. It took both Melissa and herself to manoeuvre the thing into iron brackets on the door, but it finally fell into place with a crash.

Melissa tugged at her arm.

"We should keep moving."

"You think she's going to get through that door?" Nicola asked. "She isn't any bigger than us."

"Siobhan doesn't need to be. Most of this castle is dream-stuff. She can control it."

Nicola stared at her blankly for only a moment before the implications sank in. She looked back at the door just in time to see it start to dissolve from the bottom up.

"All right, follow me."

Nicola set off, with Melissa close behind her, and did her best to remember the layout of the castle. Maybe if they could get to somewhere where there would be help, they might get out of this alive. As much as Nicola hated the thought, there was only one truly safe place that came to mind.

"We need to find the Queen."

Melissa started to shake her head, but Nicola half dragged her along.

"Who else do you think will stop her?" Nicola glanced back to where Siobhan had made it through the door and was following them at a leisurely pace. She seemed utterly unconcerned about the fact that Nicola and Melissa were getting away. Nicola didn't have time to look more than that. She pulled Melissa around a corner, then led her up a flight of stairs, and along a corridor. A couple of servants stared as they passed, but made no move to interfere.

Where were they? And where would Erithnae be? Nicola wracked her brains, trying to remember everything she could about the castle's layout. It wasn't a lot. She'd snuck through it once, been led through it by guards, and been carried through it unconscious. None of those were particularly good ways of getting to know a place. Finally, she did the only thing she could think of, and grabbed a passing chambermaid.

"Where is the Queen?"

The chambermaid took a good look at both of them.

"Quickly! There isn't much time!"

"She'll probably be in the library, ma'am, but she won't

want to be disturbed."

Nicola thought she could hear the sound of following feet.

"Just tell me where, please."

"Up the next set of stairs, left, then left again, then right out of the gallery, then up the small staircase, and it should just be along that corridor."

"Thank you."

Nicola sped back into motion with Melissa beside her.

"You stopped a chase to ask for directions?" Melissa asked.

"Yes. It's just as well you're not with Thomas. You know men never do that sort of thing."

"*No one* does that sort of thing when they're being chased."

"I just did," Nicola countered. "Now are you talking or running?"

They ran on. Nicola kept a careful watch on the turnings, making sure they followed the directions exactly. It was a bit of a shock, therefore, when the pair of them ran into a dead end. This was particularly the case since, until they were about halfway down the corridor in question, it had been perfectly normal. A wall just… appeared in front of them, letting Nicola run into it hard enough to see stars.

Nicola looked back to see Siobhan rounding the same corner at a casual stroll.

"What on earth…?"

"I said she could change this place." Melissa's matter of fact tone was at odds with her face, which held so much fear that some of it started to spill over into Nicola. Desperately, she scanned the place for ways out. There weren't any.

"Now," Siobhan said with a smile that might have seemed gentle under other circumstances, "are you sure I can't persuade you to come back, Melissa?"

Nicola saw the other woman shake her head.

"Then you're going to have to die. Both of you." She looked Nicola in the eye. "My dreams obviously weren't enough, so I'll just have to do things properly. I can't wait to see my mother's face when she learns you're gone. It will teach her to give so much attention to something so... fragile."

When Grave stalked into the little square at the centre, all eight feet of him blocking the exit, his coat flapping around his armour like a superhero with a second career in caretaking, impending victory suddenly didn't seem quite so easy. Thomas resisted the urge to look at the mirror, which he held carefully behind his back. It seemed better to have at least one surprise left.

"Look," he said, "can't we talk about this?"

Grave growled a response. Actually growled, as though human speech was momentarily too much of an effort. After a second, he punctuated the response by edging forward menacingly. Then again, given his size, there wasn't much Grave didn't do menacingly. Finally, he seemed to remember the idea of real words.

"No."

"But look, I'm sure Siobhan won't want me hurt. Doesn't she want me for her big experiment?"

The big man seemed to think about that for a fraction of a second. "Stuff her."

He took another step forward, and stared down at the banana as though trying to work out why it should be there. Grave looked up with a smile that made Thomas' blood run cold. With one precise, deliberate step, he squashed the banana into something like the consistency of baby food.

"That only works in cartoons."

Thomas' brow creased. "How do you know about cartoons?"

Grave hesitated, like a teenager who'd just realised he'd admitted that yes, the stash of magazines under the bed was his. "I see them sometimes, in your world. I like the chases." He gave a great huff of breath, as though that had used up his stock of words for the day. Thomas tried to think of something that would get him talking again. Yes, it would only delay the inevitable, but delaying the inevitable seemed infinitely better than standing there with arms wide open to welcome it. It was rather like an elderly relative in that respect.

"Why do you even want to kill me?"

The sky seemed to darken, but Thomas realised that it was just Grave looming over him.

"Why? *Why?* I am the Huntsman! Do not ask me why I hunt! Would you ask the wolf why it chases the deer? Would you ask the spider why it spins a web for the fly? Would you ask the little cartoon dog why it chases after the Roadrunner?"

"It's a coyote, and the answers to your questions are: food, food, and because the scriptwriters tell it to." Thomas drew himself up to his full height, not quite making it up to the other man's chin. "Which one of those applies here? You don't even know why you're chasing me, do you?"

"Of course I know!"

Thomas folded his arms. "Go on then. Tell me."

"I am the Huntsman, it is what I do! I chase and I chase, and when I catch, I kill. Or I did."

"But you don't now, do you?" Thomas demanded. "So why do you suddenly want me dead? If I'm about to die, I think I deserve an explanation, don't you?"

Grave's expression grew, if anything, even more thunderous. "I killed up until *your* family started telling me not to." He paused, and then smiled a smile even nastier than the one just before he'd squashed the banana. "Yes, *that* shall be my reason. You will die, because it will be almost as good as wringing the life from those arrogant bastards who call themselves my betters. You will die because like all of them, you've spent your every minute making my life more difficult. You will die, Thomas Greene, because I really, *really* want to kill you."

Thomas gulped. "Since you put it like that…"

There was no point in fighting fair with someone that size, so Thomas kicked Grave as hard as he could in the groin. There was a distinctly metallic *clang* and Thomas fell to the ground, clutching his foot in a passable impression of a premiership footballer who had just been breathed on by an opposition defender.

Grave tapped the big black breastplate he wore with a finger.

"It's called armour, boy. There wouldn't be much point to it if it left me unprotected there. Now, where were we?"

Grave loomed again for a moment, before slapping his forehead theatrically.

"Honestly, forget my own head if it weren't screwed on. Now, I had a knife here somewhere just the other day." Grave patted the outer pockets of his coat. Since there were so many of them, it took a while. "Don't try to crawl away, or I'll just beat you to death. That's always nasty. Though at this rate I might end up having to do that anyway. You know what it's like. You put something down, and immediately the whole universe seems to jump around to move it somewhere else."

Grave started to drag items from his pockets. To Thomas, they mostly seemed like junk. Grave pulled out a string of flags, and then a rather worrying looking egg, a battered notebook and what appeared to be a tea cosy. With a curse, Grave shoved his hand deeper into a side pocket. He let out an almighty roar of pain.

"Ow! Get off! Let go, you little sod!"

He started waving his hand around. On it, Thomas could just make out a tiny furry shape, a rat or a mouse or something. It had its teeth sunk firmly into Grave's finger.

Hang on, why was he sitting around watching? Taking advantage of the opportunity, Thomas darted past Grave, getting about two yards past him before his ankle made it clear that it wasn't going to do running away by the simple expedient of dumping Thomas on the ground. *Typical,* Thomas thought, *dropped like the heroine of some horror B movie.*

"Aaarr!" Grave roared, tossing the mouse from him and spinning towards Thomas. It was, it seemed, time for plan B. Except that he didn't have one. He'd been relying far too much on the mirror's stupid banana...

An idea occurring to him, Thomas pulled out the magic mirror, holding it up to catch the sun as best he could. It worked perfectly. Grave, throwing up his hands to try and block the sudden glare, didn't see the bananary mess until his foot connected with it. Whatever the slipperiness of normal bananas, a puree of banana, mud and grass definitely didn't count as a sound footing. Grave threw up his hands as his foot slid from beneath him.

It was now or never. With a cry that was partly rage, but mostly pain, Thomas hurled himself forward, shoving Grave as hard as he could. The huge man tottered for a moment longer and then toppled backwards like a tree being felled. One of his outstretched arms collided with the sundial.

There wasn't a puff of smoke. There weren't any fancy sounds or special effects. It would probably have been better if there had been, really. Those might have softened the jarring shock of it. As it was, one moment there was a large, psychotic Huntsman of the dreaming folk, and the next there was just a coat with a lump in the middle of it on the floor.

Thomas didn't dare whisk the coat away, but he didn't need to. The lump fought its way to the edge of the coat, and a feline face poked out. Slowly, and without any dignity whatsoever, a long-haired black cat dragged itself from under the thing. It hissed at Thomas. Thomas was too busy to notice. He looked squarely into the mirror.

"Can you tell me how to find Melissa and my ex-girlfriend?" he demanded.

"Of course I can! If I can answer the question, I can do *anything*!"

Chapter Twenty Seven

Nicola had never really been the sort of person who could just stand around and do nothing. That applied as much to her own impending death as to efforts to save cute little animals thousands of miles away. She'd fight, and who knew, if she got lucky, and if Melissa helped, maybe they'd even win. After all, there were two of them, and only one of Siobhan, though Nicola was having to work hard to ignore the strength and speed she'd seen in Erithnae and Poppy. Nevertheless, she was going to give it a good go.

As such, Nicola was just trying to work out the best way to throw herself at Siobhan when the air in front of her split with the sound of tinkling bells, almost blinded her with a flash of light and disgorged a figure who stumbled against Nicola in a surprisingly familiar way.

"Thomas?"

A second look revealed that it was indeed her ex-boyfriend, and Nicola found herself caught between hugging him in relief and punching him for leaving her there in the first place. Unable to decide, she did both.

"Hey! What was that for?"

Nicola didn't get the chance to explain, because Melissa also hugged Thomas. Nicola felt a twinge of something at that, but decided that, on the whole, Melissa was welcome to him. Even without the whole dumping her in another world thing, there was still the matter of breaking up with her over a job.

"Excuse me."

Siobhan stood there with her hands on her hips. On someone else it might have looked frightening. On her it just looked like a tantrum.

"When you're all *quite* finished, I'd like to get on with this. Hello again, Thomas, you're just in time to watch these two die."

"No."

To Nicola, his voice sounded different. Confident, yes, but then Thomas had always been confident. Now though, it sounded more like the edge she'd sometimes heard in the voices of people who'd volunteered in some of the worst places abroad, the one that said that whatever was going on, it wasn't as bad as what had already happened to them.

"No?" Siobhan repeated, and laughed. "Haven't you worked out yet, Thomas, that you don't get to say no to me?"

She made a gesture towards the nearest of the corridor's walls. It bulged outwards, forming a sort of stony pseudopod. That refined itself until it seemed that the wall was soft clay and some giant was pushing its hand through from the other side. An identical stony fist came from the other side of the corridor with another wave of Siobhan's hand.

"Get them."

Nicola ducked as the things rushed forward, but she needn't have bothered. Thomas threw up a hand and the things stopped, before knotting themselves together. Siobhan tried again. This time Nicola saw Thomas re-direct the fists into the floor, where they stuck.

"I won't let you hurt them."

Nicola felt the floor tremble, and started to ask what Thomas was doing, but by then she could see for herself. Chains shot out of the floors, the walls and the ceiling, too many for Siobhan to deflect all at once. They wrapped around her with frightening speed, until she looked like nothing so much as a metal sculpture of some unknown pharaoh's mummy.

Thomas turned to her and Melissa.

"I can jump us out of here before she manages to get clear

of that."

Nicola started to speak, but it was Melissa who put a hand on his arm.

"There's a woman outside who got hurt trying to protect us. We need to let someone know about her before she bleeds to death. We'll jump out straight after."

To Nicola's surprise, Thomas just nodded.

"Ok. Who do we tell?"

"We were on our way to someone when Siobhan put this wall in our way," Nicola supplied. "Do you think you can… oh, never mind," she finished as the wall disappeared, changing back into a corridor. Thomas waved them on expectantly.

"So, who is it you're planning to tell?" he asked, as they rounded the next corner. Only it wasn't a corridor there. Somehow, the passage had managed to deposit the three of them directly in what appeared to be a library, complete with oak bookshelves, comfortable chairs, and enough books to keep the average second hand bookshop going for a month. They skidded to a halt, Thomas' eyes going wide. Nicola followed his gaze, and pointed to the woman who sat calmly reading, surrounded by half a dozen Figments.

"Her."

Seeing him in the flesh for the first time was a wrench. Even having seen Thomas Greene in a mirror, even having talked to Nicola about him, actually meeting him was something else entirely. As for the circumstances of it, the last thing Erithnae had expected was for him to show up in her castle like this.

Not that he appeared to plan on staying long. Even as she watched, he moved his hands in the gestures that would open the way between worlds. That a shining breach in reality opened for him like the door to a tent was the final proof of it. Not that Erithnae needed more proof. Even so, it was enough to wring the sentence from her that she'd been putting off, whispered, but still out loud.

"I have a half-brother."

A half-brother who was getting away. Already, Nicola and the other young woman, the one Erithnae hadn't seen before, were through the portal. Nicola seemed reluctant. Thomas pushed her the rest of the way through, saying something about how someone would be found, and that they could always shout back.

That was when Erithnae closed the portal.

It took no more than the closing of her hand to make the thing shut with a faint pop. That was good to know. Erithnae had been worried for a moment that he would turn out to be more powerful than her. That would be all she needed. But no, while he had the spark, Thomas Greene didn't have the centuries of experience that went with it. He stared at the spot where the hole had been and prodded it with a finger. Erithnae watched for a moment before deciding it was time, though she still wasn't quite sure what it was time *for.*

"That won't work. This is, after all, my Court." Erithnae watched as he stopped, turning to regard her with cautious eyes. Erithnae sighed.

"You might as well come closer, Thomas, and save us from having to shout." She waited until he edged forward reluctantly to a spot about five feet in front of her chair. "There, that's better. Though now I meet you, I'm not sure what to say. Actually, I am. What do you think you're playing at sticking walls across my corridors?"

Erithnae watched his head tilt to one side as he processed that.

"That wasn't me," he said at last, and it was strange to hear his voice up close. "Siobhan was trying to block off Nicola and Melissa. I just undid it."

"You've met my daughter? Where is she?"

Erithnae wasn't surprised to see him nod the way he'd come.

"Back that way, wrapped in quite a lot of chain."

He didn't elaborate. Erithnae nodded to a couple of the Figments around her.

"Go and help her." A thought struck her. "Actually, all of you go and help her. Send her along once you're done, but don't come back until I call. I want to talk to Thomas alone."

He made a small sound, and Erithnae spared him a look.

"What is it?"

"There's a woman outside, called... Poppy?"

Erithnae nodded.

"What about her?"

"She's hurt. You might want to send someone to help her. She's under a sort of grass... thing, in the garden."

Erithnae nodded to the original pair of Figments.

"You two help Poppy. The rest of you go to my daughter."

They floated out en masse, leaving the two of them together in the library she'd moved to put in the way of his flight. It hadn't been hard. Erithnae rose, scrutinising Thomas' face.

"This is... odd, meeting you for the first time. It is all right if I call you Thomas, isn't it? And of course you know who I am?"

He nodded. "Erithnae, Queen of the Dreaming Court, Siobhan's mother. My... half-sister? Do I call you Your Majesty or just sis?"

"*Don't* make fun of me. Do you think I'm happy about this?"

"Do you think I am?"

"It isn't the same." Erithnae jabbed a finger into his chest. "I've found out that my father, the King of the Dreaming Court, broke his own Treaty and fathered you, *completely* betraying my mother's memory. You've just..."

"Found out that my mother has spent my whole life lying to me, and that she mostly married the man I thought was my dad because she wanted to give me a father? You know, what with my biological one abandoning her."

Erithnae resisted the urge to lash out at that. She'd done it with Nicola, and look where that had got her. "I had to find out about it through his love letters," she said.

Thomas shrugged in response. "I got some weird dream vision thing. All I can say is that they looked happy together."

"I know," Erithnae admitted. "Nicola said something similar, about them deserving happiness. Maybe she's right, though it doesn't make it hurt less."

"No, it doesn't."

Erithnae sighed. "But that does leave us with an awful mess now, doesn't it? I'm the one who's left trying to work out what to do when my half-breed half-brother shows up on my doorstep."

"I've got a simple answer to that, Mother."

Siobhan strode across the floor of the throne room, fury obvious in every line of her face. Her hands were clenched tightly into fists. Erithnae raised an eyebrow.

"And what's that, darling?"

"We kill him."

"Now dear, I'm sure we don't need to do that."

Thomas backed up a little. His hand closed on the comforting shape in his pocket. His insurance policy. "Um... do I get any say in this?"

Siobhan gave him a nasty smile, one he knew all too well. When he was younger, every fight with his sister Kelly would be followed by that look, the one that said *all right, you're winning, so I'm fighting dirty: I'm telling Mum.*

"Think about it, Mother. The Treaty is still in place."

"Didn't your War finish years ago?" Thomas said.

"But it was still going when you were born. If we let him live, Mother, it will tell the other Courts that we broke the Treaty."

Thomas found himself trying to swim against the sudden flood of capital letters. Even so, he made an effort.

"Do you really think they'll care? Will they want to restart a War they've only just got rid of over me?"

Siobhan moved to stand beside her mother. "Can we afford to take that risk? Can we chance losing that many lives again over this *half-breed?*"

She swept a hand in Thomas' direction. Erithnae laid a restraining hand on her arm.

"Siobhan, Thomas is our blood relative. My half-brother."

Thomas saw his chance. "Siobhan knows that."

"How could she?" Erithnae asked. "Darling, how did you know about Thomas?"

"I didn't. Not that it changes anything. He's still proof that we weren't as cut off as we should have been. He has to die."

Thomas didn't see Erithnae tighten her grip on her daughter's arm, but he saw the change in her face. First a wince of pain, and then something nastier. Erithnae didn't seem to notice.

"No, Siobhan. You're not changing the subject. You knew about Thomas before I did and you didn't tell me?"

"I didn't know who he was. I thought he was just one more half-breed." Thomas noticed the shift to an expression that would have done most hurt little girls proud. "I... I've been trying to clean up the mess."

"By which she means killing us with the aid of that psycho, Grave," Thomas put in helpfully. Erithnae gave her daughter a hard stare.

"You did this? Behind my back?"

"I didn't want you to be implicated if it went wrong!" Siobhan whined. And it was a whine. She managed to make it sound like she might break into tears at any moment. Then again, Thomas thought, that might just be Erithnae's grip on her arm. "I thought I could deal with this with no risk to you, no damage to the Court. I wanted to help. I thought you'd be proud."

The worst thing, Thomas thought, was that for a moment the Dreaming Queen actually *did* look proud. All those people dead, and Erithnae seemed almost happy about it. She actually drew her daughter into a brief embrace.

"I understand, darling," she said. "I'm not sure you should have done all that killing without asking me, though."

"Not sure?" Thomas couldn't help himself. "People died!"

He expected an angry response. Something he could argue with. He didn't get it.

"The sad fact, Thomas," Erithnae replied with just a trace

of unhappiness in her voice, "is that occasionally people have to. That's part of what being a ruler means: making the decisions that no one else should have to make. Deciding when some largely blameless person has to be killed so that a lot of other largely blameless people aren't. For a queen, it's called responsibility. It's nice to see my daughter taking some for once."

Thomas' gaze flicked from Erithnae to Siobhan and back. Siobhan gave the faintest twitch of her lips. It was enough.

"That wasn't what you were doing though, was it Siobhan?"

"I don't know what you mean."

"Thomas?" Erithnae kept an arm around her daughter.

"If her aim was to clean up this 'mess' why did she capture some of us instead of killing us? Why did she keep me in a cage?"

Siobhan looked up at her mother with innocent eyes.

"What cage? Mother, I don't know what he's talking about. Are you going to let him talk like this without even proving it?"

Erithnae drew her a little closer. "Siobhan has a point, Thomas. You might be family, but I hardly know you. I can't let you accuse my daughter without backing it up. Show me this cage."

"Um… that might be a bit difficult. I turned most of it to golden syrup on my way out."

Siobhan's smile broadened. "You see, mother. I told you it was a lie."

Thomas reached into his pocket and pulled out the piece of fruit he'd been saving there. He'd been hoping not to have to use it. But then, Siobhan had hardly done him any favours. It shone, gold and ruby and sapphire and a dozen other colours, in the clear light of the royal library.

"Where did you get that?" Erithnae demanded.

"A cave hidden away in your Orchard."

"And how did you get past Jasper… my creature on the gate?"

"Is that his name?" Thomas asked, before shrugging. "He

seemed to like me."

He saw Siobhan fume at that. "I told you the stupid thing was useless, Mother."

"Not completely useless," Thomas countered. "After all, he let me get the means to show you up for what you are."

He tossed the fruit to Erithnae. Siobhan made a grab for it, but her mother snatched it out of the air ahead of her. She took a dainty bite. Thomas treated Siobhan to a level stare.

"If you hadn't chased me, I wouldn't have gone in there, and I wouldn't have found this. Do you know what your mother's seeing now? Your dreams, Siobhan. You know the ones. The ones where she's gone, and you're in charge. The ones where she's not gone, and she has to do what you say. The ones where you've used us half-breeds to make the Court the way you want it."

Siobhan started to make an innocent face, saw that her mother still wasn't watching, and just shrugged instead. "It's no more than I deserve. Do you know what the worst part of immortality is? The absolute worst? Nothing changes. Nothing. You know that phase when you're a teenager where your parents refuse to let you grow up, refuse to let you do anything? Make that last a few hundred years and you've more or less got my life."

"So you thought you'd use us to take over?"

"I just wanted, for once in my life, for my mother to take me seriously. To have a say in how this place runs, rather than being treated like a child. It's not too much to ask, but oh no, mother knows best. She's the Queen, and I've got to run round being the dutiful daughter." Siobhan sniffed, and for about a thousandth of a second Thomas actually found himself feeling a little sorry for her. It probably wasn't very nice being stuck as a Princess forever, without ever having a chance to be Queen. Then again, it wasn't very nice being chased by large men who wanted to kill you either, and Thomas had had to put up with it. He nodded towards Erithnae. "I'm sure she'll take *this* seriously. What do you think she's going to do in a second when she wakes up?"

"Whatever it is," Siobhan snapped back, moving forward,

"you won't be here to see it."

She lunged at him, her fingers extended like claws. Thomas, who'd been half expecting it, knocked a stack of books in front of her, sending Siobhan sprawling. She started to rise, only to slump back, her eyes closing in sleep. Erithnae looked down on her with a mix of hurt and disgust. The floor seemed to open up, swallowing the Princess.

"How could she…?" Erithnae shook her head. "No. I will decide what to do with her later." She looked up at Thomas. "It seems you were right, though I wish you weren't."

Thomas shrugged. "Personally, I wish that most of the last few days hadn't happened."

"But they have. And the question now, Thomas Greene, brother, is what are we going to do with you?"

Thomas took a moment to consider it, or at least a moment to realise that Erithnae was actually waiting for an answer.

"Well, naturally, I'm not exactly happy with the whole killing me idea."

Erithnae laughed. "Relax, Thomas. I'm not going to kill you. The trouble is, in one way my treacherous little bitch of a daughter was right. We can't let the other Courts know that we broke the Treaty."

There was something about the way Erithnae phrased that which jarred with Thomas. It took him a second to work out exactly what it was.

"So, if Siobhan had just been killing half-breeds who weren't related to you, you'd have been all right with that?"

"Thomas, please," Erithnae said, "we're talking about what to do with you, not about what my daughter did. Believe it or not, I'd rather not discuss her right now."

"Then we won't, right after you answer this. Would you have had a problem with just the killing? I mean, when she told you that part, you actually seemed… happy."

Erithnae was silent for a moment, and then reached out for his hand. Thomas resisted the urge to pull away. "I wasn't happy at the deaths," Erithnae assured him, "I'm never happy to have to do that sort of thing. But it did need doing."

"Which means you'll continue looking for people like me and killing them, won't you?"

Erithnae was silent, and Thomas pulled away from her grasp, half turning before she spun him back to face her.

"Thomas, do you understand the risk I'd have to take just to protect you?"

"So, what? You're going to shove me in a nice safe room somewhere while you're busy killing off other people just like me?"

"Maybe at first. At least you'd be safe."

Thomas wished that he couldn't believe what he was hearing. Unfortunately, he was just enough of a bastard himself to know Erithnae meant every word.

"What about Melissa? And what about Nicola?"

"Melissa was the other young woman here? The one who escaped with Nicola?"

"She's like me. She would never hurt a fly. She even managed to tame those roses of yours. Are you just going to kill her?"

"If she means something to you, we'll work something out, Thomas. And of course I'm not going to hurt Nicola. I've done that too much already. Maybe they'd have to come back here, but they'd be safe too."

Thomas was sure they would be. He had no doubt that Erithnae meant every word of her offer. She probably thought that she was being kind. The worst part was that they would probably even be happy, because for all its weirdness, the Dreaming Court seemed like a wonderful place to be. Safe, happy, and protected from any Court that happened to come calling. It was probably the best offer he was going to get.

"And while we're all safe, you'll be sending out Grave or someone like him to kill off any more like us that happen to be out there. How heartless are you?"

Erithnae reached out faster than Thomas could follow, clamping her fingers around his wrist much like she'd done with her daughter. When she squeezed, the pain was enough to force Thomas to his knees.

"Don't speak to me like that! You think that because you and I happen to share a father, you know the first thing about the decisions I have to make? I have to do the right thing for my people, even when it's not a decision I want."

"And aren't the ones who are going to be killed your people too?" Thomas demanded. That was enough to make Erithnae fall silent. She let go of his wrist, and Thomas surreptitiously tried to rub some feeling into it while his half-sister thought. When she spoke again, her tone was calmer.

"Do you think I like having to do this?"

"Then don't do it."

"I have to. The Treaty, the War..."

"Have both been over for more than two decades." Thomas stood, going to the library's shelves and plucking out books at random. "This was published in 1871... this one in 1978... 1981... 2000. If someone from another Court saw these, they'd know that you had contact with our world, but you still keep them. Is it such a big deal to let a few people live? Especially when you want to anyway?"

Erithnae shook her head. "It isn't the same and you know it."

"No. Books wouldn't have families who missed them. They wouldn't beg for mercy. They wouldn't feel pain when..."

"Enough!" The force of the word was enough to quiet him. "Enough. Thomas, I'm trying to keep you alive. You, and Nicola, and this Melissa if you want. But it's all I can do. Just accept that."

"No." Thomas wasn't sure where the word came from, but once it was out, he kept going. "No. I know you think you're doing everything you can, and I know this is a chance you didn't have to give to someone who's almost a stranger, but it isn't good enough. I can't just stand there while other people are being killed. For once in my life, I'm going to try not being quite so selfish."

Erithnae looked at him and sighed. "I could just lock you up."

"And how long would that work for?" Thomas asked. "I'm

guessing you can't keep watch on me all the time. Sooner or later I'd get out."

"Do you even begin to understand what you're saying?"

Thomas nodded. He understood, all right. "I'm saying that if you want to start killing half-breeds, Erithnae, you're going to have to start with me."

Thomas stood in front of her and shut his eyes, half expecting Erithnae to do it there and then. After all, as she'd pointed out, the good of everybody had to come first. Of course, that was kind of why he was standing there.

There was no sudden pain, no drag of a knife across flesh, no wrapping of fingers around his throat. All good things, of course, but there's really only so long you can stand there waiting for death before you start to look rather silly. Cautiously, Thomas opened one eye. Erithnae had sat down in the nearest of the comfortable chairs. He opened the other.

"All right," she said, "you've made your point. If I promise not to kill them, will you stop standing there like that and sit down?"

He did.

"You said that this Melissa talked to my roses?"

Thomas nodded. "And got answers. What does that have to do with anything?"

"It means that she's probably a child of the Flower Court. Maybe, if everyone else has been doing the same things, we might, just might be able to talk things through. As you said, the War is over. Maybe it's even time to think about reconnecting with the world a little. But that's something to think about later."

"Does that mean I get to go home without getting killed?" Thomas asked.

"It means that you and I get to make a deal."

"What kind of deal?"

Erithnae gave him an appraising look. "How would you like a job, little brother?"

Chapter Twenty Eight

The rose gardens were quiet when Erithnae walked down to them. It took her a minute to find Poppy, who crouched happily beside the nearest of them, tending to it and watering it. Despite having been close to death barely a day ago, she moved freely, without any sign of her injuries. She looked up as Erithnae approached.

"Hello Your Majesty."

"Good morning, Poppy. I thought you were supposed to be taking things easy."

"I was bored. Besides, I'm almost healed now, and the roses won't look after themselves."

Erithnae reached out for one, which shivered as she ran a finger down the petal.

"Poppy, *these* roses could quite happily go out and hunt down small animals if they wanted to."

"But they've not been at their best, have they? That nasty Grave, going round feeding bodies to them. That's just... mean. Um... not that killing the people in the first place wasn't, obviously."

Erithnae smiled. Trust Poppy to see hurting the flowers as the unpleasant thing in everything that had happened. "Yes Poppy, I know what you mean."

Poppy went back to her work for a second or two before looking up again.

"Your Majesty?"

"Yes Poppy?"

"Did everything turn out all right in the end? With Nicola and that other woman and your..."

"My half-brother, Poppy. Don't be afraid to say it. I don't mind. I quite like the idea of having a little brother to push around."

Poppy raised an eyebrow. "And are you going to push him around?"

"What else are big sisters for? I thought I'd keep him busy, so for the moment, I've made him a sort of... ambassador. Yes, I think that's probably the right word for it."

Poppy moved on to another plant. "Won't that make things complicated for him?"

Erithnae shrugged. "He helped to tangle up this mess, so he can help talk us out of it with the other Courts, and maybe with the humans, given time. I get the feeling that Thomas likes to talk."

Poppy nodded. "So what about Nicola?"

"As far as I can tell, she's fine. I think she went home after arriving back in their world. I think the other girl stayed with Thomas. I'm having to work from dreams, so I'm having some trouble telling. I haven't gotten my mirror back from Siobhan yet."

Poppy rose at that, moving over to where she'd left her gardening basket.

"I think I might be able to help with that."

She pulled a small hand mirror from the basket.

"I found this on the outskirts of the maze."

Erithnae looked it over. She knew her daughter's old mirror when she saw it.

"Mirror?"

The face appeared. To Erithnae, it looked remarkably happy about something.

"Yes, Your Majesty? Are you going to ask me something? Please?"

"You're eager."

"When I found it," Poppy put in, "it was going on about

having answered some question or other."

Erithnae gave it another long look. "*You* answered *the question*?"

"Yes Your Majesty. Easy, Your Majesty. Ask me something else, anything you like. Anything at all."

"Later, little one. Poppy, this is very helpful, thank you."

The other woman nodded.

"My pleasure, Your Majesty. Um... Your Majesty?"

"Yes Poppy?"

"Have you decided what to do with Siobhan yet?"

Erithnae couldn't resist a hint of a smile. She held up the mirror.

In the dream, Siobhan squirmed in the throne she sat on, trying to get comfortable on the hard stone thing. Not that there was any hope of that. For most of the past few hours it had been like she'd been glued in place. She couldn't even move, except to show the horde of tiny Figments around her how to do the most basic of things. They were tiny, and green, and they scuttled round making a hideous cacophony as they all clamoured to be heard at once.

"Princess, Princess... please, how do you thread a needle?"

"Princess... what are we going to have for dinner?"

"The front wall is falling down, Princess, how do we re-build it?"

Siobhan had tried ignoring them, of course, but it just didn't work. With her arms glued to the arms of the throne, there was no way she could even stop off her ears for a second's respite. Worse, if she ever did the sensible thing and just told them to leave her alone, the stone beneath her got hotter and hotter until Siobhan finally screamed out an answer.

And still they kept coming.

Half the time, they'd have some task so impossible that Siobhan would have to go and see it for herself, unable to resist the urge to do so. And once she was there, of course she'd end up doing almost all the work, while the little green people fell over each other with serious faces, invariably making things worse. And somehow, Siobhan would always find herself back in the chair straight after.

"Mother!" she cried after the first few rounds. "Mother, please, I'm sorry!"

"Maybe in a year or five I'll believe it." Erithnae said, wiping the mirror clear. "The first rule of punishing people, Poppy: give them exactly what it was they wanted. In this case, to be completely in charge."

Poppy looked her over with a thoughtful expression.

"Is that what it's like for you, Your Majesty?"

"Only on the bad days."

Thomas sat with Murchall and Grey's original letter in front of him, trying to compose his reply on Kelly's laptop. She was upstairs somewhere, chatting with Melissa and his mother. To say that she was still in shock was probably an understatement, but she'd deal with it.

Compared with Murchall and Grey's letter, which he'd jumped back through the Court to collect, Thomas' wouldn't look like much. It wouldn't be an elegant, precisely addressed thing. It wouldn't have a neatly applied letterhead. It would probably be rather shorter too. On the other hand, even among all the letters a company like Murchall and Grey received, it would probably have the advantage of uniqueness. All he had to do was find the right way of saying it.

After a minute's thought, Thomas wrote a sentence, deleted it, and tried again. He deleted that too. Another pause.

"Sod it," Thomas said, and wrote the first thing that came into his head.

Dear Sirs, Thomas wrote, *in reply to your letter of the fif-*

teenth, while I am grateful for your offer of employment, I must decline. I have, I am afraid, received a better offer.

In the maze, Grave had his prey nearly in his sights. He was a great hunter. The greatest. This was what he lived for. The thrill of the chase. The moments before the kill. He padded slowly around a corner.

There. He could see it now, its little whiskers twitching as it sat beside one of the hedges. With a flick of his tail, Grave launched himself at it, only to career headfirst into the hedge as the mouse darted through it.

Grave swore, the sound coming out as "*mrrowwl!*"

Even so, he wasn't that disappointed. A really good hunt *shouldn't* be easy. And at least there was no one telling him what to do here. Not having to listen to people telling you what to do was almost the definition of what he was now, and Grave liked it. Pointedly, he sat down and started to wash himself.

A little way further on, a tiny, furry shape moved into the open, scurrying for freedom. *Yes,* the cat that had been Grave thought, *this was better than hunting people any day.*

He heard the sound of footsteps long before he saw Poppy round the corner, working on the hedges with a watering can. One part of him wanted to yell "help, get me out of this", but rather more of him wanted to walk up to her and rub against her legs, so he did. Grave wasn't particularly surprised when she picked him up and started stroking his chin.

"And where did you come from?" She asked. Grave just purred. "You're a loveable old thing, aren't you?"

A memory surfaced with those words. Hadn't Freli the witch told him something similar would happen? Damn it! The hag had *known!* Grave wanted to jump down, to race to the witch's house and... and... well, part of him wanted to tear her limb from limb, but something was telling him that he should just sit outside her window and wail every night.

"I've always wanted a cat." Poppy said, interrupting

Grave's feline thoughts of revenge. "How would you like it if you lived with me, Mr Cat? I'll look after you, and stroke you, and you can eat all the mice that try to get at my plants."

She put Grave down on the ground and picked up her watering can. She took a few steps back through the maze before stopping and looking back at him expectantly.

"Are you coming, Mr Cat?"

Grave waited a moment. He had his dignity, after all. Then, with a meow to tell the little scurrying thing in the hedge that he'd be back, he bounded after the gardener.

About the Author

Stuart Sharp was born in 1980 and lives in East Yorkshire. He went to university at one of the Three Great British Universities (according to Blackadder) where he emerged knowing rather more about long-dead people than is really healthy. He started his writing career with a couple of urban fantasy novels, but now prefers things with more jokes in them. He currently works as a ghost writer. He is easily distracted by... mmm... shiny.